THE DEMON COLLECTOR

JON MAYHEW

BLOOMSBURY

LONDON BERLIN NEW YORK SYDNEY

Bloomsbury Publishing, London, Berlin, New York and Sydney

First published in Great Britain in March 2011 by Bloomsbury Publishing Plc
36 Soho Square, London, W1D 3QY

A CIP catalogue record of this book is available from the British Library

ISBN 978 1 4088 0394 3

1 3 5 7 9 10 8 6 4 2

Typeset by Hewer Text UK Ltd
Printed in Great Britain by Clays Ltd, St Ives plc, Bungay, Suffolk

FSC
www.fsc.org
MIX
Paper from
responsible sources
FSC® C018072

www.bloomsbury.com
www.mortlockdemon.com

For Branwell Johnson,
who read my earliest ace adventures

MOLOCH, HORRID KING BESMEARED WITH BLOOD
OF HUMAN SACRIFICE, AND PARENTS' TEARS,
THOUGH FOR THE NOISE OF DRUMS AND TIMBRELS LOUD
THEIR CHILDREN'S CRIES UNHEARD, PASSED THROUGH FIRE
TO HIS GRIM IDOL.

PARADISE LOST, JOHN MILTON -

Part the First

London,
1854

'Now answer me these questions three,
Or you shall surely go with me.
Now answer me these questions six,
Or you shall surely be Old Nick's.
Now answer me these questions nine,
Or you shall surely all be mine.'

'Riddles Wisely Expounded', traditional folk ballad

CHAPTER ONE
RIDDLES

Edgy Taylor screwed his eyes shut and felt his stomach churn as the carriage wheels crunched over the boy's body. The trap rattled round the corner, its pony wide-eyed, foaming at the mouth. The young girl driving had lost the reins and leaned perilously out, trying to grab them as they flicked and trailed along the street. The horse screamed as its iron-clad hooves rolled the boy in the mud and bounced his skull on the hard cobbles.

Edgy's little white terrier, Henry, gave a yap of alarm. The boy had been looking over his shoulder and had run blind into the path of the trap. But there could be no mistaking the expression on his face when he turned back.

Terror.

Someone had been chasing him.

The trap clattered on down the street, out of control. Edgy caught a last glimpse of the ashen-faced driver and then it was gone.

Folk in the street stood motionless, staring at the groaning, twisted body. Carriages rattled distantly in other streets but silence froze this one. One or two onlookers peered cautiously, shook their heads, then broke the spell, pulling their hats or bonnets down, fixing their eyes firmly on the pavement and hurrying on. Henry gave a whine.

Edgy ran forward and cradled the boy, lifting him out of the filth that coated the street. Water leached up Edgy's trouser legs, freezing his bottom half.

The boy looked much the same age as Edgy – thirteen, maybe fourteen. Blood matted his curly brown hair and smeared his face. *Well-dressed*, Edgy thought. The quality of the boy's suit shone through the muck and dirt that now caked it. Thick material, hand-stitched, neatly crafted bone buttons. His eyes flickered and he gave a strangled gasp.

'Don't worry, mate,' Edgy said, trying to sound reassuring.

The boy gave a wet, gargling choke and glanced down at his slowly opening fist. A triangle of bone lay in his palm. The boy lifted his hand, offering it to Edgy.

'You want me to take it?' Edgy asked, frowning at the scrap.

'Keep it safe . . . Salomé . . . Moloch . . . fire . . . death . . .' the boy croaked. 'Don't . . . let anyone . . .'

Edgy took it from his slick palm. 'I'll get some help and . . .'

But the boy shook his head, his eyes widening as he looked over Edgy's shoulder. His back arched and his face contorted, then he fell slack, his head lolling.

'Someone help!' Edgy shouted, but people were quickly about their business. Henry gave a snarl.

'Problem, young man?' a voice chimed behind him.

Stuffing the fragment into his coat pocket, Edgy glanced over his shoulder. Still crouched down, the first thing he noticed was her shoes.

Pointed. Shining. Black.

How was that possible? Even on a frosty winter evening, the mud from the road splattered everyone, lady or commoner. Henry bared his teeth and crushed his body against Edgy.

Edgy's eyes tracked up from the unstained hem of her long black dress. Embroidery and lace. Waist sucked in at the middle. A fine chin, her china skin and red lips smiling at him. Black hair raked into a tight bun. And those eyes, as green as envy.

Edgy nodded to the boy in his arms. 'Ran under a trap. Didn't stand a chance, ma'am.'

'No,' she said, her smile slipping into an imperfect grimace for a second. 'He didn't.'

Edgy knelt in the busy street, twitching under the woman's steady gaze. 'I dunno what to do, ma'am,' he said, nodding to the body again. 'Can you help?'

The woman looked puzzled for a moment and then gave a short laugh. Edgy didn't like her light manner – after all, this poor lad had just been killed. It was horrible.

'Oh, him,' she said, wrinkling her nose and wafting a dismissive lace glove. 'Just drag him to the gutter. They'll collect him soon enough.'

'But . . .' Edgy said, dumbfounded. The cold pinched at his damp legs. 'I can't do that.'

'Well, you can't sit in the street all evening, can you? And are you going to bury him yourself?' Her eyebrows formed a perfect arch.

Edgy gritted his teeth. She spoke as if he were an idiot. Henry whimpered and slid behind Edgy.

'I don't s'pose I am, ma'am, but –' Edgy began.

'What do they call you?' the lady cut in. 'Your name. What is it?' Her tone was light but there was a steeliness to it.

'Edgy, ma'am. Edgy Taylor,' he replied.

'Yes,' she said, as if confirming his answer. Her head tilted to one side. 'Do you know how old you are, Edgy?'

'Well, I'm not rightly sure,' he muttered. 'Twelve, thirteen perhaps?'

'Nearly thirteen. My, my, how time flies. It's your birthday soon. Did you know that?'

'No, ma'am.' Edgy gave a shake of his head. What was she on about? How could she know when his birthday was when even he didn't?

'February the fourteenth. A very significant day,' she giggled and put a lace-gloved hand to her mouth.

'I never knew that was my birthday, ma'am,' Edgy said. *Best to humour her.*

'And what do you do for a living, Edgy?' She beamed down at him, twirling the handle of her umbrella in her hand.

'I'm a prime collector, ma'am,' Edgy muttered. He

could feel his cheeks burning as she stared at him. Into him.

'A prime collector?' She raised her eyebrows again.

'I collect dog sh— droppings, ma'am.' Even over the stink of the sludge Edgy knelt in, her perfume caressed his face. 'I sell it to the tanners, ma'am. They use it to cure the hides into leather. They mix it in a big vat, stick the animal skins in it . . .'

She raised a delicate hand. 'You collect dog droppings?' A solitary wrinkle furrowed her perfect forehead. 'This world gets more hellish every day.'

'Yes, ma'am.' Edgy's eyes scanned the cobblestones.

'Riddle me this, Edgy Taylor,' said the lady, bringing her face close to his. The scent of violets and rose water made his head swim. 'What goes up a mountain and down a mountain but never moves?'

'Sorry?' He frowned, shaking his head.

'It's a riddle, silly. What goes up a mountain and down a mountain but never moves?'

'A riddle?' Edgy knew what it was and he knew the answer. He just hadn't expected some toff to riddle him while he held a dead body in his arms. Talon delighted in beating the answers to riddles into him. 'A path. A path goes up and down a mountain but never moves!' A glow of guilty pride warmed him in spite of the cold and the dead boy. At least he was good at something.

'Very good,' the lady nodded, beaming. 'And what is it that everyone is born with, some die with, but most die without?'

'This is stupid,' Edgy spat and shuffled into a squat.

'Come on, come on.' She clicked her dainty fingers. 'What is it that everyone is born with, some die with, but most die without?' The lady straightened up, waiting for the answer. Her eyes grew wide and she flashed a row of straight, white teeth.

'I dunno, ma'am.' He couldn't think, what with the cold and the strangeness of the situation. 'A nose?'

'You're going to have to do better than that.' Her voice became flat, disappointment pulled at the corners of her mouth. 'And remember, it's dangerous to give your name out to any old stranger, Edgy Taylor. You're mine now by rights but I'll let you run free for a while longer. It won't be long now. See if you can find out the answer. Good day.'

She swept away into the hurrying crowds.

'Now what was she on about, Henry?' Edgy muttered, staring after her. Henry gave a whine.

All that talk of riddles and birthdays made him feel nervous. Riddles always reminded him of Talon. Talon. Edgy shuddered. A devil of a man. Talon took all the muck he collected. Gave him a roof, a crust and a good kicking in return. Everybody else thought he was a decent man, but Edgy knew his true nature.

A rattling of wheels snapped him back to reality as a black funeral carriage rolled up behind Edgy. A hawk-featured undertaker grinned down on him from the driver's seat.

'You keepin' 'im warm, son?' he laughed, clambering down from the carriage like a huge thin-legged spider.

'Saw 'im go,' Edgy said and laid the broken body down gently. He shivered and twitched his head as he stood up. 'Kind of felt sorry for 'im.'

'Ah well, I reckon I'll take 'im. Dressed smart. Looks like he worked for rich folks. Might feel guilty and pay for a modest funeral,' he sniffed, tapping his foot against the dead boy's thigh as if he were assessing a second-hand cart. 'Can always sell his clothes at the least.' He hefted the body up and dumped it into a coffin on the back of the carriage.

'That's 'orrible.' Edgy stared at his scuffed boots.

'That's life, mate,' the undertaker said, slamming the lid shut on the box, 'and death.' He clambered back on to the carriage and gave Edgy a nod. 'Evenin'.'

Edgy watched the hearse vanish into the twilight. Was that how it ended? Limp and lifeless on the back of a cart?

He stared down for a second. A wobbly reflection peered back at him from a shimmering puddle. It was hard to tell if his face was brown from years of outdoor life or from the muck that smeared it. The tight mouth and permanent frown line between his thick eyebrows gave him a worried, suspicious kind of look. No wonder they'd called him Edgy. Not a handsome chap, that's for sure, with his thick mop of black hair. The reflection shivered in the scummy water, twitched and licked its narrow lips.

Henry gave a grumbling whine and stretched, pressing his cheek against Edgy's calf. Edgy stroked the fur, grey from life on the streets, the brown and black patches faded.

'That's life, Henry, old chap,' Edgy said, scratching behind the dog's ear. 'Apparently. Come on then. Let's go and see what delights Mr Talon has in store for us tonight.'

He shook himself and stamped on his reflection; water had soaked through the holes in his boots ages ago.

Folks of all classes now pulled their hats – toppers or flat caps – low and turned their collars against the cold fog that drifted up from the river to fill the night. The fog muffled everything, turning passers-by into indistinct shapes. The shouts and cries from the alleys seemed closer somehow.

Images of the accident and the strange woman turned over in Edgy's mind. The sliver of bone felt warm in his pocket as he flipped it between his fingers. Why did the boy want him to take it? And what had he said? It sounded like gibberish to Edgy.

A huge square shadow parted the mist, blocking Edgy's path. He skipped sideways into the gutter to avoid being squashed. It was a cage on wheels. As the cage trundled past in the swirling fog, Edgy could make out a fox curled in one corner. A rabbit nestled close to it and a hawk rocked on a perch above them. Edgy read the sign above the cage: *Happy Families – The Lion Lies down with the Lamb.*

Hardly a lion, Edgy thought, looking at the mangy fox huddled in the filthy straw. He'd seen these street attractions before – animals that normally devoured each other caged and trained to live in peace. The rich kids loved them. Edgy would watch them pulling their mothers, fathers or nannies over to the cage, begging for a farthing to see the animals. He'd watched the indulgent smiles of the parents with a sting of envy.

Happy Families. Edgy sighed. *A mother or father. That'd be nice. Anyone who cared, really. Anyone but Talon.*

Edgy prayed Talon would be asleep or blind drunk tonight. Or better still, dead.

BETTER THE DEVIL YOU KNOW THAN THE DEVIL YOU DON'T.

TRADITIONAL PROVERB

CHAPTER TWO

A DANGEROUS STRANGER

What is it that everyone is born with, some die with, but most die without? The lady's riddle teased Edgy as he dodged the ghostly figures that emerged from the mist. He shivered and glanced around. For a moment, he had the strangest notion he was being followed.

People cursed and side-stepped Edgy as he shuffled his way across London Bridge. *Nothing like carrying a sackful of dog muck to clear your way*, he thought, allowing himself a humourless grin. His face dropped as he turned a corner and the sulphurous reek of the tanning yards clogged his nostrils worse than the stink of the Thames or the streets.

This whole part of the south bank smelt foul. Here jam makers boiled vats of sugar and fruit in crumbling workshops next to slaughterhouses and tanning yards that spewed yellow sulphurous clouds, thickening the already choking fog. The smell was a sickening mixture of sweet quince jam, meat, offal and tanning agents, and it drifted from the workshops and yards whose blackened brick walls loomed over Edgy.

A narrow alley took Edgy away from the hustle of the streets and into a shadowy maze that twisted and turned. Rough, broken-toothed men propped up crumbling walls and eyed him as he passed. He paid them no heed. There weren't many folks who would roll him in the mud to steal what he was carrying. Besides, he was fast on his feet if he needed to run.

Edgy ducked into a small yard. His shoulder ached with the weight of the bag, full and heavy. He dragged it over his head, twisting his face away from the contents. Nobody wants ten pounds of dog muck tipped over themselves. He heard the filth slither from his bag and slip into a metal vat set in the ground. It bubbled and mixed with the rest of the foul concoction. The smell caught the back of his throat. He had never got used to it. Tomorrow he would be knee deep in the cocktail of excrement and urine that he'd collected from across the city, treading the raw hides into it to soften them. *Something else to look forward to.*

The tannery building itself rose above the yard some three storeys. The red-brick front was dotted with small windows and hatches with pulleys and winches for bringing goods up to higher floors. The huge oak doors stood slightly open.

Abandon hope, all ye who enter here, Edgy thought. This was where he met the sharp end of Talon's tongue and the hard end of his boot. *Why not run away?* The thought occurred to Edgy every day. But where to? Into the darkness of the London streets to have his throat slit? Into the Thames to mudlark and be drowned? There was always the workhouse. Edgy had seen the pale, grey-faced children through the bars. Why would he go there to cough his final hours away as he died of some wasting disease? And what would become of poor Henry? No. At least they were dry and warm among the curing vats.

Edgy scurried through the wooden doors. Henry scampered close to him, the sound of his clicking claws echoing back down from the shadows of the workshop's high-vaulted ceiling. Wet hides dripped and festered on the ropes that stretched between the building's slimy walls. And there, among the piles of skin and hoof and bone, sat Talon, bottle in hand, glowering.

It was trouble, Edgy knew in an instant.

Edgy tried not to look at him. He knew what he would see. Talon's eyes burning like coals deep in his twisted face. Skin crimson and bubbling like lava. Horns sprouting from his head.

Was Edgy the only one who could see what he was? Customers didn't flinch as they did business with Talon. Once, as a young boy, Edgy had mentioned it to Bill Fager, the rosy-cheeked landlord of the Green Man Inn, who used to drop by from time to time. Edgy had told him about the horns and the hooves and the red skin.

'You've a good imagination, Edgy Taylor, I'll give you that,' Bill had said, smiling and shaking his head. Then he'd leaned forward and whispered in Edgy's ear, 'Better not go tellin' anyone else such tales, son. They'll carry you off to Bedlam.'

Edgy glanced up, snapping back to the present. Talon ran a blackened tongue around his cracked lips and beckoned with a long, taloned finger.

'Where you been all this time?' he spat. 'Talkin' to pretty ladies?' Talon wrinkled his pointed nose. *How did he know?* 'Don't try denyin' it. I can smell her on you . . . roses and violets.'

Henry trembled at Edgy's heel, ears back. He'd seen the business end of Talon's hoof before.

Talon stood up, swaying a little from the drink, towering over them. His cloven hooves clattered on the stone floor beneath his leather apron. His sinewy muscles bulged through his shirt.

'I dunno what yer mean! Don't 'urt me, Mr Talon,' Edgy yelped. 'I collected a load today, I been workin' 'ard, sir!'

'You've been answerin' riddles.' Talon cuffed Edgy with his gnarled fist, sending him sprawling. 'I can tell!'

He stooped close and Edgy could smell his beery breath, see his crooked, yellowing teeth.

'Well, riddle me this, Edgy. What has nails but can make a hammer, no rope but can make a noose?' His fingers tightened around Edgy's neck. 'A hand? That what you're trying to say? Well done. Won't help though. I'm sick of wet-nursin' you. Waste of bloomin' time anyway if *she's* gonna check up on yer every ten minutes. Dunno what she's thinkin' of, drawin' attention to yer like that.'

What does he mean? It sounded as if he knew the woman. Edgy's breath whistled through his constricted throat and the blood thundered in his head, stopping all thoughts as darkness edged into his vision.

'Stop that at once!' a reedy voice barked.

Talon's fingers slackened and released Edgy. Gasping and spluttering, he fell to the floor. Air and life flooded back into his body. Henry leapt over, licking at his face.

Talon stared across the workshop. His face was a picture – and not a very pretty one. His jaw hung slack, a string of spit drooled down his pointed chin.

'Envry Janus,' he whispered. His red face seemed to pale. 'The Stonemason . . .'

A little old man with long white hair, a tight black suit and pointy boots stood in the doorway. He wore spectacles with red lenses and held a small metal tube in the palm of his hand.

'Hello again, Thammuz. How've you been keeping?' He smiled and pointed the tube at Talon.

'No, don't!' Talon cried and turned to run, tripping over Edgy in the process. Cursing, he scrambled to his feet and grabbed Edgy's lapels. 'Edgy,' he gasped, his voice thick with fear. 'You gotta 'elp me – he'll kill me.'

Edgy's stomach twisted at his touch. 'Get off me! Leave me alone!' He slapped and punched at Talon's arms and face.

Talon threw Edgy aside, pleading with the man. 'Janus, don't, I'll do anything . . .'

'Tell me where it is then.' Janus's wrinkly face was still scrunched into a smile.

'I can't,' Talon groaned. 'If I knew I'd tell yer, I swear.'

Janus shook his head and pulled a cord at the back of the tube. A muffled bang echoed around the tannery. What looked like a dirty grey snowball hurtled from the tube and smacked Talon in the face. The groaning demon span on his heel, his red skin turning instantly grey, his movements slowing. Edgy cowered against the side of a curing vat as Talon reached out. The greyness was spreading, covering his entire body.

'Edgeeeeeeee . . .' Talon wheezed, like a clockwork toy running out of spring. Then he froze, his face petrified into a beseeching grimace, a statue of Talon.

The cheerful, kind-faced old man blew the smoke from the end of the tube, snapped the tube shut like a telescope and slipped it into his waistcoat pocket.

'What did you do to 'im?' Edgy peered at the statue that had once been Talon and gingerly tapped its solid grey mass.

'Don't worry, young man, he's ossified – turned to stone. He won't hurt you again,' he said, beaming at Edgy as if he was meant to understand. 'I'll have some men come round and pick him up later.'

'But . . . why?' Edgy picked Henry up, rolling his ear between his finger and thumb.

'He's a demon,' Janus said simply, pocketing his spectacles and turning to leave. 'I collected him.'

'A demon?' Edgy stepped towards him. His heart leapt. Then he wasn't mad after all. Henry's ears flattened back.

'That's right,' Janus chuckled as he strode into the alleyway, his arms folded behind his back. 'Now run along and do whatever it is you do.'

'Y'mean he *was* a demon? A real devil? Is that why he had horns and red skin?' Edgy called after him. Janus stopped as if he were on the end of a leash and it had just been given an almighty tug. 'I thought I was barmy but you could see the horns too?'

Janus turned slowly and, placing his red spectacles on his wrinkled face, looked Edgy up and down. 'Talon didn't just look like a man to you?'

'Sometimes when he was working or asleep he looked like an ordinary cove.' Edgy gazed at the open toes of his scuffed boots. 'But most of the time when he was angry and beat me, I could see the horns and stuff. I thought it was just me. Thought I'd lost me marbles, like.'

'Well, Thammuz *was* a demon of wrath,' Janus mumbled, rubbing his chin. 'More likely to give himself away when he lost his temper. What's your name, young man?'

'Taylor, sir,' he said, twisting the last remaining button on his ragged woollen coat. 'Edgy Taylor.'

'And you worked for Thammuz? What did you do?'

'Collected . . . stuff, went on errands, solved riddles for 'im.'

He snapped to attention and peered closer. 'Riddles?'

'Yep.' Edgy frowned and twitched under his gaze.

'Seems I'm quite good at 'em . . . usually. Talon was always asking me riddles, then scribblin' down the answers. He taught me t'read so's I could learn more. From books and such. Always on the lookout for new riddles was Talon.'

'Fascinating.' Janus paced around Edgy, looking him over like a farmer inspecting a prize bullock. He stopped and clapped his hands together. 'Tell me, how old are you?'

That question again? Edgy squirmed, shaking his head a couple of times. 'Nearly thirteen, sir.'

Janus smiled and nodded as if he were impressed with the answer. 'Well, Edgy Taylor, I think you should come with me. There's nothing for you here.' He prodded his finger into Edgy's shoulder and peered down his ear. 'I think you might be . . . useful,' he added thoughtfully.

For a moment Edgy was flummoxed and looked at Henry, who stared back with dark-brown eyes that mirrored Edgy's anxiety. 'Sorry, sir,' he stammered. 'But I think I'll go me own way, if it's all the same to you.'

Edgy ducked under Janus's arm. He ran down the alleyway, risking a backward glance. Henry clattered after him but Janus just stood and stared beyond him.

Something was wrong.

Edgy looked forward to glimpse ebony horns curling from a green forehead and orange eyes burning from the shadow of a heavy brow. At first he thought it was Talon. But it was another demon. Huge. Blocking his path. The creature towered above him, much larger than Talon ever was. Between its scowling eyes, a single red flame flickered and spat. Scrabbling on the slick cobbles, Edgy slid into it, bouncing back on to the hard ground. It was as if he had run into a brick wall.

So with his finger dipped in blood,
He scribbled on the stones,
'This is my will, God it fulfil,
And buried be my bones.'

'Childe the Hunter', traditional folk song

CHAPTER THREE
A PLACE OF SAFETY?

The demon's heavily muscled arm swung down. Edgy rolled aside, springing to his feet. It lashed out again and missed, giving Edgy a split second to duck and run. Henry yapped and snapped at the demon's ankles as it launched itself forward in pursuit.

'Can't you, y'know, turn him into stone or somethin'?' Edgy yelled, pulling at a stack of barrels that stood at the side of the alley as he ran towards Janus. They clattered to the ground, sending the demon sprawling. 'What's he got against me?'

Janus was fiddling with the tube and cursing. 'Damnable ossifier's jammed,' he spat.

The demon gave a low chuckle and pointed at Edgy. Edgy stumbled forward, tripping as the sole of his boot came off. He hissed at the sudden cold on his feet.

'Careful, Edgy, it jinxed you,' Janus shouted, stuffing the ossifier into his pocket. 'Probably did the ossifier too.'

The demon picked itself up and strode towards Edgy but Janus jumped into its path, hurling a white powder at it. With a bellow of the rage, the creature threw its arms up to shield its face. Janus's fingers gripped Edgy's upper arm.

'Come with me,' he said firmly, dragging Edgy to his feet. 'And run – I think there's more than one.'

Two more demons appeared in the otherwise empty alley, similar in size and appearance to the first. Flames danced on their foreheads. It was all the encouragement Edgy needed. Janus scattered more of the white powder in a line across the alley and then broke into a sprint.

'Come on, Henry!' Edgy yelled, chasing after Janus. Henry gave a final yap and hurtled to Edgy.

For an old man, Janus could certainly move. Edgy panted for breath as Janus clattered down the alley and into the main street, sending a party of ladies screaming as he barged into them. Touching the brim of his crooked top hat, Janus bowed and set off at a brisk stride. Edgy hurried after him, his ragged boot flapping and slapping the ground.

'They'll be more careful in this crowd,' Janus muttered, his breath billowing in white clouds and merging with the fog that still shrouded everything. 'Demons like to keep themselves secret.'

Edgy glanced back. The dim outline of one of the demons weaved and pushed its way through the mass of people that teemed around it.

'They're behind us,' Edgy hissed. ''Ow come nobody's makin' a fuss?'

'People don't see demons like you do, Edgy,' Janus panted. 'They only see some rather rough-looking workmen or maybe nothing at all. Demons often use some kind of disguise but *you* can see through it.' He looked over his shoulder. 'Come on, we need to move more quickly.'

'Where're we goin'?' Edgy called after him.

'A place of safety,' Janus shouted back without slowing.

Edgy caught up with Janus, who shoved a small sack into his hand.

'It's salt,' he said. 'Demons hate it. It burns them. If one of them gets near you, let him have it.'

Janus led them towards the river. The earthy, sewer stench of the Thames returned to mask the stink of the hide-curing yards. Something flapped overhead and Janus glanced up.

'Damn, they can fly too,' he muttered. 'Get ready for trouble, Edgy.'

The fog boiled and parted as the demon thudded to earth. It lunged at Edgy, cracked black talons raking the air in front of him. Edgy dropped to the ground and rolled between the demon's legs. His eyes caught a glimmer of something metallic in the sludge of the gutter. A cast-off horseshoe! With a grimace, he snatched at the metal shoe, pleased to feel a couple of nails still protruding sharply through it. He held it in his clenched fist so that the sharp nails poked out between his fingers.

The demon had spun round to face him now and made another lunge. This time, Edgy stood his ground. A stink worse than the Thames, worse than the tanneries, blasted over him as the creature's face drew near. Edgy noticed the cracked, scaly skin, the boils and puss sliming the demon's cheeks. Then he lashed out in disgust, punching into the hideous face with all his might.

Edgy's stomach lurched as he felt his knuckles scrape crusted flesh. The nails sank into the creature's cheek. With a howl, the demon fell back, clutching at its face. The flame on its brow faded for a moment. Henry sank his teeth into its ankle.

Janus clapped his hands together and grinned.

'Well done, lad,' he called. 'Iron. A pure element of the earth. Demons don't like that either. Now run!'

Shadows thickened and closed in as tall tenements blotted out the night sky. Every now and then they passed through an arch, sloshing their way across flooded courtyards.

'Blimey, Henry,' Edgy panted. 'We'll never find our way out of this maze!' Henry looked up and gave him a little whimper.

'Not far now,' Janus said, pausing for a moment and gasping for breath. 'But we're not out of the woods yet.'

'What do they want?' Edgy asked, bending double and leaning against a crumbling brick wall.

'You, it seems,' Janus replied, frowning. 'Though I'm not certain why. Did you see that flame on their brows? That's the Fire of Moloch. Nasty creatures.'

Instinctively, Edgy's hand slipped into his pocket and closed around the sliver of bone that the dying boy had given him. He'd mentioned the name Moloch too. *Is this what they're after?*

The sound of footsteps moving through the quiet alleys behind them startled Janus into a jog.

'Have you lived at the tannery all your life?' he called over his shoulder.

'S'pose so, it's the only place I know, really,' Edgy panted. 'And pickin' up dog muck is all I've done since the day I could walk – all I was good for, so Talon said. He always said he'd found me.'

Janus looked back again. 'Your parents?'

Edgy shook his head. 'Dunno.' *Happy families.* Edgy tried not to think about them but the thought filled his heart with longing.

'Edgy – that's a curious name,' Janus said, his speech broken as their pace took his breath.

'They called me that on account of me always lookin' nervous, twitchin', like,' Edgy called back. 'Anyone'd twitch if they lived with a demon.'

'Hmmm,' Janus said. 'I wonder why Thammuz kept you.'

'Dunno that either. Talon always said I wasn't right in the head.'

'You aren't mad, Edgy, you have a gift,' Janus said. 'Which may be why there's so much interest in you.'

Before Edgy could say anything in reply, they ran out into a square. A grimy street sign told him this was Eden Square though it didn't look like any kind of garden he'd seen before. Not a tree or a blade of grass to be seen. In the centre stood a grotesque bronze statue of Satan raising a defiant fist to the skies. A warehouse with huge wooden doors and shuttered windows rose up to his left. To his right a ramshackle tenement loomed over him. In front of him a block of a building squatted, filling one whole side of the square. In the dim light, Edgy could just make out columns and pillars standing to attention right along its front.

'This,' Mr Janus announced, waving a hand at the building as if it were the eighth wonder of the world, 'is the Royal Society of Daemonologie!' He paused for a second and then added, 'Unless you want to be reacquainted with the handsome fellows behind us, I suggest you follow me inside.'

Edgy hesitated, his eyes flicking back to the gaping door of the tenement building.

The footsteps pounded closer behind them.

Edgy followed Janus a few paces behind as he bounded up a steep flight of stone steps that led to the front of the Society. Edgy picked Henry up and hugged his warm body close. He licked at Edgy's ear and buried his head under his chin.

Two black doors stood tightly shut, their brass fittings dull and unpolished, matching the gloom of the square. Edgy read the brass plaque next to the door: *The Royal Society of Daemonologie*.

'Now if we can just get some attention,' Janus said, pulling on the bell handle several times.

'You'd better hurry, Mr J.,' Edgy muttered, glancing back down the steps.

Two dark figures had broken out of the alley opposite and were stalking across the square towards them. Janus saw them too and hammered on the door. Grinning, the hideous creatures drew closer.

As I went out to take a walk,
Between the water and the wood,
There I met with a wee, wee man,
The weest man that ever I saw.
Thick and short were his legs,
And small and thin was his thigh,
And between his eyes a flea might go,
And between his shoulders were inches three.

'The Wee, Wee Man', traditional folk ballad

CHAPTER FOUR
THE IDLE BUTLER

'Thought you'd escape us, did you?' hissed the first demon as it mounted the steps.

The second followed close behind. They glowed faintly green and veins pulsed through their wet, slimy skin. Their long faces twisted into wicked grins of pure malice.

Edgy hugged Henry to him and pressed his back against the peeling black doors of the Royal Society. Across the square, he noticed the third demon staggering out of the mist, one bloody hand over its left eye.

'The main thing to remember about demons,' whispered Janus, his face close to Edgy's ear, 'is that they thrive on fear. It gives them power. Don't show them that you're afraid.'

'I'm not,' Edgy hissed back, shivering and twitching. 'I'm terrified.' Henry gave a whimper and buried his head under Edgy's arm.

Janus turned and hammered more fiercely. 'For God's sake, Slouch. Open. This. Damn. Door. At. Once.'

'No one answerin'?' sniggered the second demon. 'Looks like you're stuck.'

'Ask them a riddle,' Janus whispered.

'What?' Edgy spluttered. 'What is it with riddles and you lot?'

The demons crept forward.

'Demons love them,' Janus snapped. 'Just do it. Quickly!'

'Righto,' Edgy muttered. He raised his voice, trying not to let it crack with fear. 'Hey, you demons! What does everything do all the time?'

The demons stopped, looking around in feigned surprise and pointing to themselves. They glanced at each other and leered. Edgy shuddered at their needle teeth, the blackened gums.

'A riddle?' hissed one.

'I hate these new-fangled riddles. What's wrong with a little bit of poetry?' said the second.

'What's wrong, can't you answer?' the third said, grinning at his friends.

'Of course! I just wanted to see if you could,' snapped the second. 'I prefer the more metaphorical riddles, that's all.'

'What is it then?' Edgy asked, his heart thumping as he glanced back at Janus, who was still battering at the door, kicking and punching it.

'Easy,' said the first demon. 'Everything . . . grows old all the time.' Then it launched itself forward at Edgy.

'Slouch, we need to come in. NOW!'

Janus's yells were cut short as the double doors swung open and he and Edgy tumbled inside. The first thing that hit Edgy was the heat from indoors. The second was the cool marble floor as he fell flat on his back. He found himself looking up at a black ceiling decorated with stars. A clawed hand gripped the tail of Edgy's coat but he yanked it back as the doors slammed shut. Edgy heard a cry of anger and a yelp of pain.

Janus was on his feet. 'Blast your eyes, Slouch. We could've been killed out there. What do you think you're playing at?'

Janus ranted on but Edgy only half heard him. He stared at the hall in which he lay. It had five sides and a door sat in the middle of each wall. Brilliantly coloured paintings twisted across the panels of the walls: demons fighting, feasting, laughing and weeping. Red skin and gold crowns blended with flame tongues and blue lightning bolts. Edgy didn't know where to look next. Every wall seemed to move and shimmer. A golden pentagram glowed in the centre of the black marble floor. Henry gave a low growl, drawing Edgy's attention to the object of Janus's rage.

'You're all right now, aren't yer?' groaned a weary, wheezing voice. Edgy's stomach lurched. An impossibly tall, thin demon loomed over Janus as he continued his tirade.

'No thanks to you, you lazy ingrate. Words fail me, Slouch. I . . . I . . .'

'Well, that'll be a first,' grumbled the demon, shoulders sagging with the effort of speaking.

Edgy relaxed a little. This one wasn't like the demons

outside. He wore a butler's suit but it was a size too small; the cuffs ended well above the wrists and the jacket would never have buttoned up. A strip of lank, black hair lay plastered over his otherwise bald head. His long face, wide nostrils and large, downturned mouth gave him a look of resignation and sadness.

'Don't get clever with me! What on earth were you doing?' Janus snapped.

'Sittin' down there,' muttered Slouch, pointing at a rather worn-out sofa that had exploded at the seams.

Janus pulled his black coat off and removed his hat, tutting and shaking his head. He offered them to Slouch, who stared at them for a long time before extending a slow, lazy finger over in the general direction of the coat stand. Janus pursed his lips and stamped over to the stand, flinging his coat and hat at it.

Slouch turned his sad eyes on Edgy. Weariness suddenly pressed on Edgy's shoulders. His eyelids felt heavy.

'You'll have to forgive Slouch, Edgy,' Janus said, fixing the demon with a glare. 'He's a demon of sloth. Not given to any exertion, if he can help it. Why the governors appointed him Head Butler, I'll never know.'

'Why does he work for you?' Edgy asked, shaking himself awake as Slouch began to snore. 'An' what's a demon of sloth?'

'*He* is.' Janus grimaced at the slumbering demon. Then he frowned and drew Edgy close. 'Some demons have joined the Royal Society of Daemonologie. Not all of them are out to get us.'

'What's wrong with him? Why's he so lazy?'

'Sloth,' Janus spat. 'Most demons are connected with a certain sin. You know what sins are?'

Edgy nodded. 'They're bad things to do . . . like stealin' or murder.'

'True, true,' Janus agreed, 'but they're also ways of feeling – being envious or greedy. Sloth is laziness. Demons enjoy encouraging these sins in mankind but often they fall prey to the sins themselves before they get that far. Slouch is a prime example.'

'If he's that lazy, why does Slouch work for you?'

'He hardly does any work for us.' Janus cast a baleful eye on Slouch. 'His own idleness keeps him here. We'd be glad to see the back of him.' The old man raised his voice so that Slouch could hear. 'He could walk out of the front door any time.'

'Couldn't be bothered,' muttered Slouch from his sofa.

The mention of the door made Edgy twitch and glance at it. Janus followed his gaze and smiled gently.

'Don't worry, Edgy,' he said. 'The Royal Society is protected. The demons can't come in. Nice work with the riddle back there, by the way. Quick thinking!'

'It wasn't that good. They got it. An' now I can't get out neither,' Edgy scowled. 'Not while they're sittin' on the doorstep.'

'Then you may as well be our guest, Edgy Taylor,' Janus laughed, gripping the lapels of his jacket and standing on tiptoe. 'A good meal inside you, a bath and bed might make you a little better disposed towards us. Follow me.'

Janus charged out of the reception hall and through the nearest door. For a moment, Edgy stood in the hall, staring after him. *What's his game then? Why all the interest in me, I wonder?*

Henry gave a whine and looked up with anxious brown eyes.

'Well, there's not much else I can do,' Edgy said to him, then scurried after Janus.

Henry barked and clattered after him across the marble floor, pausing only to cock his leg on Slouch's sofa.

'Keep up, young man,' Janus said without glancing back, as he marched up a panelled corridor lined with portraits. Edgy looked at them, shivering. Sombre old men in black skullcaps stared down at him with disapproval. Small spheres hung from the ceiling, glowing warm and red, giving a twilight feel to the place.

'Ah, you've noticed our lighting system.' Janus beamed back at him. 'Not gas, no, no. Hellfire, courtesy of the Illuminati Lighting Company. Burns for a thousand years. Can't see why they haven't caught on . . . might be the smell, of course.'

Edgy sniffed at the slightly eggy smell that hung about the corridor. Every now and then a door interrupted the dark oak panelling. Pipework coiled and swerved around the doorframes, the gentle hissing cutting through the silence. No one passed them or came out of the doors. Janus seemed unconcerned by it all and strode ahead with the same fixed smile.

'Don't like this place one bit, Henry,' Edgy muttered

as he hurried after Janus. 'As soon as them demons have shifted, we're off.'

Henry gave a low whine, his ears alert as he scanned the walls.

'A bit safer than outside, eh?' Janus said, throwing a smile over his shoulder at Edgy. 'And warmer. We'll swap those rags you're standing in for something a bit more presentable.'

Edgy glanced down at his ragged torn trousers and coat, sniffing at the dog smell that emanated from them. His boot flapped where the sole had come off and holes gaped at his knees and elbows.

'Here we are,' Janus said and stopped, taking a sharp right into a small room lined with shelves. Clothes lay neatly folded in piles on each one. A little blue-skinned demon, half Edgy's height, sat on a stool in the corner of the room darning a sock. He jumped up when Janus entered.

'Ah, Professor Janus.' The man bowed low, his long nose almost touching the floor. Pointed ears sprang out from the side of his large head. He wore striped trousers and a tailcoat that touched the ground at the back.

'Evening, Trimdon. This is Edgy Taylor. He's stopping for the night, maybe longer. I'd like to show him around.' Janus beamed. 'I want him scrubbed, fed and kitted out for me. Back in half an hour.'

Janus disappeared out into the corridor. Trimdon slicked back his hair with his fingers and beamed at Edgy.

'Pleased to meet you, Master Taylor.' Trimdon bowed low again.

'Yeah, charmed,' Edgy said, eyeing the little man.

'And this is?' he said, smiling down at Henry. To Edgy's surprise, the dog wagged his tail and licked the back of Trimdon's hand.

'Erm, Henry,' Edgy said. If Henry trusted this strange little demon, he thought that maybe he should too.

'Pleased to meet you, Henry.' Trimdon nodded and then bowed to Henry. 'If you go through that door behind you, you'll find a tub of warm soapy water awaits.' Trimdon bowed again, then narrowed his eyes as he looked Edgy up and down. 'You get a wash and I'll pull out some suitable clothing for you.'

Edgy backed through the door and found himself in a tiny cupboard room. A tub of water filled the room and a three-legged stool stood beside it. He peered at the steaming tub and dipped a hand in the water, pulling it out quickly.

'Blimey, Henry, 'ot water,' he grinned. 'I can't remember the last time I 'ad a wash, let alone a full soak!'

Henry jumped up, forepaws on the side of the bath, dipping his nose in the foam. For a second, Edgy thought about the vats at the tannery – a knee's depth of urine and excrement. He sniffed at the fragrant bubbles that swayed on the surface of the water.

A cough from behind startled him. Trimdon had his head round the door. 'You get undressed and climb into the water. Use the soap and the scrubbing brush to get the dirt from your skin.' He gave a brief smile. 'Don't worry, you aren't the first young man to be frightened of a bath – and you won't be the last, I'm sure!'

The door clicked shut and Edgy undressed, piling his crusty clothes on to the stool. He pulled out the sliver of bone and the bag of salt Janus had given him and put them behind the bath out of sight.

Henry watched with tilted head as Edgy lifted a cautious leg and dipped his toes into the water. Edgy's skin prickled and tingled. He wasn't sure if he liked it at first. He inched in, gasping at the warmth that engulfed him.

'Lord above, I've never felt so hot in all my born days,' he panted.

Gradually, his breathing returned to normal. Aching muscles stretched and relaxed in the heat. He blew a few bubbles at Henry, who jumped and snapped at them.

'You're as mucky as me,' Edgy said with a laugh. He grabbed the little dog and dragged him in. Henry gave a yelp and sank under the water, only to bob up again, fur spiky, tail wagging, splattering suds and water everywhere.

Edgy slipped his whole head under, revelling in the feeling. When he came up for air, Trimdon must have been and gone as a suit of black wool hung on the back of the door, along with a shirt of thick cotton and a pair of boots that shone in the candlelight.

'Maybe this ain't such a bad place after all,' he said to Henry, climbing out and rubbing at his tingling skin with a clean, dry towel.

The terrier gave a muted bark and sniffed the air, licking his lips. The smell of warm, meaty gravy drifted into the room. Edgy's mouth watered.

'A feast, Henry,' he whispered, pulling on shirt and trousers, drawn by the aroma of food. He snatched up and pocketed the salt and bone fragment.

When Edgy emerged, Trimdon stood holding a plate of pork chops, mashed potato and gravy.

'Tuck in, Master Taylor,' Trimdon said, his pearly teeth gleaming even in the red glow of the hellfire lamps.

Edgy smacked his lips. He sat with the plate on his knee, devouring the feast, throwing Henry chunks of the chops whenever he pawed the air for more. Edgy had never tasted anything like it. Food at the tannery was stale crusts, cheese and gruel. Now and then, Talon would get a few bones and boil them up but Edgy had never had such succulent meat.

'So, Mr Trimdon,' Edgy said, his voice thick with gravy, 'you been with this Royal Society long then?'

Trimdon smiled and inclined his head. 'About a hundred years.'

Edgy's eyes widened.

'I know, I know,' Trimdon smiled, patting his little beer belly, 'I hardly look old enough. The Society has been like a family to me.'

'What kind of demon are you, Mr Trimdon?' Edgy asked. 'If you'll pardon the question.'

'A domestic demon.' Trimdon puffed out his chest. 'I watch the hearth and keep a fire burning. We're not all about pitchforks and hellfire. Why I –'

But Trimdon was cut short by Janus, who popped into the doorway and stood there beaming.

'Perfect fit, Trimdon, another job well done,' he smiled, testing the quality of Edgy's suit material with his finger and thumb.

'Thank you, sir.' Trimdon seemed to grow another inch as he stood tall, hands behind his back. 'Hand-stitched, finest quality.'

'Right then, young man,' Janus said, taking Edgy's shoulder and leading him into the corridor. 'Let's show you to your room. You'll soon feel at home.'

'Now listen, Mr Janus –' Edgy started to say.

A blur of red hurtled down the passage. It seemed to Edgy that the hellfire lights had detached themselves from the ceiling and were flying towards him.

'Vandal! Thief!' someone screeched.

Edgy felt a dull pain in his stomach and found himself rolling backwards across the floor as long red fingers closed around his throat.

THERE WAS AN OLD FARMER IN SUSSEX DID DWELL,
THERE WAS AN OLD FARMER IN SUSSEX DID DWELL,
AND HE HAD A BAD WIFE, AS MANY KNEW WELL.
THEN SATAN CAME TO THE OLD MAN AT THE PLOUGH:
'ONE OF YOUR FAMILY I MUST HAVE NOW.
IT IS NOT YOUR ELDEST SON THAT I CRAVE,
BUT IT IS YOUR OLD WIFE, AND SHE I WILL HAVE.'

'THE FARMER'S CURST WIFE', TRADITIONAL FOLK BALLAD

CHAPTER FIVE
THE UNWELCOME

A glowering red face snarled down at Edgy, its long nose pressed against his. Orange eyes burned with fury and stubby little horns butted his forehead. The fingers tightened and, for a moment, it was as though he was back in Talon's merciless grasp.

'Give them back, you thief!' snarled the demon, pinning him to the floor. 'Where have you hidden them?'

'Spinorix!' Janus yelled. 'What's the meaning of this?'

'Ask the little worm!' Spinorix spat. 'He can tell ... Owwwwww!'

The demon suddenly loosened his grip on Edgy's neck and turned. With a snarl, Henry had sunk his teeth into the demon's tail. Edgy, feeling the creature's balance shift, pushed forward, sending him sprawling on to the polished floor.

A small demon with large, floppy ears lay before Edgy.

He was red from head to foot – red skin, red suit and tie, red hair greased back and plaited in a ponytail. His eyes were wide and he panted heavily as he tried to stand up. Sweat trickled down his furrowed brow and round his short horns. Spinorix tumbled sideways, his tail still firmly gripped by Henry's teeth. He writhed and wriggled, swatting at Henry ineffectually.

'By the sweetbreads of Cerberus! Call him off, call off this hound of hell!'

'Don't see why I should,' Edgy snapped.

'Please, I beg you. Professor Janus, tell him to release me!' Spinorix whined.

'That's up to Edgy. What were you thinking of, attacking him like that?' Janus said, putting his hands on his hips.

'Ow, oh, owww,' Spinorix moaned.

Edgy shook his head and clicked his fingers. Henry dropped the tail immediately. Spinorix jumped up, tears coursing down his red cheeks.

'Well?' Edgy demanded, copying Janus's pose.

'I'm sorry, I thought you were the other boy,' Spinorix began.

'Other boy?' Edgy said, frowning. 'What other boy?'

Janus gave an embarrassed cough. 'We had an errand boy –'

'A thief!' Spinorix hissed, massaging his tail. 'He's been taking things from the exhibition hall.'

'Now you can't be sure of that, Spinorix,' Janus said, pursing his lips. 'Perhaps you've just mislaid . . .'

Spinorix went a deeper shade of crimson. 'With respect, sir, I do not "mislay" valuable artefacts.' He trembled and gripped his tail tightly. 'Things have gone missing and where's the boy now?'

'You'll have to forgive Spinorix, Edgy, he's an imp and as such is prone to melodrama. As for the boy, he'll turn up, I've no doubt,' Janus murmured, frowning at Spinorix. 'Anyway, who's watching the collection now?'

The imp's colour drained. With a squawk, he turned on his heel and clattered down the corridor. Janus gave a chuckle and watched him vanish.

'A dedicated imp but a little excitable, I think. Spends far too much time in the exhibition hall,' Janus said. 'I'll take you to your room now.'

Edgy thought of the boy he'd seen die only hours before. He had a smart suit. Black. Woollen. Perfect stitching. Just like his new one.

'Ah, good evening, Madame Lillith,' Janus smiled, looking beyond Edgy.

Edgy turned. A round lady, her hair pulled up in a tight bun, swept the tiled floor behind him. She looked up from her work with narrowed eyes. Her brush scraped the tiles with short, vicious strokes, her green silk dress swishing in time to them. She watched them pass.

Henry's head flicked back and forth with the brush; his tail wagged to the same rhythm. He gave a playful yelp and snapped at the brush. Madame Lillith stopped and glared at him.

'Sorry.' Edgy smiled as her eyes bored into him. 'C'mon, Henry. Leave it.'

Edgy heaved a sigh of relief as they turned a corner and left her behind. For a moment he forgot the boy in the street. As they walked, Edgy felt the floor slope downwards. The lower they went, the plainer the decor became. The walls in this part of the Society were plain plaster rather than wooden panelling. *Servants' quarters.*

'She's a demon of envy,' Janus explained as they walked on. 'Anything you have, she wants it.'

'Didn't you say that demons are meant to make *us* sin?' Edgy wondered aloud.

'You're absolutely right, Edgy, but, like Slouch, most demons fall prey to their own weaknesses first. Madame Lillith is so eaten up with jealousy that she's practically human. It's only a matter of time before mortality sets in. It happens to a lot of demons. Ah, here we are . . .' Janus said, swinging open a rough plank door to reveal a small room with a table, wash-basin and jug.

On the bed sat a pale young girl, rubbing her hands and fingers as if she were trying to get warm. She jumped up, startled.

'Sally, what're you doing in here?' Janus frowned.

The girl folded her arms defiantly. She was about Edgy's age and quite pretty, he thought, though very pale. Edgy would have called her long, wavy hair blonde but actually it was white. Her dress, which was tied up with a ribbon around her thin waist, was white. Her boots and stockings were white too. Everything about her was white but not a clean-laundry kind of white. It was more of a bleached, faded white.

'Just resting,' she sniffed, sounding quite cheeky to Edgy's mind. 'I *do* rest sometimes, you know.'

'Well, you can't rest in here, young lady. This is Edgy Taylor. It's his room now,' Janus said with raised eyebrows.

Sally's eyes widened and Edgy couldn't help noticing the dark circles underneath, as if she hadn't slept for a week. She stamped her foot.

'It's *my* room – it has been since 1735,' she yelled, stamping again. 'Why can't he go somewhere else?'

'You know full well that we're short on beds, Sally, and you don't actually need yours.'

'It's not fair,' she snapped and punched her hands down at her sides. 'Just because I'm dead –'

'Dead? Is she a ghost, Mr Janus?' Edgy whispered, hugging Henry, unable to take his eyes off her. Now he came to think of it, she didn't look quite right. A bit too thin and gaunt.

'I am here, you know,' Sally said with a gasp. 'And, no, I'm not a ghost. I'm a revenant – there is a difference!'

'Well, whatever you like to call yourself, go and haunt some other chamber,' Janus snapped back at her.

With a squeal of outrage, Sally flew into the passage and Janus shut the door on her. Edgy could hear her yelling and raging outside as Janus scratched his head.

'Sorry about that, Edgy,' he smiled. 'I'd forgotten about Sally.'

'But she said she was dead,' Edgy whispered, looking sidelong at the door, trying to ignore the curses being hurled at its other side.

'She's right, really – she's a revenant. A returned one. Not a spirit or phantom as we might imagine but one who has died . . . and then come back.'

'She can't walk through walls or anything then?' Edgy asked, eyeing the door again.

Janus shook his head and sat on the bed. 'She's flesh and blood . . . kind of. Sally was brought back over a hundred years ago by Glassten Lustenbrück during his investigations into the afterlife. A very clever man – I still have his notes, some of his experiments were quite ground-breaking.'

'Don't suppose Sally was particularly impressed,' Edgy murmured, feeling sorry for the girl.

'What?' Janus muttered. 'No, I suppose not. I'd not really thought of it that way.' He sat in silence for a moment, as if ruminating on the idea, then shook himself and jumped up. 'Anyway, it sounds as if she's gone for now. If she bothers you again, just let Trimdon know. Try and get some sleep – you'll need all your strength tomorrow. Oh, and I got you this.'

He pulled a small book from his pocket and presented it to Edgy. He took a deep breath. Nobody had ever given him anything apart from harsh words and cruel blows. Now here he was – clean, clothed, fed and being given a gift.

'That's all right, sir,' he said quietly. 'You've been too kind already.'

'Nonsense, my boy.' Janus beamed at him, placing the book on the bed. 'I'll leave it here. You get some sleep and we'll talk in the morning.'

Janus left, closing the door gently behind him.

Edgy picked the book up and shivered. It felt warm in his hands. Not like the warmth that came from being in someone's pocket but warm like a living thing.

'*Everyday Daemonologie*,' he read aloud, '*Or a Demon a Day*.'

The book, covered in black scales, glistened in Edgy's hand. The shifting colours within it reminded him of the swirls of oily blue and purple he'd seen on the wings of black beetles.

He glanced out of the small window and into Eden Square. Three dark figures sat hunched around the statue of Satan.

Edgy lay on the bed but sleep didn't come. He flicked through the book. It wasn't like any book he'd seen before – not that he'd seen many. Edgy wasn't sure he liked it but it fascinated him. Certain articles jumped out at him again and again. Others he skimmed through once and then they couldn't be found again no matter how hard he searched.

He flicked through woodcut pictures of huge demons locked in combat, armies of devils bearing cruel weapons, assembling on vast plains. Titles such as *Getting the Best out of Imps* and *Asmodeus Proposes* jostled with *The Role of the Governing Body at the Royal Society*, until his head whirled with jumbled-up facts.

'*Imps are the most minor of demons,*' he read aloud, totally engrossed. '*Usually the lost souls of unbaptised children or babies kidnapped by demons. Imps are the workforce of hell. They make fiercely loyal friends and annoyingly obstructive enemies.*' Edgy thought about Spinorix and his anger about things going missing.

Another passage caught his attention:

In 1797, Hector Corvis, seventh Earl of Rookery Heights, invited a hooded stranger to install panelling to the Royal Society. Bizarrely, once this stranger had finished, fellows of the Society soon found themselves lost in their own building. It was the associate demon Asmodeus who discovered that because of the demonic decor one had to think of the appropriate location to find one's way there, as he was often fond of saying, 'Just think where you might be tempted to stray and you'll find yourself there . . . but one still has to walk.' Typical demon capriciousness.

Edgy looked down at Henry, who lay curled at the foot of his bed. 'Well, that settles that,' he murmured. 'This place is a nuthouse. First thing tomorrow, we're off, demons or no demons. It's all well and good livin' like this but I'll take me chances, I think, Henry, old chap.'

Henry gave a contented whine and buried his muzzle in his chest. Gradually the events of the day took their toll on Edgy and he fell into a restless, dream-filled sleep, chased by demons and dead boys, carriages and the grinning face of Janus.

DEVILS CAN'T BE DRIVEN OUT WITH DEVILS.

TRADITIONAL PROVERB

CHAPTER SIX

THE EXHIBITION HALL

Grey shafts of morning light coaxed Edgy out of his sleep. He stretched. Normally at this time of day he'd be shivering at the cold and rubbing his hands together, but every inch of the Society glowed with heat. Edgy felt good – well fed, clean and dry. He'd never been able to say that. Henry yawned and shook himself, jumping off the bed. Edgy rubbed the condensation off the tiny windowpanes and peered through.

Mist made the surrounding buildings grey and indistinct. A white frost cloaked Eden Square but the three demons had stayed close to the Satan statue. Edgy could see steamy breath clouding around their curling horns as they stamped out the cold. One of them glanced up, making Edgy pull back from the window, his unease creeping back.

'Still there, Henry,' Edgy murmured. 'How are we goin' to get away from this place?'

He picked up the book and stuffed it in his pocket. The heat stifled him, made him feel trapped. Edgy reached for the latch of the door.

'Let's go an' find a way out, shall we?'

He opened the door and gave a yell. Sally stood right in the threshold, making Edgy fall back. She must have been standing with her face pressed against the door to be so close when he opened it. Henry barked and scampered off down the corridor into the gloom.

'Henry!' Edgy called, but he had vanished. 'Look what you've done now!'

'Well, you shouldn't have taken my room!' Sally's ice-blue eyes burned and she stood glaring, hands on hips.

'I 'aven't taken your stupid room – I'm not stoppin'.' Edgy picked himself up from the floor. 'But if Henry comes to any harm, you'll wish you were properly dead!'

Sally's face crumpled. A sadness swept across it. She turned and stalked off down the passageway.

'I already do,' she said, without looking back. Edgy could hear the tears in her voice but he hurried in the opposite direction in search of Henry.

If Edgy hadn't seen the daylight through his bedroom window, he wouldn't have known whether it was day or night in the gloomy corridors.

'That dog's got himself lost, good and proper,' he muttered as he crept through the tangling passageways.

Remembering that reference in the book, he tried to think his way towards Henry. He hissed with annoyance

– why did the exhibition hall that Janus had talked to the imp about yesterday keep slipping into his mind?

The corridor twisted to the left and a bulky shadow twisted its way around the curved wall. A scraping, swishing sound followed it.

Edgy stopped dead. His heart pounded.

The noise became louder. *Swish, scrape, swish, scrape.*

Edgy started to back away from the corner.

The swaying green bulk of Madame Lillith appeared behind the grotesque shadow, sweeping with vicious strokes as she went. She froze and glared at him.

'Give 'im to me,' she muttered, though her mouth remained a tight line in her round prune of a face.

'What?' Edgy stammered. 'Who?'

'Your dog.' She craned her neck forward, leaned on her brush and jabbed her thumb behind her. 'I want 'im. Give 'im to me.'

'Henry?' Edgy said. He barged past her and ran round the corner.

A round hallway opened before him and Henry cowered in the centre, looking from right to left.

'Henry!' Edgy called, crouching to meet him as he came bounding forward. He leapt into his arms, licking his face and battering the floor with his tail. 'That 'orrible old bat ain't havin' you!'

Edgy looked up. Two enormous doors stood before him. Golden rivets held thick, polished planks together. A brass plaque shone out on the left-hand door.

'*Exhibition Hall*,' he read out loud. 'Well, I'll be . . .'

He thought better of finishing the sentence and gripped the huge, round handles. Dragging one of the doors open, he poked his head round it and yelled in terror.

A huge skull with curling ram's horns leered down at Edgy with teeth like six-inch nails. He stumbled backwards, tripping over Henry, and lay in a ball, eyes squeezed shut.

Henry's bark echoed around the hall but all else was silent. Edgy opened an eye. The skull hovered over him as still as a statue. Chancing both eyes, he peered up and fell flat on his back, laughing at his own cowardice.

'It's some kind of exhibit,' he said to Henry, who cocked his leg on a statue of a dragon that flanked the door to show how concerned he had been. The wired-together bones of some long-dead demon loomed over them, claws outstretched, jaws wide. 'It had me fooled.'

Beyond the skeleton, rows and rows of glass cases, display cabinets, statues and vases dotted the enormous hall. Various gargoyles and fiends dangled from the ceiling, suspended by steel cable.

'Fascinating, isn't it?' Janus said, appearing from behind a display cabinet. Edgy gave a start and put a hand to his thumping heart.

'Mr Janus, you frightened me 'alf to death,' he said, clearing his throat. 'Look, I'm sorry an' all that but I've got to go. It's a bit . . . mad round 'ere.'

'Let me show you around first.' Janus smiled as if reading Edgy's mind. 'It may answer some of your questions and make more sense.'

Janus led Edgy further into the hall and stopped at a huge fireplace. No fire burned here but a portrait of an unsmiling man hung above it. His eyes fixed Edgy with a sombre glare. In one hand he held a skull, in the other a crown. He was sitting on a golden chair draped with an ermine cloak. Piles of books towered behind him.

'King James I of England,' Janus said, 'founder of the Royal Society of Daemonologie. He gave it the Royal Charter in 1605.' Janus waved his hands around the hall. 'We collect and study demons of all kinds, their habits, their history, their biology, everything about them.'

'What for?' Edgy muttered, glancing sidelong at a leering ossified demon.

'Knowledge, Edgy,' Janus said, raising his eyebrows. 'Knowledge is power. King James realised that. To defeat your enemy, you have to know him. James I was a great scholar and was keen to defeat the powers of darkness.'

'So you fight demons?' Edgy murmured. 'Then how come there are so many wanderin' around the building?'

'Not any more.' Janus smiled and shook his head. 'Ours is a scientific cause now. We study, observe and sometimes collect them.'

'Like you did with Talon?' Edgy grimaced as he remembered Talon's twisted, ossified face.

'That was regrettable,' Janus said, sighing. 'More often we encourage demons to join us and become "associates".

That way we can work with them to understand their nature.'

'What about the demons who don't want to be collected or join up?' Edgy asked.

Janus shrugged. 'There was a time when it was all-out war. Demons didn't like the Society at first. And the early fellows saw themselves as the last crusaders. They could afford to – the Society was stronger then. These days, we can usually reach a compromise.'

They wandered among the display cases and statues. Janus stopped every now and then, pointing out an arte-fact or a specimen.

'The more we find out, the more questions there are,' Janus murmured, his eyes shining. 'Riddles and complexity, Edgy. Riddles and complexity.' He traced his finger across the handle of an ornate dagger. 'Demons love riddles. Life is a game to them, dangerous – often fatal – to mortals, but that doesn't bother them.' He lifted the dagger, its blade flashing red in the hellfire light. 'In fact, they envy our mortality sometimes.'

'Righto,' Edgy said, unsure what to say.

His head began to spin as Janus showed him skulls and spears, enchanted talismans and fragments of bone, telling the story behind each one. Edgy forgot about the demons waiting for him outside, his need to leave or the last boy.

'Can't demons die then?' Edgy asked at last.

'They can be turned to stone with our ossifiers. The

ball they fire is a combination of salts and pure elements of the earth, whereas demons are creatures of fire and light. We don't know how ossifying works and we don't know if it truly kills. In theory, you could chop demons into a million pieces and then put them back together again and they would come back to life.'

'And what about this?' Edgy murmured, touching a demon skeleton on a stand. It looked human apart from the skull, which displayed razor teeth and long spiral horns. The chin came to a sharp point too. There was a hole in the top of the skull. A perfect triangle.

'Oh, that.' Janus waved a dismissive hand. 'Just the bones of Aldorath. Nothing much . . .'

Edgy looked more closely at the skull. Something bothered him but he couldn't think what. Janus's voice lowered and he spat his next words out, making Edgy jump.

'My illustrious brother found them. Such a fuss over nothing. They made him chancellor on the strength of those mouldy old bones. Chancellor!'

'Your brother?' Edgy muttered, raising his eyebrows.

'Yes, Lord Mauldeth.' Janus spoke through gritted teeth. 'Not happy with just our family title, being the eldest and all that. Oh no, he has to muscle his way into the Royal Society.' The fire died in his eyes. 'Anyway they're just the bones of a demon, that's all.'

'Righto,' Edgy murmured.

'There was a time when demons ruled the earth . . .' Janus's voice became distant and he looked far beyond

Edgy. 'The great arch-demons waged war, multiplied, built huge cities. Do you want to hear a story? A story from the dawn of time, passed down from the mouths of demons themselves?'

Edgy listened, spellbound by Janus's sonorous voice.

THE FIELDS WERE GREEN, AS GREEN AS COULD BE,
WHEN WE FROM HIS GLORY FELL;
AND WE HIS CHILDREN THEN WERE BROUGHT
TO DEATH AND NEAR TO HELL.

'THE MOON SHINES BRIGHT', TRADITIONAL FOLK CAROL

CHAPTER SEVEN

THE LEGEND OF SATAN AND MOLOCH

'Many ages ago, before Man was turned away from the Garden of Eden, the earth was fresh and blue-green, sparkling in dew so fresh that God wasted many a foolish hour smiling down on His creation.

'But beneath all this, in Stygian depths, Satan ruled supreme in the kingdom of hell. He sat on his throne of obsidian in his palace of beaten gold, basking in the searing heat of the lava flows, enjoying the spit and hiss as molten rock poured over ash flows and pooled around him. His queens and consorts huddled, adoring, at his feet.

'Demons sang his praises in beautiful, haunting voices. Have you ever heard a demon song, Edgy Taylor? Its beauty would break your heart and drive you mad. They fought each other to be in his presence, plunging one another beneath the seething, flowing earth, to Satan's delight.

'Men and demons are like fires in the dark – bright and hot. Every now and then a spark of anger or hatred would flare up, then flicker into the blackness and die. But one demon, Moloch, caught hold of his spark, a smouldering ember that he clutched to his heart. He blew on it with a bitter breath, whispered his grievances to it and it grew into a furnace cupped in his gnarled palms. The fire of hatred burnt into his veins and consumed his heart.

'When God had thrown Satan and his rebellious angels down into the pits of hell, it was Moloch who had wanted to continue the battle, to rise up once more and crash like a fiery tide upon the walls of heaven. But Satan had counselled deviousness and trickery, knowing that they could never beat the Almighty.

'"Better to confuse and corrupt man, the Almighty's pride and joy," Satan had said and set off to tempt and torment humankind.

'"Better the field of battle than to skulk in the shadows, whispering obscenities into the ears of village idiots," Moloch hissed to himself.

'Day after day, Moloch crouched in his dark cave of ash and stared out.

'Week after week, Moloch wondered, *why should Satan sit upon that throne?*

'Month after month. *What gave him the right to be worshipped by the other demons?*

'Year after year. *He is no better than the one God, demanding our tribute and adulation!*

'Century upon century added heat to Moloch's anger, until one day he burst forth and threw himself at the startled Satan.

'Demons howled in despair as Moloch plunged the great Satan into the molten lava. Satan had never been challenged. He never expected to be. He was unprepared. Moloch cast Satan into his dark cave of ash and sealed him in.

'Satan hurled himself at the dark cave walls. Mountains threw themselves up into the sky. Satan pounded his prison confines. Hills rolled across the earth's crust like waves. Finally, Satan threw himself to the floor and despaired, weeping bitter tears that flooded from his cavernous gaol, leaving salt seas between the mountains.

'In his grief, Satan tore at himself and gouged at his flesh. In his madness, Satan shaped the skin, blood and nail he ripped from himself. He fashioned limbs and eyes, horns and teeth. He laughed and tormented the creatures in the darkness and they grew to hate and fear him, even though he had fashioned them from his own body.

'The demons hated and feared Moloch too. He had thrown down the great Satan. He was preparing them for a war against heaven, a war they could never win. He was leading them to their destruction.

'Yet who could oppose Moloch? The demons were all too afraid, too craven to stand against him. They crawled at his feet, begged for his favour and mercy.

'All except one.

'Salomé. Satan's queen. She stood proud in the blue-green world and defied Moloch – until he decided to cast her into Satan's pit.

'"Do what you wish," she cried. "At least I'll be with the true master."

'In a rage, Moloch broke open the seal of Satan's cave. Sensing freedom, all the creatures of the pit spewed forth, blinded by the daylight, battering into Moloch's face. Seeing his weakness, Salomé plunged her fist deep into Moloch's chest and tore out his heart.

'"You have been loyal," Satan said to Salomé. "You can have any gift you wish."

'"Give me Moloch's heart that I may keep it hidden and separate from his foul body," replied Salomé. "That way he will never rise again."

'"Very well," Satan agreed, "but you must protect it and every thirteen years you must show me that you still have it safe."

'He knew that if she wished she could replace Moloch's heart and bring him back. So Satan hid Moloch's body from prying and disloyal eyes. And to this day, nobody knows where the body lies.

'Salomé, her wish granted, feared Satan's distrust. She knew that only if she held the heart of Moloch could she keep the ear of Satan. So Salomé hid the heart where nobody would ever find it. Not even Satan himself.'

*

A spell of silence hung over the exhibition hall. Janus sighed and lowered his head as if exhausted by telling the tale.

'So has anybody found them? Moloch's heart or the body?'

Edgy whispered. The names echoed in his mind. He could still hear the boy gasping them out with his dying breath.

'Some say it's only a story,' Janus muttered, his gaze distant. 'Fools! I've worked long and hard to prove that Moloch exists and to find his body. But recently my investigations have become more than academic.'

'What d'you mean?' Edgy said, frowning.

'Salomé,' Janus whispered. 'She exists. I've seen her. She wants Moloch's body. I think she seeks to bring him back, to destroy this world and the next.' He grabbed Edgy's wrists, squeezing them until they hurt. 'And I think you can help me stop her –'

A short cough interrupted Janus and made Edgy jump. He turned to see a grey, sullen old man huddled in a long coat. His lined, wrinkled face seemed to be losing the fight with gravity, so droopy were his jowls. His eyes looked dull and watery. Not a curl of hair grew on his head; he reminded Edgy of a boiled egg that had gone off.

'Who's this, Janus?' he murmured, stooping over Edgy and looking him up and down.

'Edgy Taylor. I brought him in yesterday,' Janus said. 'Edgy, this is Mr Sokket, a fellow and one of the governors of the Royal Society.'

'My God,' Sokket muttered, making an even longer face than Edgy thought possible. 'Your last employee's not cold in his grave and you find a replacement. Let's hope he lasts a bit longer.'

'I'm not workin' for 'im, sir,' Edgy said, trying not to twitch. 'I'm just waitin' for a chance to leave.'

'Very wise, boy,' Sokket said. 'And don't forget the governors' meeting later, Janus. I think your presence will be required after yesterday's excitement.'

Sokket walked out of sight, leaving Edgy staring after him, open-mouthed.

'Don't worry, Edgy,' Janus grinned as Mr Sokket's final mutterings faded down the corridor. 'Mortesque Sokket is one of life's eternal pessimists, never disappointed when everything goes wrong. Mortesque has a taste for the macabre. And to think he's on the board of governors when I'm not! It makes my blood boil, Edgy.'

'But he said something about the other boy,' Edgy said. 'Is he dead?'

'Sadly, yes. We found out this morning. But it's nothing for you to concern yourself about.' Janus smiled back at him. 'The poor lad was a bit careless, that's all. Didn't keep his wits about him. Now you strike me as an alto- gether more . . . cautious kind of chap.'

'Damn right I am,' Edgy snapped and stalked off towards the main doors to the exhibition hall. 'I've been strang- led by an imp, called a thief, seen ghosts an' demons an' governors who tell me I'm gonna die, an' you tell me it's nothing to worry about?'

'Edgy?' Janus called after him. 'Where are you going?'

'Out of this madhouse,' Edgy called back. The clicking of Henry's claws echoed off the high ceiling of the hall.

'But the demons at the front,' Janus shouted urgently, 'they're still there.'

'There must be a back door,' Edgy said.

'Stop! It's too dangerous out there,' Janus called after him.

'An' it's safe an' sound in 'ere?' Edgy called back and stalked past the displays and demons out of the hall and into the corridor. 'I'll take me chances with the demons if it's all the same to you, sir.'

FALSEHOOD IS THE DEVIL'S DAUGHTER,
AND SPEAKS HER FATHER'S TONGUE.

TRADITIONAL PROVERB

CHAPTER EIGHT

THE SNAKE
AND THE LIBRARY

Edgy strode down the corridor, trying to orientate himself so he was walking towards the rear of the building. He twitched and blinked in the gloom. He wanted to be out of this strange place with its jealous demons and dead girls who yelled at you. Janus had clothed and fed him, true – but the boy he'd seen die had worked here, he was sure of that now.

'Not goin' to end up like that,' Edgy murmured to Henry. 'Nah. Let's get out of 'ere while we still can, I reckon.'

Edgy stopped. The corridor ended in tall, thick double doors. He squinted at a brass plate on one of them.

'*Library*,' he read aloud. Henry gave a low growl. 'Well, we don't want that – we want a way out. What did that book say? "Think where you might be tempted to stray"? Somethin' like that.'

Edgy doubled back and took a left turn but more double

doors blocked the way. Another sign read: *Library*. He turned back again, walked right. More doors.

'Another library. Somethin' is goin' on 'ere, Henry,' he muttered. 'I think we're meant to go in.'

Edgy pulled open the door and stepped through.

'Blimey,' he gasped, staring open-mouthed at the scene before him. *How did I not notice this from outside?*

A vast dome curved above him like St Paul's Cathedral. It glowed with a deep translucent blue like a midsummer night sky. The walls reached up to the dome into the distance, lined with bookshelves. Ladders and walkways zigzagged higher and higher, vanishing into the shadows. Edgy's head spun just looking up. A maze of bookshelves also filled the floor of the hall. Each shelf looked to be composed of living branches, twisting themselves into compartments that housed thousands of books. Dark leaves sprouted from the bookshelves and trembled in the warm breeze. Black apples clustered among the leaves. A thin mist drifted around them. Edgy wandered further into the library, Henry trotting at his heel, panting.

'Funny library, this, old chap,' Edgy murmured, leaning on a nearby desk.

He shivered as the sound of gentle weeping drifted out of the mist. Hazy white human figures darted from shelf to shelf, pulling books out or running skeletal fingers down the spines. A spectral man floated over to a pile of volumes and ran milky white eyes over the titles. He was dressed like a gentleman but all colour had drained from him. He reminded Edgy of Sally except the outline of the bookshelves, desks and tables shimmered through his transparent body. Tears coursed down his long, scarred face and he ground his teeth in anguish as he turned over cover after cover.

'They seek one book. They will never find it,' hissed a voice above Edgy.

He turned with a start. Henry gave a yap and Edgy followed his gaze to the top of the nearest bookshelf. A huge, black snake hung from the gnarled branches of the bookcase. It curled and looped around the branch time and again but its tail vanished into the shadows.

'Why not?' Edgy asked.

'I do not wish it,' the snake hissed, shifting its coils. 'They are my lost souls. They sold themselves to me in life. Now they pay their debt. What do you seek, human boy?'

'Erm, nothin'. I couldn't get away from 'ere, that's all. It seemed like I had to come in,' Edgy muttered. 'I'm looking for a way out of this place.'

'I know but are you sure that's what you want?' the snake whispered, flicking its black tongue out. 'You are full of questions, boy. I can taste your curiosity – and your uncertainty. What do you want to know?'

Edgy glanced at the apples and the leaves.

'Do you see the fruit?' the snake said, slipping down the trunk that made the side of the bookcase. 'Not many can. Few can see me unless I allow it. But what better place to house books than in the Tree of Knowledge?'

'The Tree of What?'

'No,' the snake's wide mouth formed a grin, 'the Tree of Knowledge. You know . . . Adam and Eve, the Garden of Eden, biting the apple and all that nonsense. If you choose to believe it, of course.'

'And this is that tree?' Edgy asked, hardly able to believe it. 'Are you . . . *him*? The devil?'

The snake weaved across the dusty, woodblock floor towards Edgy but still its tail never left the shadows of the shelves.

'It could be that tree and I suppose I'm old enough to be him,' the snake said, as if it hadn't considered that before. 'But who I am doesn't matter. I am the library, I bring knowledge. A little knowledge is a dangerous thing and that's just how we like it. A little piece at a time.'

'Righto,' Edgy said, trying to look like he understood.

'So you want to leave?' The snake stopped at his feet. 'What about Salomé?'

'What d'you mean?' Edgy said, trying not to give anything away.

The snake swayed his head from side to side. 'Oh, come along, Edgy Taylor. Do you think you're here by accident? Mr Janus needs your help. Why are those demons outside so keen to catch you? Don't you know?'

'Do you?' Edgy said. 'I thought you brought knowledge.'

'I do,' the snake snapped, rearing up. It looked like Edgy had hit a sore spot. 'I knew you were curious, Edgy Taylor. The answer might be here. Care to look for it?' The snake's eyes narrowed. 'I could find the information for you if you've got something to . . . exchange . . .'

A lost soul drifted by, blinded by tears, battering through the pages of a book in a desperate search. *For what?* Her white hair billowed, blown by a spectral breeze, her sobs echoing in Edgy's ears. He shook himself. How did the snake know his name? Did it know everything?

'No,' he said. 'I'll work it out for myself, thanks very much.'

'Well, call in any time. I like you, Edgy Taylor. You've got a sharp mind. You're always welcome.'

Edgy watched the snake uncoil and slide back into the shadows, merging with the books in the shelves so that it became part of them. Soon it was invisible but for a pair of amber eyes burning from the bookshelf.

'I'm sure you'll find a way out, one way or another.' The eyes faded and vanished.

The huge hall echoed with the muted cries and sobs of the lost souls as Edgy trekked back towards the great main doors and out into the corridor.

A small window hung open, allowing a rare draught of cold air to cut through the stuffiness of the Society. Edgy peeked through the thin, leaded frame. He looked out on to a narrow alleyway. *Probably the side of the building.* With a bit of a squeeze he could be through it and away before anyone at the front could see him.

'Whatever the answer is,' Edgy murmured to Henry, 'I've 'ad enough of demons an' devils an' snakes.'

He leaned out of the window, lowered Henry on to the ground, then straddled a leg over the sill of the window and flipped into the gloom.

LIE THERE, LIE THERE, LOVE HENNERY,
TILL THE FLESH ROTS OFF YOUR BONES,
AND THAT PRETTY GIRL IN MERRY GREEN LEA
THINKS LONG OF YOUR COMING HOME.

'YOUNG HUNTING', TRADITIONAL FOLK BALLAD

CHAPTER NINE
TAKING CHANCES

Every noise made Edgy shiver and twitch as he crept down the alleyway. Mud squelched loudly under his boots; his breath sounded to him like a blacksmith's bellows. He glanced left and right, waiting for the hideous demons to pounce on him from every shadowy doorway, to come snarling through every blackened window, but nothing moved.

Edgy reckoned it was mid-morning but the grey twilight of the winter streets was as confusing as the ruddy glow of the lights in the Society. The alleys here twisted and doubled back on each other. Henry trotted ahead, leading Edgy deeper into the tangle of claustrophobic streets. The occasional cry made Edgy flinch but he saw nothing more threatening than ragged children trying to snatch morsels of stale bread from each other.

He stepped into a small yard littered with planks of

rotten wood and old barrels. A rusted pump stood in the centre, surrounded by a puddle of green water.

'I think we've done it, Henry,' he muttered, still on the lookout. 'I think we've left them demons back at the Society.' He allowed himself a brief smile.

Henry gave a fretful whine and peered up, his eyebrows knitted with concern. Edgy scanned the courtyard for any signs of life or movement.

The windows stared down on him, black and lifeless. A few bubbles popped on the surface of the scummy puddle. Edgy stepped forward, craning his neck to see to the bottom. It was inches deep. Nothing could hide under there. He sidled along the side of the yard, pressing his back against the walls of the slums that formed the square. The water bubbled again.

Then, in a fountain of slime and scum, something burst up out of the puddle as if it were as deep as a lake. Henry gave a bark and Edgy froze as the demon hovered above them, flapping its bat-like wings and splattering water all around.

It was one of the creatures that had chased Edgy yesterday. Green and glowing slightly, the flame flickered between its thick eyebrows. The Flame of Moloch. Edgy shuddered and twitched, wiping the spots of slime that rained down on to his cheek.

'Be brave,' he muttered to himself. 'Don't show yer fear. That's what old Janus said . . .'

The demon gave a deep chuckle and lowered itself to the ground, the beat of its wings ruffling Edgy's tousled hair.

'On second thoughts,' Edgy said, 'run!'

He launched himself away from the wall as the demon lunged forward. Edgy twisted his body to avoid collision. With a hiss of frustration, the creature smacked into the wall. Edgy clattered out of the courtyard and down the nearest alleyway.

Left, then right, Edgy ran without thinking where he was going. Henry panted at his side. Behind them powerful wings pounded the air. With a breathless sob, Edgy doubled his efforts. The downdraught of the flying demon chilled his sweaty neck. He could feel its claws graze the back of his head as he ducked forward.

And then, suddenly, Edgy burst out into the main street and the crowds. He risked a backwards glance, clipping the shoulder of a protesting gentleman as he did so. It was enough to show him that the demon stood at the mouth of the alleyway. *Why has it stopped?*

With a groan, Edgy crashed to the ground, just managing to shield his face with his hands. The dirt and gravel between the cobbles scoured his palms and took the air from his lungs. For a moment he lay still, gasping to breathe.

'Did you forget to count?' snarled a fierce voice. Edgy looked up to see the other demon leering down at him. 'There's more than one of us, remember?'

Edgy bit his lip. He should have realised. Only one had chased him – the others must have been heading him off all the time. He'd been tricked. But he could still only see two of them. Henry barked and snarled, snapping at the demon's ankles, but the creature ignored him.

'You 'ave something we want,' said the first demon, catching up with them.

'I don't know what yer mean,' Edgy gasped. 'What could I 'ave that you'd be interested in? Why don't you leave me alone?'

But the demons weren't looking at him now. Instead they stood to attention, jaws slack, eyes wide. Henry was staring too, body rigid, one paw raised, a low rumbling growl sounding in his throat.

'Why, if it isn't Edgy Taylor,' a voice chirped. 'I hardly recognised you in those fancy clothes.'

Edgy, still sprawled on the floor, looked up to see the same young lady he'd met yesterday. Black hair tumbling down her shoulders, cheeks dimpled by a crimson-lipped smile.

'The Royal Society *is* looking after you, isn't it?'

'Salomé,' gasped one of the demons, falling to one knee. The second demon appeared reluctant but his companion pulled it down as well and it didn't give too much resistance.

'Leave us,' the woman said, snapping her fingers and waving her hand impatiently. 'Go.'

'But the boy . . . we have spent many days hunting him. We –' the first demon began.

'I said leave.' Salomé's perfect smile fell, her lips tightened. 'Or do I have to tear your hearts out and feed them to this mutt?'

Henry bared his teeth at Salomé and the two demons. They rose and bowed slowly, then backed off into the crowd and vanished.

'Not the same as it used to be,' she sniffed, pulling a black lacy glove on to her hand. 'But they still show some respect.'

Edgy twitched as he clambered to his feet. His heart pounded. Pressing his hand to his pocket, he felt the pouch of salt that Janus had given him still nestled there next to the shard of bone.

Salomé, the Demon Queen. She's after Moloch's body but what does she want with me? Edgy pondered for a moment. *Whatever it is, it can't be good.*

Salomé spoke again, cutting through his thoughts. 'Names are valuable currency, young Edgy, I told you that last time we met.' She giggled, pacing around him. Wherever she stood, the crowds parted like a stream around a rock, staring ahead, oblivious of her. 'The fools at the Society give their names like loose change. I never give my name freely but you know who I am by now, I suppose.'

Edgy muttered, 'Well, I could have a good guess', then pushed the nearest passing gent into Salomé and darted off in the opposite direction. Henry's claws clattered alongside him. His new boots slapped the cobbles, hobnails sparking as he stumbled round a corner and into a dark alley. He slammed his back against the wall, panting for breath. After his previous chase, Edgy had little energy left.

'Have we lost her?' Salomé said, appearing right next to

Edgy and imitating his wide eyes and heaving chest. She giggled like a young girl playing kiss chase.

Edgy bolted back into the crowds, rolling through mud, scurrying under barrows. He pitched into another alleyway.

'This is so exciting,' she said with a squeal and a skip.

Again he ran, dodging around walkers and street sellers, sending a juggler flying, skittles and balls bouncing into the street and startling horses. Edgy's body ached. He couldn't run any more. He dived into a deep porch at the side of a shop.

Salomé appeared behind him once more.

'You are funny, Edgy Taylor.' She beamed, slapping her hands to her knees. 'Much more fun than that other boy. He didn't last ten seconds.'

So the boy had been running from Salomé. Now Edgy knew what had happened to the other boy and that was not going to happen to him. He stuffed his hand into his pocket and grasped Janus's pouch of salt. He needed to get close if this was to work. He remembered the woman's riddle. Janus had said that demons love riddles. Talon had taught him so many . . . maybe that would distract her just enough.

'What can cure but is no remedy, white as snow but melts it, invisible in water unless you taste it?'

'A riddle, Edgy? Oh, I love riddles! Have you found out the answer to mine yet? It would fascinate you.' Salomé still bent towards him as if she were playing with a toddler, hands on her knees.

'What's the answer to *mine*? Or is it too hard for you?' Edgy taunted, taking a step closer.

'Hmmm.' Salomé tilted her head and put a gloved hand to her dainty chin. 'It can cure but isn't a remedy? Cure must mean to preserve, like a ham.' Her face was close, Edgy could smell her perfume. 'It's white and melts snow and you can taste it. Of course I know! It's s—'

Edgy didn't let her finish but lashed out his fist and gave her a faceful of the answer.

'Damn your black heart, Edgy Taylor!' Salomé screamed, throwing her hands to her eyes.

Edgy turned and ran, not waiting to see how much damage he'd inflicted. He hurtled up the street, fear powering him along. Faces blurred as he flew past countless gentlemen and ladies. The cries of the street sellers flew by as he dodged and weaved among the crowd, desperately trying not to look back.

Finally, he slowed. It seemed safe. Henry's sides heaved as he looked up, his tongue dangling from his mouth, puffing hot breath like a steam engine.

'I know,' Edgy sighed, sitting down on a shop door-step and stroking Henry's ear. Henry was right to feel nervous. It seemed that Salomé could find him whenever she wanted. The demons would soon be on his trail again and he couldn't escape them. 'I 'ate to admit it but we're stuck, good an' proper.' Edgy looked up. His stomach tightened. 'An' it looks like we've got company again.'

Grinning with anticipation, the two demons pushed

their way through the pedestrians towards Edgy. Edgy sat, all his energy spent, and watched as they advanced. With a grimace, he pulled himself up, clinging to the frame of the shop window as the world began to spin.

THE ELFIN KNIGHT SITS ON YON HILL,
BLOWING HIS HORN LOUD AND SHRILL.
'I LOVE TO HEAR THAT HORN BLOW;
I WISH HIM HERE THAT OWNS IT AND ALL.'
THAT WORD IT WAS NO SOONER SPOKEN,
THAN ELFIN KNIGHT IN HER ARMS WAS GOTTEN.
'YOU MUST MAKE TO ME A SHIRT,
WITHOUT THREAD, SHEARS OR NEEDLEWORK.'

'THE ELFIN KNIGHT', TRADITIONAL FOLK BALLAD

CHAPTER TEN
A DECISION

Henry's shrill bark echoed in Edgy's ears. Sharp talons dug into his shoulder and he felt himself being dragged to his feet. The crowds in the street bustled by, oblivious to the demons.

'Take him,' hissed a demonic voice. Edgy couldn't distinguish between the two demons. Their twisted faces swam before him, merging, leering, gnashing their razor teeth. The flames flickered on their brows, dancing as if in victory.

'Our names will be forever on the lips of Lord Moloch,' said the other, 'if this is the child –'

A muffled thud cut the demon's sentence short. Edgy blinked, shaking the stars from his dazed eyes. The demon stood before him still gripping him by the shoulder of his jacket, but a puzzled frown creased its pock-marked brow as it wiped grey sludge from its upper arm. The creature's eyes widened in horror as the grey stain spread up its neck. Edgy tried to pull away but the demon's grip on his coat tightened. Gradually it froze, the demon's eyes becoming marbled, then lifeless and blank.

A second bang sounded in the street. Glancing left, Edgy watched as the second demon writhed, trying to escape the dirty snowball that splattered wetly on to its back. Little by little, its movements died down to a slow dance, then it too froze altogether. A statue.

Edgy hung by his coat, half suspended from the ossified demon's closed fist. He wriggled to get free but the jacket was pinched tight around his armpit. The demon statue rocked on its heels, threatening to fall forward and crush Edgy. One or two passers-by began to stop and stare, open-mouthed, at the spectacle that had appeared before them.

'Just popped outta thin air,' shrieked a flower girl, craning her neck at Edgy as he tugged at the trapped fabric of his jacket. 'It's a blimmin' miracle.'

'Garn! Some kind o' trick,' sneered a passing street cleaner, leaning on his brush and spitting into the gutter. 'Chuck 'im a coin.'

The growing crowd parted and Janus appeared, placing the smoking ossifier back into his waistcoat pocket.

'Now you have to decide, Edgy Taylor,' he said, sawing furiously at the shoulder of his coat with a penknife, 'what you're going to do. You've put me to a lot of inconvenience today, not to mention a small amount of personal danger. It wasn't easy tracking these demons down, you know.'

The thick material gave way with a ripping sound and

the statue keeled backwards, shattering into pieces on the unforgiving cobbles. Edgy flinched.

'I-I'm sorry, Mr Janus,' Edgy stammered. His head swam and his thoughts jumbled up on top of each other.

'Apology accepted, lad, though what the governors will make of three ossifications in two days, I don't know.' Janus shook his head and pursed his lips for a second. Then he snapped his head up and fixed Edgy with a flinty glare. 'Now what's it to be? Are you going to take your chances here on the streets? Or are you willing to come back to the Society and work for us? I need your skills, Edgy.'

'Work for you?' Edgy asked, his jaw sagging. 'Y'mean like a job?'

'Exactly,' said Janus, pocketing his knife. 'Your abilities would be invaluable to the Society and you've proved yourself to be fast and resourceful, if a little headstrong. I was going to offer the position to you this morning but you waltzed off – and ruined a perfectly good jacket. What do you think?'

Edgy didn't get a chance to reply. The third and final demon sprang up from behind Janus. Its long, warty fingers closed around his neck and yanked him off the ground, sending the penknife and ossifier clattering from his pockets to the ground.

'I'll wring this devious old buzzard's neck, then rip your heart out,' it sniggered.

A tall gent stepped forward to challenge what he saw as a large ruffian taking hold of an old man. The demon swatted him away with its free hand as if he were a fly.

Edgy lunged forward and snatched up the ossifier. It felt clumsy and alien in his hands, like a collapsed telescope. He wracked his brains. *How did Mr Janus open it? Which way does it point?*

Janus made a gargling sound.

Edgy tugged at the tube and it opened with a metallic click.

A trickle of blood oozed from Janus's mouth.

Edgy aimed the tube and a cord tumbled from the back. *Did Mr Janus pull this?*

The professor's face bulged blue as he kicked feebly for his freedom.

Edgy yanked at the cord and the ossifier produced a bang, winding Edgy and sending him stumbling back, away from Janus.

The grey sludgeball whirled through the air. For a moment, Edgy feared he had missed as the ball arced left but the demon was huge and still in its path. It splattered on its shoulder. Janus's eyes widened as he realised what was happening. Edgy ran forward. If the demon ossified with that grip then Janus would surely die. If he could break the grip, all might not be lost.

Edgy pressed down on the demon's greying thumb. Its eyes grew milky as life ebbed away. He could feel the stoniness creaking up its arm through its wrist. The creature slackened its grip slightly as it solidified and Edgy pulled at the fingers. Janus slumped to the ground, blood rushing to his face.

The demon stood, arm extended, solid. Stone.

Edgy crouched down. 'Come on, Mr Janus, don't die,' he muttered, cradling him and slapping his cheek.

Janus coughed and spluttered, spraying Edgy as his eyes flicked open. He struggled to his feet, propped up by Edgy.

'That was close, Mr Taylor,' he said, his voice hoarse. 'You need some target practice with the ossifier but thank you. You saved my life.'

'We're evens, then. You saved my life, I saved yours,' Edgy said, extending his hand. Janus shook it weakly and nodded. 'Now that it's up to me if I stay or go, I'd like to accept that job if it's still on offer?'

Once more, Edgy lay on the rough bed in Sally's room. Something had changed when he had saved Janus's life. He didn't feel trapped now. The demons outside had gone but Janus had given Edgy the impression that the danger was far from over.

'This woman you told me about,' Janus had said as he limped back to the Society. 'The demons called her Salomé?'

'They did, sir,' Edgy replied. 'They bowed to her. Is she really the Demon Queen?'

'She is,' Janus had said, his voice barely a whisper. 'Things are shaping up, Edgy. Rumours abound among my demon sources. They say she seeks the corpse of Moloch. She already has the heart. Think of the havoc she could wreak if heart and body were reunited.'

A prickle of dread had run up Edgy's spine. 'What do we do, Mr Janus?'

'We find Moloch's body first,' Janus said, then frowned and chewed his lip. 'But do me a favour: don't mention Salomé to anyone. The governors won't believe us until I have proper evidence and we don't want anyone questioning your sanity again, do we?'

Edgy shook his head. 'No, I've had enough of people doin' that.'

Now Edgy rolled over on his bed and sighed. He had never been praised before. No one had ever told him he was useful and now Janus thought he was needed to stop Salomé from destroying the world. Maybe the Society could become his family, like it had Trimdon's. Edgy smiled. *I won't let Mr Janus down.*

He flicked through *A Demon a Day*, trying to find any reference to Moloch. However, the book was being obstinate. Every time he turned a page, it seemed to be the same story. With a sigh, Edgy rolled on to his stomach, flattened the page and began to read.

The Hunt

In the early days, when the blue-green world was fresh and sparkled in the morning sun, Satan wandered among the forests, whistling and planning his next outrage against the Lord.

As he stood in a glade dappled with sunlight, the sound of baying dogs shattered his thoughts. A wild boar burst out of the undergrowth beside him and fled through the trees. Soon the bark and howl of the pack grew nearer. Satan's eyes glowed. There was bloodlust and excitement in that sound and in the bellow of the human voices urging them on.

A pack of hounds surged into the glade, filling it as the sea drowns a rockpool. They leapt around Satan, almost knocking him off his feet. He laughed and stroked the lashing tails as they swished past him.

Three men in furs came close behind. They held spears, sharp and pointed.

'Forgive my dogs, sir,' said the tallest and strongest looking of the men. 'They did not see you in their excitement.'

'You are gracious.' Satan nodded. 'I would have cursed anyone who dragged my dogs from the scent.'

The man merely nodded and smiled back. 'It is wise to befriend strangers, for sometimes they prove to be devils or angels in disguise. Join us in our hunt, sir, and share the spoils.'

So Satan joined the hunt and after many hours of scrabbling through bushes, clambering over rocks and splashing across streams, they cornered the boar in a narrow ravine deep in the forest. The beast's sides heaved for breath. Blood streamed down its sides and matted its fur. The men's eyes glittered dark and deep. They held their spears as steadily as they could.

And Satan watched in envy.

The men closed in as the boar snorted and stamped the ground ready to charge.

Satan knew why this was exciting.

With a last roar of rage, the boar hurled itself forward. The men stood firm, hurling their spears.

They could die, Satan thought. *That's what makes this exciting. They have a game. They have danger.* He himself – a creature of light and flame – could never die. Nothing could hurt him.

That night Satan sat at their campfire and shared their meat but it tasted like ash in his mouth. How could he enjoy anything again? For him, everything was so easily gained. To these men, every moment was precious because it could be taken away in a second by the turn of a stag's antler or a stumble of their horse. That's what made life sweet.

He took the hunter's dagger and held it above the flame.

'I swear that whoever uses this dagger against me shall find that it can take my life,' he declared and handed it back to the hunter. 'But whosoever kills me will also die.'

'I will guard it,' said the hunter, staring wide-eyed at the stranger at his campfire. 'I shall keep this dagger a secret. None shall take arms against you, sir.'

'Oh they will,' muttered Satan, glancing around at the hunter's men. Some glanced down, unable to meet his gaze. 'For men talk. Men boast. Rumours spread. And there will be those who seek the Devil's Dagger. Those who would gladly die to slay me. Whether for fame and glory or for their weakling God, they will seek that dagger and seek to kill me. That dagger will bring misery to every generation of your family unless you throw it away. For men brag. And none will brag more than those who have supped with the great Satan and lived to tell the tale!'

And with that, he leapt up and ran into the night. Suddenly, Satan felt alive again. Excited. He was mortal – slightly. What a game was this! He could be killed and that made everything sweet.

Edgy frowned. What did this have to do with anything? He turned the book over in his hands. Its cover glittered in the ruddy light. Snakeskin.

A banging at Edgy's door made Henry bark. Edgy leapt off the bed and swung the door open to be greeted by Sally, pale and serious, arms folded, her head to one side.

'Look, if it's about this room –' Edgy began.

'Never mind that,' Sally muttered, giving a cruel grin through clenched teeth. 'You're to come with me. The governors want to see you and it's trouble. I reckon I'll have me room back within the hour.'

ALL SAINT WITHOUT, ALL DEVIL WITHIN.

TRADITIONAL PROVERB

CHAPTER ELEVEN
THE GOVERNORS

Edgy followed Sally through the silent corridors. Stuffy portraits stared out from the shadows. Henry kept at Edgy's heel, his ears back, glaring at Sally as she stalked ahead of them. One portrait caught Edgy's eye. It was filled by a portly-looking gentleman with serious eyebrows and a black fur cloak. The shadows seemed to swirl behind him, shifting somehow as if something lurked there.

Sally glanced back. 'Don't gawp at them,' she snapped. 'There's trapped demons in them paintings. Look too hard and the creature inside might leap out and drag you in.'

'Blimey,' Edgy said and threw his eyes to the floor. He fell quiet for a while, trying not to look at anything.

'Oh yeah.' Sally gave a bitter laugh. 'Full o' surprises is the old Society of Daemonologie, I should know. Some charmin' customers walked these corridors in days gone by, I can tell you.'

Edgy's stomach turned over. *What are these governors like? What are they going to do?*

They stopped at yet another oak-panelled door. Edgy had lost track of the twists and turns of the passages.

Sally drew a breath and knocked twice. A muffled voice bid them enter. Edgy sat Henry down outside and went in.

The governors sat around a long, polished table laden with food. Three men and one woman. He recognised Sokket from their encounter in the exhibition hall, sitting there pulling a sour face at a bunch of grapes. The others were murmuring to Janus, who stood in front of the table. More portraits dotted the panelled walls of this grand room. A large one hung over the glowing fireplace. The sober features of James I stared down at him.

'The boy, Lord Mauldeth,' Sally said to the tall, dark gentleman at the centre of the table. She gave Edgy a sharp shove, making him stumble.

'Thank you, Sally,' Lord Mauldeth said, looking down his long nose at Edgy. A cat sat on Mauldeth's lap, as haughty as the lord. 'Now, boy, tell us your name.'

'His name's Edgy Taylor –' Janus began but a fat, red-faced man sitting next to Mauldeth cut him off.

'Can't he speak for himself, Envry?' the man bellowed, huffing and puffing. 'He's got a voice, what?'

'Very well, Plumphrey.' Janus inclined his head but Edgy could see flashes of red on his cheeks.

'My name's Edgy Taylor, sir,' he said, his voice sounding

dry and squeaky. He felt stupid and small in front of these grand people. Maybe Talon was right and picking up dog dirt off the street was all he was good for. He twitched his head.

'Can't you keep still, boy?' Mauldeth said, as he scratched the cat behind its ears.

'No, sir. Sorry, sir. It's just something I do,' Edgy said, avoiding Mauldeth's gaze. Edgy didn't like him already.

'Probably brought cholera in with him off the street,' grumbled Sokket, heaving a huge sigh. 'Or some other malady. Wouldn't be surprised if we're all dead by dawn.'

'Don't be so melodramatic, Mortesque,' said the lady next to him.

She easily filled her end of the table, looking taller and wider than any of the men in the room. Her wiry brown hair stuck out in all directions, a wild curly mass that she had obviously tried but failed to contain with pins and bands. She struck Edgy as being brown in every way – brown eyes, brown skin, brown tweed clothes. She reminded him of a huge tree.

'Don't worry, Edgy. We're pleased to meet you,' she said. 'I'm sure Envry has a very good reason for ossifying three demons and bringing you into our midst.'

'He always does, Professor Milberry,' Plumphrey said, slapping the table, his moustache bristling. 'That's the trouble!'

'Yes, little brother, do tell us.' Lord Mauldeth's sharp features twisted into a smirk. He snapped a biscuit in half. 'Why did you compromise the security of the Royal Society so flagrantly?'

'I believe the boy may be useful,' Janus said, ignoring Mauldeth's accusation. His neck was red too now, Edgy noticed.

'Hmmph,' snorted Sokket. 'You said that about the last one and look what happened to him –'

'Bernard.' Milberry's brow creased into concerned furrows.

'What?' asked Sokket, obviously confused.

'He had a name,' Milberry snapped back. 'Bernard Green.'

Edgy's stomach churned again as he thought of the boy crumpled in the mud of the street. *Bernard Green.*

'Yes, well. A simple case of carelessness crossing the street,' Janus said, shaking his head. 'That wasn't my fault.'

'No, it never is,' Sokket muttered, 'but someone always ends up dead, don't they?'

'That's not fair,' Janus said.

The room fell silent for a second. Edgy tried to swallow but his throat felt so dry that he ended up coughing and spluttering.

'And then there's the budget,' Plumphrey said, sitting back heavily in his chair and making Edgy jump. 'We'll have to pay for the last one's funeral, y'know. And then can we afford to feed another mouth? Do you realise the size of the food bill for this month alone?'

'Yes, well, if you insist on collecting demons of gluttony,

then we will be eaten out of house and home, won't we?'
Janus said. His whole face glowed red now. 'You only
collect them because it's so easy. All you do is invite them
to a slap-up meal and then clap the irons on them!'

'How dare you?!' Plumphrey roared, jumping to his feet
and knocking his chair backwards. The cat leapt from
Mauldeth's lap. Sokket just shook his head and threw the
grapes down in disgust.

'Gentlemen.' Milberry held up her hands, casting a
shadow over Plumphrey. 'We should conduct ourselves
as fellows of the Royal Society. This is not some public
house to brawl in.'

'Apologies, Anawald,' Plumphrey coughed. 'But he's
always mocking my collection.'

'Envry.' Milberry raised her eyebrows at Janus. 'You
said the boy might be useful. Tell us how.'

'Yes.' Janus straightened his waistcoat down and gave
an embarrassed cough. 'I found the boy, having tracked
down Thammuz, Scourge of the Innocents, captain of
twelve demon legions.'

Edgy frowned at Janus. He'd never heard Talon
described in that way.

'We are aware of Thammuz's status,' Mauldeth cut in,
picking up a glass of port. 'The boy was with him?'

'He was,' Janus said, 'and – what's more – Edgy has
demon sight.'

Edgy stared, blank-faced, at the panel of governors who
leaned forward as one and raised their eyebrows at him as
if they'd been told he could juggle live canaries.

'So you can see demons, can you, boy?' Plumphrey asked, twisting his moustache.

'I think so, sir.' Edgy's voice sounded croaky again.

'Can you see *all* demons?' Mauldeth said, rotating his glass and staring at it through the candlelight.

'Well, I could see Mr Talon, the one you called Tha . . . mmuz, all red like and with horns. He'd get proper angry and beat me, you see, sir.'

'Well, well, a demon with a bit of respect for discipline at last.' Mauldeth grinned.

Edgy didn't see anything funny. He looked away from Lord Mauldeth, trying to ignore the sting of tears in the corner of his eye.

'And the ones that chased me,' Edgy said, coughing roughly. 'I could see them quite plain, sir.'

'Ah, yes, Janus ossified them too.' Mauldeth raised an eyebrow at his brother.

'One thing at a time, Mauldeth. How do you think he's come by this talent, then, Envry?' Sokket's codfish mouth drooped as he sniffed in Edgy's direction.

'I don't know yet.' Janus shrugged. 'He's not a demon himself, so far as I can tell.'

Almost in unison, the panel donned the red-lensed spectacles that Edgy had seen Janus wear earlier. They stared hard, looking him up and down. He coughed and looked at the floor, trying not to meet their gaze.

'These are Hades Lenses, Edgy,' Milberry explained, smiling and lifting her spectacles so he could see her warm brown eyes. 'Some demons disguise themselves as humans

– well, as all kinds of things really, cats and goats, even teapots and saucepans. The lenses can see through most glamour spells that demons use. We don't need them inside the Society as most demons reveal their true nature to us here but outside it's a different matter.'

'He doesn't look like a demon,' Plumphrey muttered, pulling off his specs.

'*Are* you a demon?' Sokket leaned over the table and squinted through the lenses at Edgy.

'No!' Edgy snapped. 'Erm, no, sir, I'm not.'

'He says he used to help Thammuz solve riddles too,' Janus said, nodding and pointing a finger in the air.

'Good at riddles, eh, lad?' Mauldeth sneered. He raised one eyebrow and smiled triumphantly. 'Tell me then, what is as ancient as the earth but only one month old?' He sat back in his chair, looking sidelong at his fellow governors with a self-satisfied grin.

'The moon, sir. Beggin' your pardon, sir,' Edgy muttered. He felt awful answering so quickly but it was an old riddle and simple really.

Mauldeth's neck went red this time and Janus beamed at his brother's discomfort.

'He has you there, Mauldeth,' Plumphrey chortled. 'How do you do that, lad?'

'I don't know, sir. Tal . . . Thammuz taught me to riddle as a nipper, sir.'

'Riddles are the basic currency of demons, Edgy. They greet, trick and challenge each other with them, trade with them, all kinds of things. Demons love complexity and challenges. It is said that a demon can never resist a riddle,' Milberry said, noticing Edgy's confused expression and taking pity on him. 'Being good at riddles is a must when dealing with demons.'

'Either that or being a good shot with an ossifier, eh, little brother?' Mauldeth said, sipping at his port and shooting a barbed smirk at Janus. 'Four in two days. It's getting to be like old times.'

'I had no choice.' Janus gave Edgy a meaningful glance. 'I had to ossify them.'

'You *had* to?' Milberry asked, narrowing her eyes.

'They were threatening the boy,' Janus said. 'I suspect they would have killed him.'

'You know we only use ossification as a last resort, Envry.' Milberry looked stern. 'How can we encourage more associate demons if you go around killing them?'

'One almost killed me,' Janus said quietly. 'If it wasn't for Edgy, it would have.'

'So the boy saved your bacon, eh?' Mauldeth said, regaining some of his composure.

Edgy could see Janus's jaw muscles tighten as he bit back a retort.

'Well, I for one would be happy to see more of these blasted creatures turned to stone,' Plumphrey muttered, breaking the tension. 'I remember Thammuz. Very fond of sending plagues of buttock boils to make people miserable.'

'Could he do that?' Sokket went a lighter shade of grey.

'He's nothing more than a stone gargoyle now,

Mortesque.' Mauldeth shook his head. 'Your buttocks are safe . . . from him, anyway.'

Sokket shuffled in his seat and glanced sideways at Plumphrey. 'It's just that, well, remember the curse of the whistling flatulence back in thirty-two? Most embarrassing . . . and inconvenient.'

'Lasted a month.' Plumphrey's red face faded to a mild pink and a haunted look came into his eye. 'The shame . . .'

'You think we can use the boy?' Milberry gave Janus a hard stare.

'Think of it: he could detect demons without them knowing. They get wise to the Hades Lenses. One sniff of a pair of red spectacles and they're off!' Janus said. 'And he's a sharp wit with the riddles.'

'But the budget –' Plumphrey began.

'Give over, Roland,' Mauldeth yawned, filling his glass again. 'We're rolling in cash – hardly anybody in the government even knows we exist.'

'But if there was an audit?'

'When was the last one?' Milberry cut in.

'Not sure, really,' Plumphrey said, glancing around the room and shuffling through some dusty old documents in front of him. 'Ah, here we are . . . 1703,' he said, drumming his fingers on the table.

'Go on then, Envry.' Mauldeth raised his glass to Edgy. 'Have your servant boy. All agreed?'

'But try to avoid any more ossifications,' Milberry said. 'We simply must get away from our past reputation.

We are scientists, observers and recorders – not demon hunters.'

The panel grunted and murmured in a fairly positive way. Janus nodded, grabbed Edgy's elbow and steered him out of the door.

'Shouldn't we record it in the minutes?' he heard Plumphrey say.

'When were the minutes last taken, Roland?' Sokket asked with a weary roll of his eyes.

'Oh, er, 1705 . . .'

A smirk crept across Edgy's face.

'Try to keep him alive this time, Envry, there's a good chap,' Sokket called after them.

Edgy's smile faded.

Trotting after Janus seemed to be becoming a habit. Edgy looked down at Henry, beginning to understand how he must feel as Janus stamped down the corridor.

'Well, that went better than I expected,' he said over his shoulder. 'But did you hear the pompous oaf?' Janus put on a nasal drawl that sounded surprisingly like his elder brother. '*Have your servant boy.* You see why I don't tell them my concerns about Salomé, Edgy? They wouldn't understand. I was so pleased when you guessed his riddle right off. Ha! That put his nose out of joint!'

'Just doin' what comes natural, sir,' Edgy said, blushing with pride. Mauldeth deserved the humiliation, he thought. Janus was right. Mauldeth was a snob. At least Janus treated Edgy with some respect.

'Good man.' Janus grinned over his shoulder. 'Right,

get some rest and report to me first thing tomorrow. You're now officially an employee of the Royal Society of Daemonologie! And our first mission is to find out where the corpse of Moloch lies.'

O, WHERE ARE YOU GOING TO?
I AM GOING TO MY SCHOOL.

O WHAT ARE YOU GOING THERE FOR?
FOR TO LEARN THE WORD OF GOD.

I WISH YOU WAS ON THE SANDS.
YES, AND A GOOD STAFF IN MY HANDS.

I THINK I HEAR A BELL.
YES, AND IT'S RINGING YOU TO HELL.

'FALSE KNIGHT ON THE ROAD', TRADITIONAL FOLK BALLAD

CHAPTER TWELVE
THE FIRST ERRAND

'Thought you weren't coming back,' Sally muttered, standing by the door to his room one morning. For all her saying she wasn't a ghost, Sally did a grand job of haunting Edgy's bedroom.

'Yeah, well, it's not that bad, is it?' Edgy snapped, barging past her. 'Three good meals a day, indoor work an' clean clothes. An' I don't have to do anythin' more dangerous than climb a ladder to get a heavy book from a high shelf.'

'That's what *he* said too,' Sally hissed.

Edgy froze as he closed the door. He could feel the cold draught of her gaze. 'Who?'

'Bernard,' Sally whispered. 'Thought it was all beer an' skittles until he got his skull caved in . . .'

Edgy twitched. 'That won't happen to me,' he croaked, trying to sound brave.

*

Although he'd been there less than a week, Edgy already had a rough idea of the layout of the upper floors of the Society. By day, he kept busy, carrying books for Janus and cleaning his study, and the fellows sent him scurrying about the passages with memorandums and letters. By night, he would sit beside Janus as he pored over ancient manuscripts, searching for any clue as to the whereabouts of Moloch.

'Take this to Professor Plumphrey and be quick about it,' Mauldeth would snap. He glowered at Edgy whenever they met and, to make matters worse, Henry was banned from Mauldeth's quarters because of the chancellor's bad-tempered cat.

'Tell Trimdon that I need more roast chicken,' Plumphrey would bluster, barely acknowledging Edgy, while Sokket would just stare at him or leave notes as if he couldn't bring himself to actually talk to him.

Milberry was different, though. While the other fellows' rooms – and even Janus's study – were dull, with leather seats and book-lined walls, her office teemed with all manner of plants and flowers. It was like a small forest. Vines tumbled from pots on shelves, huge palms sprouted from massive vases. Small finches even flitted among the branches of some of the larger specimens, and in the centre of all this sat Professor Anawald Milberry.

She had been writing at her desk when Edgy first entered the room. She stopped and smiled at him. Edgy smiled back.

'And how are you settling in?' she said, taking the memorandum from Edgy.

'Fine, ma'am,' he replied, glancing around at the thick foliage that filled the room. Had he just seen a pair of emerald eyes glaring out from one of the bushes to his left?

'Don't worry, Edgy,' Milberry smiled, running her stubby fingers through her brown wiry hair. 'The demons I collect are friendly on the whole. They're nature spirits. Quite harmless unless provoked.'

'Right, ma'am,' Edgy nodded. He wasn't convinced. Looking more closely, he could see that some of the plant specimens actually had eyes and mouths deep within their foliage.

'They're my family,' she said, picking up a watering can and pouring its contents into the nearest plant pot. She turned and frowned, looking at Edgy with kindly concern. 'Do you have any family, Edgy Taylor?' she asked.

'No, ma'am,' he said, scraping the toe of his boot on the tiled floor. He looked up. 'Have you, ma'am?' He flinched. The question had just come out. He hadn't meant to ask. She would think him so impertinent.

Milberry gave a sigh and a shrug. 'Only these,' she said, waving her hands at the plants that surrounded her.

'I'm sorry, ma'am. I shouldn't have asked,' Edgy said, blushing under her gentle gaze.

Her face crinkled into a kind smile. 'Not to worry, young man, you and I are in the same boat, it would seem. We can look after each other,' she said. Her expression became serious. 'So tell me, have you been out yet?'

Edgy frowned. 'No, ma'am.'

'Well, just take care when you do,' she said, with a look of concern. 'Don't get drawn into any of his mad schemes . . .'

'No, ma'am,' Edgy said, backing out of the room.

Janus had shown Edgy nothing but kindness since he'd taken him in. Only yesterday, he'd spent a whole morning showing Edgy the exhibition hall in more detail, telling him stories of arch-demons and sprites, of angels and devils. Spinorix had followed them around, eyeing Edgy at first but his cold stare seemed to thaw as Edgy's interest became apparent. And Edgy *was* becoming more interested.

'It's a fascinating world, Edgy,' Janus said, his eyes gleaming. 'There's more to discover than we ever can and stranger things than we can imagine.'

'D'you think I'll be able to make a discovery one day, Mr Janus?' Edgy asked, his heart pounding with excitement.

'If I have anything to do with it, young man.' He nodded, patting Edgy's back. 'You'll be at the heart of the greatest discovery yet.'

Two weeks later, Janus summoned Edgy to the entrance hall on an errand. Edgy hurried up there to find Janus pacing back and forth by Slouch's sofa. Slouch's feet poked up over the arms of the chair. Loud snoring echoed around the hall.

'Now, keep your wits about you,' Janus said, rummaging in his jacket pocket. 'I have a letter here. I want you to take it to a business associate of mine.'

'Right, sir.' Edgy swallowed hard.

Outside. Janus was asking him to venture outside, where Salomé and the Cult of Moloch were. He glanced down at the address.

Evenyule Scrabsnitch
The Emporium of Archaic Antiquities
13 Jesmond Street, London

Evenyule Scrabsnitch? What kind of a name is that?

'Is it safe, sir?' Edgy gulped.

'You don't need me to tell you that it mightn't be a straightforward task. You know that not everyone is well disposed towards the Royal Society. You might meet a bit of . . . mischief on your way. But you've proved yourself to be resourceful and quick on your feet.'

Edgy gave a brittle grin. 'Don't worry, Mr Janus, I can handle meself in the streets.'

'I know you can, Edgy, but if you meet Salomé again . . .' Janus's voice dropped to a near whisper '. . . then run. Run for all you're worth and don't let her see that letter.'

'No problem,' Edgy said, trying to sound casual, but he couldn't help shuddering. He felt the blood drain from his face.

Janus had spent long hours questioning Edgy about his encounter with Salomé. He wanted to know what she looked like. How she moved, spoke, laughed. How she dressed. What she said. Everything.

'You did well to escape her last time. She is a truly

crafty demon. We know what she wants and she might be curious about what we know.'

'I wouldn't give nothin' away, Mr Janus, trust me.'

'Don't even talk to her, Edgy, just throw your salt and run,' Janus continued, stuffing a small leather sack of salt into Edgy's hand.

'Righto, Mr Janus,' Edgy whispered, pushing the letter and pouch into his jacket pocket.

A gloomy silence hung over the dilapidated Eden Square. Edgy shivered at the bronze statue of Satan, its face contorted with rage. He looked at the letter again. The address would take him back over the river. He hadn't been north since the day Bernard died.

The busy streets soothed Edgy's nerves. Here he was one of many. Part of the crowd. Harder to pick out.

When he reached it, Jesmond Street buzzed with mid-morning activity. The busy throng of shoppers, beggars and costermongers squeezed past each other trying to keep safely away from the carriages and carts that clattered up and down the cobbles.

'The place is heavin',' Edgy muttered to Henry, side-stepping a portly gentleman who tutted and swished him away with his cane.

The shops stood proud and well kept. Edgy spotted a milliner's shop, all lace curtains and glossy, painted woodwork, and a tailor's, dark and respectable. Halfway up the street, wedged between these buildings like a drunk at a temperance meeting, stood Scrabsnitch's Emporium of Archaic Antiquities.

'Blimey, Henry,' Edgy said. 'I dunno what sort of place this is, but it don't look very high class.'

Wooden planks shuttered the windows to Scrabsnitch's shop and pedestrians tiptoed through the shards of glass that littered the pavement. The place looked like someone had set about it with a sledgehammer. Edgy made his way to the door and pushed it inwards with a loud scrape followed by a tinny *ping* as the rusty bell announced his arrival. The inside of the shop looked no better. Edgy's feet crunched on more glass. He lifted Henry up and picked his way past wrecked display cabinets, smashed chairs and scattered, torn books.

'Hello?' he called. 'Mr Scrabsnitch?'

Cold metal pressed at the back of Edgy's neck. Circular. *The muzzle of a gun?*

'Don't move,' creaked an old voice behind him. 'This musket is loaded with silver. Sees off most supernatural types, I've found. Now, tell me who or what you are.'

CALL NOT THE DEVIL, HE WILL COME FAST ENOUGH UNBIDDEN.

TRADITIONAL PROVERB

CHAPTER THIRTEEN
EVENYULE SCRABSNITCH

'Mr Scrabsnitch?' Edgy said hoarsely, his whole body shaking and twitching.

'Who wants to know?' asked the voice behind him.

'My name's Edgy Taylor. I'm from the Royal Society of Daemonologie.'

'I've not met you before,' croaked the voice. 'Any proof?'

'I-I have a-a letter,' Edgy stuttered, desperately trying not to twitch too much in case the gun went off. 'It's in my jacket pocket, sir.'

As a hand snaked round Edgy's stomach and reached for his pocket, a growl rumbled in Henry's throat.

'Henry, no,' Edgy hissed, but Henry snapped at the hand.

With a yelp of pain, the hand was snatched back and Edgy heard a crash as whoever it was stumbled backwards. Flinching, Edgy turned to see who had been holding him at gunpoint.

Amidst the wreckage of a glass cabinet sat a thin-looking man. He wore a faded silk smoking jacket and carpet slippers. His hair billowed out from his head in wild grey wisps and he looked as devastated as the shop. A silver candlestick dangled from his free hand, the other was rammed firmly in his mouth, covering the bite.

'I'm sorry, sir,' Edgy muttered, eyeing the candlestick. 'Henry was just watchin' out for me.'

'No, no, it is you who must forgive me, young man,' he said with an air of slight embarrassment. He stared at Edgy with sad, droopy eyes. 'I am Evenyule Scrabsnitch. I was bluffing, as you can see, but I have to be cautious.' He shook life back into his bitten hand.

Edgy sighed with relief – Henry hadn't drawn blood.

Scrabsnitch continued, 'My emporium is usually a little unkempt, but not this bad. I've had some unwelcome visitors recently. Goes with my line of work.' He glanced around, looking for a suitable home for the candlestick he held, then shook his head and dropped it on the floor. 'It's taken me weeks even to get it back to this state. I think I may be getting too old for it all.'

Edgy spluttered on the dust that mushroomed up from the floor and handed Scrabsnitch the letter. Henry gave a low growl but Edgy held his muzzle.

Scrabsnitch looked down at the letter. 'So, you're the Mr Taylor that Envry Janus has been talking about.' His eyes twinkled over the top of the letter. 'I've heard good things about you, young man.'

'Oh, well,' Edgy said, casting his eyes down and hiding his blushes.

'You're a talented chap,' Scrabsnitch said. 'Tell me, can you see demons everywhere?'

'Most places, I reckon,' Edgy said. He felt uncomfortable talking about it. Until not long ago, he'd thought himself to be insane. 'But they don't seem to be everywhere.'

'Not as many of them as there were, I suppose.' Scrabsnitch's face drooped once more and he fell silent for a moment. Edgy wasn't quite sure what to say. Scrabsnitch snapped his attention back and said, 'Anyway, I believe you're a bit of a whizz at riddles too?'

'Mr Janus exaggerates,' Edgy smiled. 'It was just somethin' Talon, the, erm, demon I worked for, somethin' he insisted on.'

'Why, I wonder?' Scrabsnitch frowned thoughtfully. 'Was he preparing you for something, do you think?'

'I dunno, sir.' Edgy shrugged. 'He used to come back from the pub sometimes, quite uppity, like, wakin' me up an' demandin' the answer to a riddle he couldn't solve. Used to get a rare beatin' if I couldn't solve it.'

'You poor boy.' Scrabsnitch looked genuinely appalled. Edgy thought of Mauldeth's cynical retort at the governors' meeting. 'Which public house did he frequent?'

'The Green Man, it was, sir,' said Edgy. 'He owed the landlord Bill Fager a few bob, so I believe.'

'Who?' Scrabsnitch narrowed his eyes and peered at Edgy.

'Fager, Bill Fager,' Edgy said. 'He was always in debt to Bill. Never shut up about it. Why, sir?'

But Scrabsnitch had jumped up and was ransacking a tabletop full of junk. Eventually, he found a blank sheet of paper and began scribbling feverishly. 'I think Mr Janus might be interested in the name you just gave me, Edgy,' he murmured as he wrote. 'There is a rather powerful demon called Belphagor whom your employer might be eager to meet. Bill Fager, Belphagor? Quite a coincidence, don't you think?'

'Old Bill Fager, a demon?' Edgy mumbled as Scrabsnitch straightened up and handed him the hastily scribbled message. 'But I'd 'ave seen him, y'know, horns an' all that, wouldn't I?'

'There are demons and there are demons, Edgy,' Scrabsnitch said, raising his eyebrows. 'Some are more powerful than others. Maybe Belphagor's magic is stronger than most.'

'What would Mr Janus want with this Fager bloke?'

'It may just be part of the puzzle that Janus is trying to solve, Edgy. Now, the book he ordered.' Scrabsnitch turned and with surprising ease for a man his age clambered up a ladder that leaned against a bookshelf. 'A puzzle laced with danger ... *The Legends of Moloch*,' Scrabsnitch muttered. A hush fell over the room for a moment. Henry whined and Edgy shook himself.

'Begging your pardon, but why danger?' Edgy whispered, glancing around the wrecked shop as if eavesdroppers crouched behind every display cabinet.

'An arch-demon. A destroyer,' Scrabsnitch replied. 'Moloch is a demon of obsession and possession. He was the one demon who would wage total war on God, even though he knew it would end everything. Association with him seems to bring a certain compulsion and fanaticism. It's not by chance that the Cult of Moloch has so many adherents.' Scrabsnitch paused, staring through Edgy. Then he shook himself and said, 'I have the volume up here – fortunately it wasn't damaged.'

'Righto,' Edgy murmured, looking up at the old man and shielding his eyes from the dislodged dust.

'You tell Mr Janus to tread carefully,' Scrabsnitch said, heaving down a thick, leather-bound book and passing it to Edgy. 'Moloch can take hold of the wariest soul. And it is becoming something of a favourite topic for Mr Janus.'

'Well, forgive me for sayin' as much, sir, but I reckon Mr Janus, bein' a collector an' all, knows what he's doin',' Edgy said. A stab of annoyance made him twitch and shake his head. 'He's been good to me.'

Scrabsnitch paused, mulling over Edgy's words. 'Yes, I suppose you're right,' he said, nodding. He took the book and wrapped it in thick brown paper, then slid it into a sack. 'But I've met a few obsessives in my time. They never come to a good end.' The old man stared off into the darkened corners of the emporium.

Edgy shivered. 'Well, if you'll excuse me, sir,' he said, teasing the sack out of Scrabsnitch's fingers and slinging it over his shoulder. 'Mr Janus'll be keen to see me back.'

Scrabsnitch's eyes snapped back to Edgy, making him jump. 'Wait,' he hissed, pushing Edgy down behind a three-legged display cabinet. 'Someone's peering through

the window, hard to see through the grime . . . A woman
. . . dark hair . . .'

'Salomé,' Edgy gasped. 'Mr Scrabsnitch, I've got to
hide!'

'Salomé?' he said, his eyes widening.

'I've no time to explain,' Edgy said. 'But she seems to
be after me.'

'The back door,' Scrabsnitch said.

'No, she'll be on to me like a flash,' Edgy muttered,
remembering the chase in the alleyways.

'Upwards then,' Scrabsnitch snapped, looking to the
ceiling.

'But Henry –' Edgy began.

'Put him in the sack with the book,' Scrabsnitch said,
guiding Edgy across the shop to a side door. 'Go up the
stairs to the attic. You can make your way along the
rooftops there – it may just give you a head start.'

With a shove, Scrabsnitch sent Edgy staggering
through the door and up the first few steps. As the door
shut behind Edgy, he heard the muffled tinkling of the
bell and started up the stairs as fast and as silently as he
could.

Edgy didn't have time to take in his surroundings as
he hurried upwards. He had a vague impression of fusty
decay, worn carpets, peeling walls and then he was in
an attic room cluttered with more junk, packing cases,
stuffed animals and rusted suits of armour. He squeezed
through the room and bundled Henry into the sack before
lifting the groaning sash window and gasping at the cold

wind that slapped his face. Henry yelped and squirmed in
the sack as Edgy tied the top with some curtain cord and
secured it over his shoulder. He would need free hands
for this.

Edgy had seen some children on the rooftops last
year. They'd been thieving lead from church roofs and
had escaped from the peelers that way. Edgy had been
impressed and had imagined himself skipping across
narrow alleys and sliding down slick slates.

Now his head spun and his feet felt like they'd been
cemented on to the narrow brick causeways that ran
along the eaves of the buildings. Henry wriggled, making
the sack feel leaden and pulling Edgy in every direction.
He teetered on the edge of a grey slate roof. Something
gave way under his foot. A loose brick tumbled down
through the air below him. Edgy windmilled his arms,
bending double and straightening time and again.

And then he slipped.

With a yelp, Edgy slapped his hand out to catch hold
of the black line of the gutter. Fire seared up his shoulder
and he heard his knuckles crack as his descent jerked to a
halt. For a moment, Edgy dangled by one arm, dazed and
yelling in agony. The cord holding the sack and Henry cut
into his shoulder. He swung his other arm up and grasped
at the cast-iron gutter with both hands. It was cold, full of
moss and slime. How long could he hold on for?

'Edgy Taylor, what *are* you doing, you silly sausage?'
Salomé peered over the edge of the roof, leaning on
an umbrella. Her face split into a childish grin. 'You ran

away from me and that funny Mr Scrabsnitch tried to shoot me with a candlestick. What larks we're all having!' She hitched up her lemon-yellow skirts and squatted down close to him. 'I remember this rooftop being built. Oh, it must've been thirty, maybe even forty years ago.'

The cold metal gutter numbed Edgy's knuckles.

'The man who laid that brick – you know, the stone that fell from under your feet? He was a lazy, careless worker. I made sure of that.'

Edgy's breath grew ragged as his head fell forwards, crushing his own windpipe. His shoulder felt ablaze as he struggled to hold on. Salomé frowned and put her dainty finger to her red lip.

'Oh, and the man who fixed this gutter ran out of screws but couldn't be bothered going back down for more so he missed a few out.' Salomé's red lips pursed into a neat smile. 'I made sure of that.'

With a metallic groan, the brackets holding the gutter buckled, snapped and swung out away from the wall. Suddenly Edgy was dangling in mid air high above the ground. Sweat trickled down his back.

'Ooops.' Salomé's eyebrows rose in perfectly plucked arches, her mouth a round 'o' of pretend surprise. 'But the man who worked down there – the one who fitted the pointed iron railings directly beneath you – he was a God-fearing man. He did a good job.'

The street beneath Edgy swung to and fro as the gutter creaked and shifted again. The lines of the paving slabs, the edge of the road, the railings rocked and see-sawed.

The gutter sagged. Henry's weight in the sack dragged at him, burning his shoulder.

Salomé's face screwed into a hard scowl. 'You see what you're up against, little boy?' she hissed. 'Whole lifetimes of corner-cutting, settling for second best. All to serve me. That was a nasty trick, throwing salt in my face. I was very disappointed in you.'

Salomé beckoned with her finger and, as if it were alive, the gutter began to swing back to the wall of the building. Edgy lost his grip, slipping along the slimy iron-work towards the broken end of the gutter. Then his head hit the wall and, for a moment, all was darkness and weightlessness.

This is it, he thought. *I'm going to die.*

FAIR ELEANOR, SHE SAT STILL.
IT WASN'T LONG TILL SHE SAW
HER OWN DEAR SEVEN BRETHRENS
ALL WALLOWING IN THEIR OWN BLOOD.
FAIR ELEANOR, SHE SAT STILL.
SHE NEVER CHANGED A NOTE
TILL SHE SAW HER OWN FATHER'S HEAD
COME TUMBLING BY HER FOOT.

'EARL BRAND', TRADITIONAL FOLK BALLAD

CHAPTER FOURTEEN
CUTTING CORNERS

A sudden jerk opened Edgy's eyes.

Salomé had his waistcoat scrunched in her fist, her arm outstretched supporting him as though he were weightless. A button from his jacket vanished to the street below. Edgy heard it clink against the railings that speared up beneath him and felt sick.

'Wait,' he gasped. 'Wh-what clings tight to hand or nose, from toady slime it grows, as quick as it's here, it goes?'

'A riddle?' Salomé's eyes glowed a deeper green. Slowly she eased Edgy back on to the rooftop and dumped him flat on to the tiles. 'Oh, Edgy, you are naughty. You know I can't resist a riddle.'

'If you can't get it,' Edgy croaked, straightening up and sitting next to her on the roof's edge, 'you must let me go.'

'Oh, you are clever, Edgy Taylor,' Salomé smirked at

him. She dangled her booted feet over the edge of the
roof and kicked them like a child on a grown-up's chair.
'But I know it, you see. It's a wart. A wart clings to face or
hand and then one day it's just gone!'

Edgy's heart plummeted. He felt as though he were
falling all over again.

'Just give me the letter, silly,' Salomé giggled. She
leaned over and pulled out the letter from his pocket.
'That's twice you've lost to me. Have you solved my first
riddle yet?' Her eyebrows rose as she scanned the letter.
'Oh, I see. Mr Scrabsnitch suggests a revitalising pint of
ale at the Green Man Inn, does he? Fascinating.' She
carefully folded the letter and slid it back into Edgy's
pocket. 'What's Mr Janus going to think when you tell
him about our meeting?' She smoothed Edgy's hair and
whispered, 'You could lie. Say you managed to run away
or tell him you out-riddled me.'

'You mean,' Edgy said in a hoarse voice, 'you're gonna
let me go?'

Salomé laughed and wrinkled her nose. 'Of course
I am. You're the best fun I've had in centuries. I only
wanted to look at the letter. I could have tortured it
out of that old goat Scrabsnitch but where's the fun
in that? Just don't get too interested in Moloch – it's
not healthy.' She jumped to her feet and, putting her
hands behind her back, skipped up the roof. Edgy sat as
if cemented to the roof edge, slack-jawed, watching her
vanish over its apex.

*

It took Edgy a full hour and a half to clamber down from the rooftops. His feet seemed to slip with every move and each step was torture. His body ached with dangling from gutters and his clothes were covered in soot and bird muck from the slates. Shame burned in his gut like a furnace. He'd wanted to please Janus. How could he tell him that Salomé had taken the message from Scrabsnitch so easily? Henry tumbled from the sack with an indignant yelp and shook himself.

'Sorry, old friend,' Edgy said. Henry gave another shake and licked the back of his hand.

Edgy should have run from corner to corner, hiding behind fruit barrows and slipping into shop doorways. But what was the point? Salomé could kill him with the flick of her finger. A tall lady passed by, laughing out loud, making him flinch. Tears stung his eyes.

A grey rain pelted down on Edgy as he trudged across Eden Square and up the steps to the Society.

'Been busy?' Slouch muttered from his sofa as Edgy staggered into the hall, soaking and dishevelled.

'Yeah,' he muttered. 'How 'bout you?'

'Rushed off me feet,' Slouch yawned. He stopped and a frown slowly spread across his wrinkled brow. 'What's in the bag?'

Surprised, Edgy pulled the book from the sack and showed him *The Legends of Moloch*.

Slouch gave a shudder. 'Read *The Legend of Aldorath and Moloch*,' he said. 'It's my favourite bedtime story.'

Edgy grimaced, slumped on the floor and rested his

back against the sofa. The book fell open at the chapter
he wanted. Edgy began to read silently to himself.

'Not like that,' moaned Slouch from deep within the
sofa. 'Read it aloud. Like I said, it's my favourite.'

Heaving a sigh, Edgy began to read to the dozing demon.

The Legend of Aldorath and Moloch

Aldorath was a young demon who loved nothing more
than making mortals dissatisfied. It was all he lived for. He
was never happier than when whispering into a new bride's
ear, pointing out how her new husband snored so loudly at
night and belched at the dinner table. He revelled in making
young children dream of the toy their parents could never
afford. Any misery Aldorath could think of, any reason to
be miserable, he would whisper into mortal ears. As far as
he was concerned, life was good for him when it was not
satisfactory for mortals.

Then one day he woke from a particularly poor slumber.
He scratched his backside and belly as he wondered who
to discontent today.

And something strange happened.

As he stood thinking, an emptiness, a feeling that
something was missing, overcame him. Yes, he could
go down to the old woodcutter in the forest and make
him wish his son wasn't such an idiot. But what was the
point? Yes, he could visit the bakery and make the baker
raise his prices and put chalk in his flour so he could make
enough profit to buy a wig. But where was the challenge
in that? Was this all life had to offer?

Aldorath had made himself discontented and there was nothing he could do.

Or so he thought.

One day, as he sat on a tree stump, sighing, Satan chanced by.

'And what is your complaint, my fine demon fellow?' Satan asked.

'I'm fed up and bored,' said Aldorath, not recognising Satan, who never sat still long enough to have his portrait painted. 'I'm tired of making mortals discontented. I want a challenge!'

'Well, if it's a challenge you want,' laughed Satan, 'then a challenge you shall have.'

'Anything,' said Aldorath, 'if it will make me happy again.'

'Very well.' Satan gave a toothy grin. 'Somewhere in this blue-green world, I have hidden the body of Moloch. Find it. That is your challenge.'

'And what if I find it?' Aldorath asked, worried now because he'd realised who he was dealing with.

'You won't,' Satan said, raising his eyebrows at such a stupid question. 'I have hidden him well. You'll never find him.'

'Oh, won't I?' Aldorath loved a challenge as much as the next demon. 'But just supposing I did? What would you do then?'

'I'll probably skin the flesh from your body and scatter your bones across this blue-green world, so be sure you don't.' And with that, Satan vanished.

Aldorath pondered Satan's challenge. On the one hand, he couldn't resist such a quest. On the other, he could never win. Common sense told him to forget about it and carry on being discontented, but demons are weak creatures and victims of their own vices. After much anguishing and agonising, Aldorath decided to search for Moloch's body.

Long years passed and stretched into decades. Aldorath wandered the blue-green world hunting for the lost remains of the arch-demon Moloch. He swam among strange sightless fish in the blackest, deepest ocean ravines. He crawled and hacked his way through the thickest jungle floors.

But he didn't find Moloch.

Long decades past and stretched into centuries. Aldorath stumbled through blinding white blizzards, feeling his way with icy blue claws. He flew over mountain tops, soaring with eagles as he scanned remote passes and valleys.

At last, after many lifetimes of Man, he found the Demon Lord Moloch, though nobody knows where that was.

Satan was furious when he found out that Aldorath had found Moloch. He sent his fleetest demons to catch him, ordering, 'Stop him before he speaks to anyone and bring him to me. Tear out his tongue before he can speak to you or you will perish too.'

The demons flew faster than arrows and caught Aldorath, tearing out his tongue as they were commanded. Satan threw Aldorath into the deepest caverns of hell.

I'm doomed for sure, Aldorath thought to himself. *Satan doesn't want anyone to find Moloch, but I'll show him.*

And while Satan held him captive, Aldorath carved a map deep into his own flesh, into the very bone of his skull. A map showing where Moloch's body lay.

I can't tell anyone myself, thought Aldorath, *but one day someone will find my bones and then they will know.*

True to his word, Satan had Aldorath's flesh hacked from his body and scattered his bones across the blue-green world.

No one has found them to this day.

'Until Lord Mauldeth, that is,' Edgy muttered to himself, remembering Janus's outburst. He pictured the skeleton as he had seen it the other day, standing in the exhibition hall.

A perfect triangle cut out of its skull. Edgy's eyes widened as he realised. He dropped the book. A perfect triangle where the map would be. He rummaged in his pocket and pulled out the sliver of bone that the dying boy had given him. It was a perfect triangle and it had marks and squiggles on one side. Part of a map. The skull had a map on it. A map showing where the body of Moloch lay. Or at least part of it. He'd been carrying it all the time! The rest was carved into the top of the skull. All Edgy had to do was link the two together and they would have the location of Moloch's body. For a moment he sat there, imagining Janus patting him on the back. The thought was so sweet after his bitter humiliation at Salomé's hands.

Trembling, Edgy scrambled to his feet, but a blur of red rocketed into the entrance hall, knocking him back down.

'Spinorix!' Edgy snapped. 'What the 'ell are you playin' at?'

'I didn't know who to turn to . . . Mr Janus would tell the governors and Sally just laughed.' The imp's face was streaked with tears. He gripped his long red tail in his fists and twisted it like a dishcloth. 'It's happened again,' he sobbed.

'What has? What are you on about?'

'Something else has gone missing, Edgy.' Spinorix stared up at him with wide eyes. 'The skull of Aldorath. It's vanished and when Lord Mauldeth finds out, he'll ossify me!'

TRUE THOMAS LAY ON YON GRASSY BANK,
AND HE BEHELD A LADY GAY,
A LADY THAT WAS BRISK AND BOLD,
COME RIDING OVER THE FERNY BRAE.
TRUE THOMAS, HE TOOK OFF HIS HAT,
BOWED HIM LOW DOWN TILL HIS KNEE.
'ALL HAIL, THOU MIGHTY QUEEN OF HEAVEN!
FOR YOUR PEER ON EARTH I NEVER DID SEE.'
'O NO, O NO, TRUE THOMAS,' SHE SAYS.
'THAT NAME DOES NOT BELONG TO ME;
I AM BUT THE QUEEN OF FAIR ELFLAND,
AND I'M COME HERE FOR TO VISIT THEE.'

'THOMAS RHYMER', TRADITIONAL FOLK BALLAD

CHAPTER FIFTEEN
SUBTERFUGE

The great arched ceiling of the exhibition hall echoed with the sound of Spinorix sobbing. Edgy looked down at Henry, who looked back with furrowed brows. They stood before a perfect skeleton, the bones wired together into a standing position. Perfect but for the fact that its head was missing. Two strands of thick wire stuck out from the top of the spine where the head should sit.

'Well, it wasn't me who took it so yer can get that idea out of yer head,' Edgy said, giving a rough cough while Spinorix sat and bawled like a baby. Edgy noticed a hand-kerchief in his breast pocket and handed it to him.

'Thank you,' Spinorix sniffled and blew his long nose into the hanky. He seemed to blow for ages and then offered the slimy remnants back to Edgy.

'No, no, keep it,' he smiled, trying not to wrinkle up his nose. 'My pleasure.'

'I don't know what I'm going to do,' Spinorix sighed,

his eyes wide and expectant as if Edgy was going to jump up with a solution. Edgy stared back awkwardly.

'Look, Spin, you've got to pull yourself together,' Edgy said at last. 'Lord Mauldeth won't ossify yer.'

'He will,' he groaned. 'Or worse, he'll send me down to the boiler room and I'll stoke coal for eternity.'

'They have imps stoking up the boilers?' Edgy raised an eyebrow. No wonder it was so stuffy and warm all the time. Edgy could imagine imps zealously piling coal into the boilers down below as if they were stoking the furnaces of hell itself.

'Never mind that,' Spinorix wailed. 'Do you know how many decades it's taken me to work my way up to be curator of this collection? I hope Lord Mauldeth does ossify me – better that than the shovel!' The little imp threw himself down and beat his crimson fists on the tiled floor.

'How often does he come down here for a start?'

'What?' Spinorix stopped sobbing and stared up at Edgy.

'Well, does he come every day? Once a week? Will he notice, is what I'm askin' yer?'

'Will he notice?' Spinorix began wailing again. 'Of course he'll notice. He doesn't come down very often, but when he does, he'll see. I mean, you can't miss it. If it were a toe or a vertebra . . . But the head!'

Edgy gazed around the hall, desperately scanning the room for some inspiration. Finally, his eyes rested on a display cabinet full of horned skulls. He strode over and wrenched open the door.

'How about if we use one of these?'

Spinorix jumped to his feet, his eyes so wide Edgy could barely make out any of his other features. 'Use one of those?' he spluttered. 'Just slap another skull on top of the body of Aldorath? Just like that?'

'Yeah,' Edgy said. Henry whined, licking his lips as Edgy rocked the skull in his palms.

Spinorix groaned. 'It was bad enough when that horrible boy cut a hole in it . . .'

'What did Lord Mauldeth say about that?' Edgy said, thinking of the piece in his pocket.

Spinorix gave an embarrassed cough and twiddled his fingers. 'Well, you see, I hadn't quite plucked up the courage to tell him about that.'

'I reckon you have a choice,' Edgy said. 'You can go and tell Lord Mauldeth –'

'No,' Spinorix gasped. 'He'd never forgive me.'

'Well then, you can either leave it as it is and hope nobody notices or,' Edgy tossed the skull to Spinorix, who gave a shriek as he caught it, 'you can stick that on, which'll buy us more time to figure out who is nickin' all this stuff and get it back!'

Spinorix jumped up and down on the spot, the points of his ears wobbling. 'Oh, you mean you'll help me find them? Thank you so much! I knew it wasn't true what they said about you,' he gabbled, shaking Edgy's hand.

'Who? Said what?'

'Oh, I just heard Sally grumbling to Slouch, that's all.' Spinorix went a deeper shade of red, if that were possible.

'I didn't join in. Backbiting isn't my style.' He glanced away from Edgy's gaze. 'But she said you were just the sort to go waltzing off with someone else's head.'

'I bet she did,' Edgy said, rolling his eyes to the ceiling. 'What did Slouch say?'

'Not much,' Spinorix sniffed. 'Couldn't be bothered.'

'Right, let's get started,' Edgy said. 'We need to find the skull that will fit the best. An' we'll need a pen an' ink . . .'

It took longer than he'd hoped. Spinorix took ages rummaging around in drawers for a pen and once that was achieved, some of the skulls they selected wobbled on the wired spine and fell off. One clipped Spinorix's toe, making him curse and hop around the hall. Finally, Edgy stood back and admired the new head. Spinorix bobbed and weaved nervously around him, jumping up on his shoulder at one point to get a better view.

'There,' Edgy said, trying to keep his voice bright. 'Looks like the real thing to me.'

'How would you know?' Spinorix muttered. 'No one's going to be fooled by that scribble on the top of it.'

He did have a point. The skull they'd chosen was a little small for the body and Edgy's attempts at drawing a map on the top of the skull were smudged and clumsy.

'It's hard to draw on a curved surface,' he said, stiffening at the complaint. 'Anyway, it doesn't have to be perfect, just less obvious it's missing so we've got a bit of time.'

'And how are we going to catch the thief?' Spinorix's eyes glowed and he grabbed Edgy's sleeve. 'Have you worked it out?'

Edgy glanced at Henry, who cocked his head as if he wanted to know the answer too. Things had just got a bit more complicated. Edgy had imagined himself fixing the triangle of bone back into the skull and presenting it to Janus with a flourish. But now he had to find the skull first – and whoever had taken it. Edgy's eyes widened. *And if Mr Janus reads the book, he'll find out about the skull and want to see it!*

Before Edgy could speak, Janus came striding into the exhibition hall.

'Ah, there you are,' he said, ignoring Spinorix. 'Did you get my book?'

'The book?' Edgy twitched and nodded to the volume. He had set it on top of a display case right next to the bones of Aldorath.

'Yes, that's what I sent you for, wasn't it?' Janus said, peering at Edgy. 'Is something the matter? Did you have any trouble on your errand?'

'No, no,' Edgy lied. He couldn't stop Janus getting the book. 'It's there, sir. Sorry, I was goin' to bring it straight to you but Spinorix distracted me.'

Spinorix's knees buckled. He clasped his hands together and looked despairingly at the false skull. Janus seemed oblivious.

'Never mind, never mind,' he snapped, skipping over to the book and flicking through the pages. He clenched his fist and shook it triumphantly in the air. 'This is excellent. Excellent!'

'There was this too, sir,' Edgy said, pulling Scrabsnitch's message from his pocket.

Still staring at the book, Janus took the letter. Long seconds crept by. He was lost in *The Legends of Moloch*. Edgy stood, glancing sidelong at Spinorix, who just stared at the skull. Edgy gave him a swipe with his foot, making him yelp.

Janus looked up, startled, and gave a grin. 'This is superb news, Edgy,' he said, scanning the letter. 'I think we should pay a visit to the Green Man Inn tonight!'

'Righto,' Edgy said, giving a thin smile.

The story of Aldorath was halfway through the book. At least Janus wouldn't have time to read up to that point today. But it was only a matter of time. Edgy had to find the skull before then or Spinorix would be in deep trouble – and so would he.

SATAN COULDN'T GET ALONG WITHOUT PLENTY OF HELP.

TRADITIONAL PROVERB

CHAPTER SIXTEEN
THE GREEN MAN INN

The Green Man public house stood at the end of a narrow, twisting alley near the leather market. Tall warehouses flanked it, making it look like a drunk hanging from the shoulders of two friends. The roof sagged, the windows slanted. Everything looked as if it would slide into a stagnant heap at any moment. Dark shadows crossed and weaved across the grey of the pub's misted-up windows. A magic lantern show of drinkers and merrymakers. The murmurs, cheers and laughter rose and fell from inside.

Janus tapped his foot impatiently as he stood in the shop doorway opposite the pub.

'Scrabsnitch should be here by now,' he said, pulling a fob watch from his pocket and squinting at it.

'What're you goin' to do, Mr Janus?' Edgy said, huddled behind him, staring across the road at the glowing windows. He wished Henry was with him but Janus had insisted he stay at the Society. 'Are we going to try to capture Mr Fager? Will you ossify 'im?'

'Ideally, we'll just chat to him,' Janus muttered, tapping his watch. 'We don't have to ossify him. There are other ways, you know.' He rummaged in his pocket and pulled out a round pebble, blood red and pulsing with a gentle light.

Edgy stared, bewitched by the crimson glow. 'What is it, Mr Janus?'

'This is a demon pearl. If you throw it at the right moment, you can trap a demon inside it.'

'Inside?' Edgy said, his eyes widening. 'How's that possible, sir?'

'The pearls are collected from oysters that cling to the bottom of the marsh fed by the River Styx.' Janus rolled the pearl between his finger and thumb. 'The theory is that pearls are formed around impurities and demons are the ultimate impurity. Throw the pearl at a demon and it absorbs him. Once trapped inside the pearl, the demon is in debt to anyone who frees him.'

'But why,' Edgy began, wondering if it was a wise question, 'why not use them instead of ossifying demons?'

Janus pursed his lips for a moment. 'I don't like ossifying demons, Edgy, but sometimes even a pearl won't do. Besides, demon pearls are rare to find and so are not cheaply spent.' He paused as the muffled, shabby figure of Scrabsnitch emerged from the shadow on the other side of the alley. 'Anyway, why ossify or use a pearl when I have Riddle Master Edgy Taylor at my side? Sharpen your wits, Master Taylor, we're going to meet Belphagor.'

Edgy's heart sank. Him? Riddle Master? Not after his terrible performance with Salomé on the rooftops.

The scrunch of Scrabsnitch's boots on the rough ground of the alley brought Edgy back to attention.

'Good evening, Mr Janus,' Scrabsnitch said, raising his top hat. His voice was muffled by the scarf that covered his face.

'Good evening, Mr Scrabsnitch,' Janus replied. 'Care for a flagon of strong ale and some demonic banter?'

'Very much so,' Scrabsnitch murmured. 'I need some strong drink after my encounter with her ladyship.' Janus stared blankly at Scrabsnitch. 'Didn't Edgy tell you of our close call today? Salomé herself, I believe, came into my shop after this young man, but he was too fast for her and took off across the rooftops!'

'No,' Janus said, narrowing his eyes at Edgy. 'He didn't mention it at all . . .'

'I didn't want to bother you, Mr Janus an' I got away, no problem,' Edgy lied.

'I fear the boy is just being modest, Mr Janus,' Scrabsnitch grinned.

Janus gave a smile and ruffled Edgy's hair. 'You may be right, Scrabsnitch,' he said. 'Now let's get inside and see this demon. We'll watch Edgy in action!'

Edgy groaned inwardly. *Why don't I just tell them the truth?* He'd thought he was so clever at riddles but Salomé had beaten him twice now. What made him think that this Belphagor would be any easier? He was a fraud and now this demon would show him up. Before killing him or taking his soul, that is.

The heat from the crush of bodies in the pub hit Edgy as Janus pushed the door open. The wave of noise and the smell of unwashed bodies, gas lamps, tobacco smoke and ale jostled his senses, making him screw his face up.

Most of the drinkers appeared human but Edgy noticed the odd hoof or tail poking out from the mass. Edgy stood flanked by Scrabsnitch and Janus. The hubbub stopped and all eyes turned on them as they stepped further into the single room of the pub. The crowd parted before Janus like the Red Sea before Moses, a corridor of craned necks and curious eyes with, at the end of it, the burly, red-faced Bill Fager leaning behind the bar.

'Evening, gents,' he said, grinning through his bushy, handlebar moustache. 'How can I help you?'

Is Janus wrong? This landlord looked human to Edgy. But, as Janus had said before: 'There are demons and there are demons.'

'What d'you see, Edgy?' Janus asked, donning his Hades Lenses. 'Looks ordinary to me. His glamour spell must be strong.'

Edgy shrugged. 'Just old Bill, sir.'

'Look harder, really peer at him,' Janus whispered.

Edgy squinted at the landlord. The burly man's outline blurred for a moment and a shadowy horned silhouette flickered briefly into view.

'Wait a minute, sir,' Edgy muttered. 'I can see somethin' now.'

'Is that you, Edgy Taylor?' Fager said, frowning and straightening up from the bar. 'Didn't recognise you with those fancy clothes on. Where's Mr Talon these days?'

'Ask him a riddle,' Janus hissed, elbowing Edgy.

'Excuse me, Mr Fager,' Edgy said. 'Could you tell me, what walks around all day on its head?' Fager looked blankly at him. Edgy turned to Janus and said under his breath, 'See, he must be human. He hasn't got a clue what I'm talkin' about.'

'A horseshoe nail, that's what walks about all day on its head,' Fager said, making Edgy turn back.

The man's outline shimmered and flickered again. Edgy glimpsed spiral horns, furnace eyes.

'He's our man, Mr Janus. Or not, as the case may be,' Edgy said out of the corner of his mouth.

Janus beamed and turned to address the creature at the bar. 'Belphagor, we know who you are. We would like to talk to you. To ask you some questions and invite you to join the Royal Society of Daemonologie.'

Belphagor stepped back from the bar, seeming to grow, his outline indistinct and flickering. 'Royal Society, eh? And how d'you propose I join? As one of your statues to decorate your precious exhibition hall?'

'Believe me,' said Janus, holding up a hand, ignoring the growing murmur of the crowd at Belphagor's shimmering change, 'we no longer ossify demons.'

'Try telling that to Thammuz, Janus,' Belphagor spat. A ram's head replaced his slicked-back hair and chubby face.

'Or should I say, Janus the Stonemason. That's what they used to call you, wasn't it?'

Janus slipped his hand inside his pocket. 'All we want to do is talk.'

But Belphagor's attention had shifted to Edgy. 'And you seem full of yourself, Edgy Taylor. Riddling's a dangerous game. Never know what you might lose. Now you'll riddle with me.'

My father left me three acres of land,
Sing ivy, sing ivy.
My father left me three acres of land,
Sing holly, go whistle and ivy.
I ploughed it with a ram's horn,
And sowed it all over with one peppercorn.
I harrowed it with a bramble bush,
And reaped it with my little penknife.
I got the mice to carry it to the barn,
And thrashed it with a goose's quill.
I got the cat to carry it to the mill;
The miller, he swore he would have her paw,
And the cat, she swore she would scratch his face.

'Acre of Land', traditional folk ballad

CHAPTER SEVENTEEN
RIDDLE MATCH

Edgy's heart pounded. Belphagor meant business, that was for sure.

'Riddle me this, Edgy Taylor,' the demon hissed. 'What runs but never tires?'

'Water,' Edgy said.

Mustn't get distracted, he thought. He had to fire another riddle back. This was how Talon used to do it. Back then if Edgy lost he got a beating. This time it could be worse.

'What eats but is always hungry?'

'Fire,' Belphagor hissed back. 'What sings a song that spells disaster?' He cupped his hands in front of him. A pile of writhing maggots appeared in his palms.

'Wind,' Edgy said.

Belphagor blew into the wriggling pile before him. A whirlwind of maggots and flies filled the pub, blasting Edgy off his feet and sending the drinkers into chaos.

'Lord above!' howled a bargirl, half stumbling, half blown towards the door.

''Ere, what happened to Bill?' yelled a toothless old man, gripping his hat and rolling under a table.

Screams and shouts deafened Edgy as tables overturned and glasses shattered. Chairs whirled around in the putrid storm, crashing through windows, shattering mirrors. Edgy curled into a ball, covering his face. Bodies fell over him, voices swore as people struggled to get out of the pub.

And then silence, punctuated by the odd groan or curse.

Edgy peered up.

The pub looked like an explosion had gutted it. Chairs and tables lay splintered in pools of spilt beer. Long shadows flickered in the light cast by small fires started where gas lamps had been smashed. A thin mist of smoke gave the whole room a hazy, dreamlike quality. Most of the patrons had stampeded out of the door, but one or two bodies lay scattered like the wrecked furniture.

Belphagor sat cross-legged on the remnants of the bar, his spiral horns and ram's head raised imperiously over them. His muscles flexed under a glistening blue skin. Edgy picked himself up, dragging mushed-up maggots out of his hair and ears. He retched and wiped the back of his hand across his mouth.

Janus staggered to his feet, rubbing his head and groaning.

Scrabsnitch stood in the corner of the room, extracting a crushed beetle from his frizzy beard. 'I'm getting too old for this, that's a certainty,' he grumbled.

'Don't worry, old man,' Belphagor said, his voice deep and rumbling. 'Your miserable life will soon be at an end.' He strode on cloven hooves towards Scrabsnitch, who cowered in the corner.

'But it's my turn!' Edgy yelled. 'What can you catch many times but once it's let out, you can't catch again?'

Belphagor stopped, looked at Edgy and frowned. 'Say the riddle again,' he snorted. Edgy repeated it. Belphagor's eyes flamed. 'Give me some time,' he said.

Edgy remembered the first time he had met Salomé and clicked his fingers like an impatient schoolmaster. 'Come along!' he snapped, trying to keep the quaver out of his voice.

'No! Wait, let me think. A cold, a tiger . . . I don't know,' Belphagor roared, his eyes wild as his guesses. He stamped back and forth in front of Edgy, punching his blue fist into his palm. 'Tell me the answer. You'll have cheated somehow, that's for sure!'

'It's breath,' Edgy said, risking a grin. *I've done it. Outsmarted the demon.* 'You can catch your breath but once you let it out, you can't catch the same breath again.'

'So simple. Yet it defeated me. You are sharp, boy.' Belphagor stared down at him, nodding. Some of the fire had left his eyes, but his ram's head still made Edgy shudder. 'Very sharp. Watch you don't cut yourself, young man.'

'And now, Belphagor, you must submit to us,' Janus said, stumbling forward through the wrecked tables and chairs. 'We seek the body of Moloch.'

Edgy frowned and turned, blinking at Janus.

'My debt is to the boy,' Belphagor said.

'And the boy works for us,' Janus snapped back. 'Now tell us where it is.'

'Is that what you want?' Belphagor asked, his orange eyes boring into Edgy's. 'You could have riches, more than you can imagine. You would never be hungry again.'

'The Society keeps me fed,' Edgy said honestly. 'And Mr Janus 'ere looks after me. Tell 'im what he wants ter know.'

'Well said, Edgy,' Janus beamed, clapping his hands.

'A poor choice,' Belphagor said. 'I don't know where Moloch's body is. Only the great Satan knows that. But I've heard tell that it lies frozen in a land of snow and ice.'

'That's all?' Edgy murmured.

But Janus's eyes grew wide and excited. 'It certainly narrows things down a little, Edgy.'

'You aren't the first to ask this,' Belphagor said. 'A certain demon queen by the name of Salomé was riddling me this very afternoon. I imagine she wanted to know much the same thing. Honestly, the number of times she sent that dolt Thammuz in here, trying to out-riddle me.'

Edgy's heart skipped. *Salomé sent Thammuz?*

But before he could speak, Belphagor leaned close to him, making him flinch. 'You'll not beat me again, boy,' he hissed, throwing himself forward through the pub window.

Janus fumbled in his pocket and hurled the demon pearl after Belphagor, but it flew wide and bounced feebly off the blackened frame.

'He's gone,' Scrabsnitch said, peering out into the empty alley.

'But we're another step closer,' Janus whispered.

'All he said was that Moloch's body was frozen in a land of snow and ice,' Scrabsnitch replied. 'That could be either end of the earth.'

'It takes time, Evenyule, my friend, but sooner or later the pieces of the puzzle will all fit.' Janus stared out into the darkness. 'And then imagine the excitement, the glory. To have not only proved the existence of arch-demons, but to have a specimen. Can you imagine the look on my brother's face then?'

Edgy felt like a conquering hero as he made his way back to his room in the Society. He'd out-riddled a demon as easily as he'd shown up that snob Mauldeth.

He was so lost in his daydream that he turned a corner and almost ran into the man himself. Mauldeth loomed over him, glowering. Edgy's mouth went dry.

'You look very cheerful, Mr Taylor,' Mauldeth sneered. 'A fruitful trip out with my little brother?'

'Er, yes, sir. I mean, no, sir. I mean, nothing much to report, sir.' Edgy nodded and bowed. Why did he feel like some kind of village idiot when he was in front of this man? Janus didn't make Edgy feel like that.

'Well, something's put a spring in your step. Probably

feeding you too much,' Mauldeth said. He lowered his face close to Edgy's and whispered, 'Just be careful. Don't get too involved with my little brother's madcap schemes. You can always come to me if you have any concerns.'

'No, sir. I mean, yes, sir,' Edgy said, trying to nod and shake his head at the same time.

Mauldeth strode past Edgy and off down the corridor. Edgy stood and watched him disappear. *Stuck-up toff*, he thought. They'd show him. Madcap schemes indeed. Their discovery would make the scattered bones of Aldorath look so pathetic that Mauldeth wouldn't be able to hold his head up at the Society again. As if Edgy would go scurrying to him at the first sign of trouble!

Henry greeted Edgy at the door with a wagging tail.

'All we 'ave to do now, Henry, old chap,' he muttered, stroking the dog's ear, 'is find that bloomin' skull before Mr Janus reads about it in the book and we're made.'

THE NIGHT, THE NIGHT IS HALLOWEEN,
OUR SEELY COURT MUST RIDE
THRO' ENGLAND AND THRO' IRELAND BOTH,
AND ALL THE WORLD WIDE.

'TAM LIN', TRADITIONAL FOLK BALLAD

CHAPTER EIGHTEEN
HELL TURKEYS

The following morning found Edgy deep in thought about the skull and where to find it. In his mind it all seemed connected. Whoever had stolen the skull didn't want Janus to find Moloch. Why else would they take it? Once he'd completed his morning tasks, he would go straight down to the exhibition hall and talk to Spinorix about any suspicions he might have.

He opened his bedroom door to find Sally standing there as usual.

'Haven't you got anythin' better to do than to 'ang around 'ere?' Edgy said. Henry cowered behind him.

'There's no law against it, is there? Besides, I'm good at houndin' people – you wanna watch out,' she retorted, folding her arms and slumping against the wall. 'An' anyway, Trimdon wants you to deliver the hell turkeys.'

'Hell turkeys?' Edgy repeated, forgetting his grudge for a second. 'What're they?'

'Disgusting's what they are,' Sally snorted. 'Don't you know nothing? The imps down below eat them.'

'Down below?' Edgy liked the sound of this less and less.

'Yeah, in the boiler room.' Sally screwed her face up. 'It's where you belong, if you ask me.'

'Well, I didn't ask you,' Edgy snapped and stamped past her, followed by Henry, who crushed his belly to the floor and pressed his ears back as he passed her.

The smell of the turkeys greeted Edgy before he actually saw them. Ammonia, stripping the skin from his nostrils only to make way for the aroma of rotten eggs and decaying meat. Only worse. It filled the corridor as he approached Trimdon's room. The little demon stood with three cages stacked on a trolley and his fingers squeezing his pointy nose.

The creatures inside looked as bad as they smelt. Fat, featherless bodies squeezed together behind the bars, wrinkled skin dotted with a few downy quills as if they'd already been plucked. Their long, scaly claws clicked on the floors of the cages, their big heads bobbed and long, bubbly wattles wobbled as they crushed to the sides of the cages to stare at Edgy. Their large, liquid eyes and cruel, curved beaks made Edgy shudder.

'Hell durkeys,' Trimdon said, holding his nose. 'Don't doe how ibs cad eat dem.'

Henry jumped up at the trolley, licking his lips and making the turkeys cry out – a cross between a *hoot* and a *kark*.

'Where are they from?' Edgy asked. The smell was bad but he'd experienced worse in his prime-collecting days.

'Hell, ob course,' Trimdon said.

'Is it a real place?' Edgy asked. 'Is that where you go if you've, you know, been wicked?'

'Is hard to exblain wib by dose blocked,' Trimdon said, evading the question. 'It is a blace though, kind of.'

Edgy shook his head, wondering if he would ever get a straight answer from a demon. The turkeys gave a startled cry as he lifted the trolley, their cries increasing as he moved off.

'Where do I take 'em then?' he asked.

'Down below.' Trimdon pointed to the floor with his free hand and then to the pipes that clustered along the roof of the corridor. 'Follow the red pipe. Oh, and be careful – the lower lebels of the building are less, erm, well-policed, shall we say. And you're going to the lowest lebel.'

Edgy had become quite familiar with the upper levels of the Society but he had not yet ventured downstairs. Many of the upper rooms lay empty and shrouded in dust sheets, slowly decaying and out of use. The lower chambers were mainly for storage and the archiving of materials. The functional part of the building. He wondered what Trimdon meant by 'less well-policed'. Were there marauding demons down there? He followed the red pipe.

'Keep an eye out, Henry,' Edgy muttered. Henry licked his lips and stared at the hell turkeys. Edgy shook his head. 'How can yer? They're 'orrible.'

Hoot, the hell turkeys cried. *Kark*.

The pipe veered right into a long, twisting flight of stairs that led downwards.

'Oh joy,' Edgy murmured, looking from the wheels of the trolley to the stairs.

CLUNK! Hoot! BANG! Kark! Deeper underground, further down he went, banging the trolley and making the turkeys jump. Henry snapped at them as they squawked. Edgy cursed, sweating with each step.

At the bottom step, Edgy leaned on the trolley, panting. The corridor before him sloped down even further.

'No more steps though, boy,' he said. Henry wagged his tail and trotted ahead.

The gloom increased as he descended; the hellfire lamps seemed feeble in these passages. Rough-hewn flagstones replaced the usual black-and-white marble floor tiles of the ground floor. Everything here seemed much older; the doors that led off the corridor were studded with iron and topped with stone arches. The echo of Henry's panting and the *hoots* and *karks* of the turkeys bounced off the bare stone walls, which felt dry and coarse when Edgy put his hand against them.

He stopped in front of a huge iron door twice his height. Rivets the size of Edgy's fists reinforced the dull metal and held it on two hinges as thick as his thighs. The words *BOILER ROOM* had been etched into a brass plaque. He reached out and grasped a large handle. The door felt hot. Edgy pulled and the hinges squealed as it opened.

The heat hit Edgy first, followed by a bright red light

and the stink of burning coal. It was like opening an oven door. He shielded his eyes and peered in. Seven imps, very like Spinorix in appearance – small and red – scurried around a huge metal fire box. Inside a furnace roared loudly. The imps took it in turns to shovel coal from a mountainous pile into the box. One rammed his shovel into the black heap while another heaved his coal into the small doorway in the front of the box. Sweat glistened on their ruddy skin. Their horns and tails reflected the infernal glow. Every now and then Edgy heard the hiss of steam as it blasted from a valve in the pipes that snaked their way from two massive boilers that filled half the room. The imps didn't pause for one second.

'Hello?' Edgy called over the din.

'Can't stop,' one imp yelled back. 'Break our rhythm. Gotta keep this thing boilin'.'

'Dump 'em there and then get out,' snapped another imp as he threw his load into the furnace. 'And move it – you're letting all the heat escape! Don't want the governors to freeze, do we?'

The imps gave a wicked cackle in unison but never stopped scooping and throwing the coal into the furnace.

Edgy raised an eyebrow but wheeled the turkeys into the room. Their cries were lost in the rumbling of the furnace. The heat seared his cheeks and hurt his eyes. He tipped the turkey cages off the trolley and dragged it out. With a grunt, he swung the door shut and leaned heavily against the wall, panting for breath. Henry looked longingly towards the door and the turkeys behind it.

As he rested, a breeze blew across his cheeks. Edgy closed his eyes and savoured the cool caress. It felt so welcome. And was there something else – a sound, singing? Edgy strained to listen. Distantly, he heard a wordless song, slow and mournful, yet beautiful too. It called to him.

A smile played on Edgy's lips as he drifted down the corridor. The singing grew louder, more distinct; a slow melancholy tune, a single voice.

Wordless.

Hypnotising.

The breeze felt refreshing, soothing. Edgy's smile grew. He loved the singing. He loved the chill of the breeze. He noticed, with mild curiosity, a brass door set into the rough wall that marked the end of the corridor. It was slightly ajar. The song came from beyond it. It invited him in. Henry whined and growled, making Edgy frown.

'Quiet, boy. Listen – it's calling me.' Edgy took a step forward. The singing grew louder. 'I have to go. I want to go . . .'

He was being drawn and there was nothing he could do to stop himself.

FROM A CLOSED DOOR, THE DEVIL TURNS AWAY.

TRADITIONAL PROVERB

CHAPTER NINETEEN
THE PORTRAIT

Professor Milberry appeared from behind the door and clanged it shut behind her. Edgy started as if he'd woken suddenly from a dream.

'Edgy, what are you doing here?' She stared down at him, her brow furrowed with concern.

'I was deliverin' turkeys. I heard . . . singin'.' Edgy shook himself. His head felt fuzzy and vague. Slowly he came to his senses. Milberry bent down and brought her face level with Edgy's. She ruffled his thick black hair.

'You must never go through that door, Edgy,' she said. 'It is highly dangerous.'

'Why? What's behind it?' Edgy asked, peering over her shoulder at the door.

'Tunnels,' she replied. 'Miles upon miles of tunnels, in fact. A Maze. Once you go in, you'd never find your way out.'

'But that singing – it was beautiful.'

'The creature doing the singing is not so pretty,' Milberry said, shuddering. 'The Echolites – for that is what they are called – inhabited these underground caverns eons before the Society excavated and extended them. Though, usually, they tend to lurk in deeper passages. What's bringing them to the surface, I couldn't say.'

'The Society dug the tunnels?' Edgy asked.

Milberry gave a wry grin. 'In the early days, the first fellows believed that hell lay beneath the earth. They thought the best way to wage war on evil was to find it, to dig it up.' Her swarthy face grew grim and pale. 'All they found were the Echolites. Hideous creatures who lure the unsuspecting into the dark and then devour them. In the end, the Society lost so many fellows it was decided to seal the tunnels up.' Milberry nodded to the door behind her.

'It's a huge door,' Edgy said.

'It has to be. The Echolites aren't the only things lurking in those tunnels,' Milberry said. 'It was fortunate I happened to be down here when you came. Who left the door open like that, I couldn't guess. Now let's get you back up to the more respectable levels.'

She turned a huge key in the lock and took Edgy back up.

The rest of the day passed without event, but Edgy had no opportunity to visit Spinorix until early evening. However, on his way to the exhibition hall, he bumped into Mortesque Sokket.

'Ah, so you're there, are you?' he muttered. 'I need you to polish the furniture in my office – getting frightfully dusty. Hop to it now!'

Edgy cursed under his breath. Tiny artefacts littered every surface of Sokket's office and everything wore a thick coating of dust. As he wiped and cleaned, he imagined Janus reading the book with widening eyes and then rushing to the exhibition hall.

Edgy's hand swept over the cover of a book from the library. It lay on the desk, the snakeskin cover smooth and glistening. The title shone out in silver: *The Legends of Moloch. Why does Sokket have a copy? Is he trying to find the arch-demon's corpse too?*

'What are you doing?' Sokket appeared behind Edgy and planted a hand firmly on the book, covering the title. 'You aren't paid to read the books, boy. You're here to clean.'

'Yes, sir.' Edgy nodded and twitched his gaze to his feet. 'Sorry, sir.'

'Should think so too,' Sokket sniffed. 'Now clear off.'

Edgy ran from Sokket's study back to his room.

Madame Lillith shuffled around the corner, swishing her broom as she went. She glared at him, her amber eyes aflame. She looked down at Edgy's boots.

'Wish I 'ad a pair like that,' she spat and swept on past him.

Edgy stared after her. He shook his head as he found himself at his bedroom door. This whole building and everyone in it was beyond him.

A picture stood propped up against his bed. Its gold

frame glimmered in the feeble light of the room. It looked like one of the portraits from the corridor walls. A stern man with a long, scarred face sneered at him. He didn't seem quite so grand staring up from the floor instead of down from the wall. Edgy peered harder. Henry whined and scraped at the door. Edgy ignored him. Something about the man in the picture looked familiar. *Where have I seen that long face? Why would someone put a picture in my room? For safe-keeping?* Henry barked.

'Quiet, boy, I'm thinking. Just wait,' he snapped. Maybe the portrait had fallen off and someone wanted him to put it back up in the morning. Then it struck him.

Edgy had seen the man in the picture haunting the library. He was one of the lost souls drifting among the books. The dark background behind the man rippled. Edgy blinked. A chill realisation wrapped itself around his shoulders, prickling his scalp. *How stupid can I be?* Sally had warned him not to look too hard at the portraits and here he was staring into one. But now he couldn't move his eyes.

The blackness at the man's shoulder swirled like water down a hole. Edgy's heart pounded. Two huge luminous eyes glowed from the centre of the spiral. Edgy stood transfixed in the middle of the room. A clawed finger wriggled through the opening gap in the picture, then another. Soon a whole hand and a hideous face poked out of the portrait. Henry barked and clawed at the door. Edgy stared at the emerging creature, fascinated, unable to look away.

Expressionless orbs dominated the head. Sabre-like teeth poked up from a thin, downturned mouth. A few strands of lank green hair drifted from its scabby, green head. Henry growled and barked at the creature but it kept its gaze on Edgy. It pushed a skinny shoulder through and started to wriggle its way free from the picture. The canvas clung to it like a thick mud. All this time, the creature fixed him with its gaze.

A terrible stench of stagnant water filled the room and Edgy noticed that the scene behind the man in the picture was a black pool with dead reeds poking from its slick surface. *This must be where it lives,* he thought.

It slapped one foot on the floor of the room, leaving a puddle of stinking black water. It reached forward with long, clawed fingers and Edgy caught a glimpse of the pool behind it. Pale faces beneath the surface. Bloated with staring eyes. A strange calmness came over him. Henry's barking faded into the distance.

It'll drag me into the picture and drown me in the pool too. There's nothing I can do.

The bedroom door flew open with a bang, waking Edgy from his stupor. Henry yelped, spinning round. A cold hand gripped Edgy's arm at the elbow and yanked.

'Get out of there!' Sally yelled, pulling at him.

Edgy felt wet fingers slap around his other arm at the wrist. Edgy struggled against the creature's grasp. A sickening, sabre-toothed grin cracked its face. Sally heaved again and his shoulder burned with the strain. Edgy wrenched back again. The creature's face fell as it slid on its slimy feet and they inched back, but its grip remained as firm as iron. Edgy's shoulder felt as if it would come out of its socket. Sally and Edgy pulled again but the creature just slid closer. Edgy lashed out with his foot only to have that grabbed too.

'Don't let go, Sally,' he sobbed.

His calmness had quickly evaporated. Now Edgy wriggled and pulled with all his might as the creature tried to edge back towards the picture with him in tow.

Henry darted and yapped at the creature. For the first time it snarled down at him. Henry snarled back and it lashed out with its webbed foot. At the same time, Sally gave a huge tug. Edgy screamed as pain lanced up his shoulder. The creature tottered and fell to the ground with a wet slap, losing its grip. Sally and Edgy tumbled out through the door and into the passageway. Edgy lay there, stunned, feeling Sally's cold breath on his cheek, her icy fingers still gripping his arm.

The creature unfolded its skinny body, preparing to spring forward, but Sally leapt up. Edgy just glimpsed Henry bounding towards the monster, teeth bared, and then Sally threw herself forward, slamming the door shut.

'No!' Edgy panted, scrabbling to get up. 'Henry's still in there!'

An unholy howl filled the air. Edgy could hear Henry yelping and barking. Something smashed against the door.

Then all fell silent.

He who sups with the devil should use a long spoon.

Traditional proverb

CHAPTER TWENTY
A STRANGE BARGAIN

Pushing Sally aside, Edgy ripped the door open. Darkness filled the room. The creature had gone. The picture lay on the floor ripped to pieces, its frame snapped and bent double against the wall. Henry lay on his side, his ribcage heaving. A little trail of blood trickled from his mouth. He didn't get to his feet but his tail flicked feebly as Edgy crouched by him. He hugged the wounded terrier, feeling the dog's heart beat weakly against his chest.

'Henry, poor Henry,' Edgy sobbed.

'Is he badly hurt?' Sally said, her voice faint.

'Can't see any cuts but he can't move and his breathing's getting weaker,' Edgy said, scuffing at his eyes with his sleeve. 'Who could help him?'

'I don't know.' Sally bit her lip. 'Professor Milberry works a lot with nature spirits but I don't think she knows much about animals.' She kicked the frame of the picture with her foot. 'What were you doing with the picture in the first place?'

'It was in the room when I arrived. Someone must've put it 'ere,' he muttered. 'Anyway, there's no time for that. What am I going to do about poor Henry?' The dog gave a whine and lapped at Edgy's cheek.

'I told you, I don't know. There's nobody in the Society with that kind of knowledge.'

'Knowledge,' Edgy said. *The snake will know what to do.*

He bundled Henry up close to him and ran out of the room. Sally ran behind, her feet tapping as Edgy's boots rang on the tiles.

'Where are you going?' she called after him.

But Edgy didn't answer. Henry's breathing grew shallower with every clattering footstep.

'Come on, old chap,' Edgy panted, trying to cushion him in his arms from the jogging up and down. 'Hold on.' Henry's eyes flickered and closed. His breathing became more rapid. 'Hold on, boy, hold on.'

Edgy gritted his teeth and tried to remember his way. But suddenly the door to the library loomed before him. Edgy slammed against it, dashing into the blue twilight of the hall, and stopped so abruptly that Sally crashed into his back.

After the tumbling rush down the passages, the library seemed tranquil and quiet. Edgy glanced from bookshelf to table, desperate to find the snake.

'Hello? Snake?' Edgy yelled. What should he call the creature who presided over the library?

'Back so soon, Edgy Taylor?' a voice hissed to his right. The leaves shivered and the snake slithered from between two large volumes. 'What have we here? A canine. In bad shape.'

'Can you make him better?' Edgy said, easing Henry down on to the floor. The dog's breath came out in wheezing gasps now.

The snake's eyes glowed brightly. 'Probably but what point would there be in that?'

'Well, I . . .' Edgy didn't know what to say. He'd expected the snake to make Henry better. He hadn't thought he'd say no.

'What I mean to say,' the snake slid closer, circling Henry, 'is, what's in it for me?'

'Edgy –' Sally said, grabbing hold of his arm. He shook her off.

'What do you mean?' he said. The snake slid around Edgy's ankle and stared up at him.

'I mean, Edgy Taylor, if I save this scruffy hound,' he hissed, 'what can you offer me in return?'

'Don't listen to him, Edgy.' Sally's voice sounded full of fear. 'He'll take your soul.'

'His soul? Now there's an idea,' snapped the snake. 'I hadn't thought of that. Full of good ideas, your friend. Lucky she just happened to turn up when the creature came out of the picture.'

Edgy stared down at him. How could he possibly know what had just happened in the bedroom?

'I am knowledge, Edgy Taylor. I know. So do you want

me to save the mutt?' the snake hissed, curling up his knee.

Henry gave a strangled sigh. A little froth bubbled from his lolling tongue. Edgy ran his fingers over Henry's smooth ears. He and Henry had been firm friends through the worst of times. Edgy had lost count of the number of kickings Henry had received trying to stop Talon from beating him.

'Yes,' he said, staring at the snake. 'What do you want in exchange?'

'Edgy, no!' Sally ran forward and grabbed his elbow again. 'Don't do this. If he takes your soul, you'll end up like . . . like . . .'

'Like who, missy?' The snake coiled itself around Edgy's waist, its tail still lost in the depths of the shadows. 'Like you? I did you a favour in return for your silence many years ago. Look at you. A lifeless husk, eaten up with jealousy and hatred. Who did put the picture in Edgy's room? Didn't it used to be *your* room?'

'Stop it.' Edgy pushed Sally away. *Did she try to get rid of me?*

The snake reared its head up level with his eyes. Henry gave a shudder and his back leg lashed out in pain.

'What do you want?' Edgy repeated.

'Not your soul, that's for sure – give it a few more years yet. No, it's a promise I want. Promise that you'll never hurt me and you'll never mention my presence here to anyone. That's all.'

'Hurt you?' Edgy murmured. 'How could I hurt you?'

'I don't know. You make me nervous.' The snake
darted around his head. 'Call it an old snake's whim.
It's a bargain: your old friend back for a promise not to
do something you can't do anyway. Money for old rope.
What do you say?'

Edgy glanced at Sally. She clasped her hands together,
her eyes wide, begging him not to agree.

Henry gave a sad whimper.

His sides rose, then fell.

His breathing stopped.

'Done,' Edgy said. 'I promise never to hurt you. Now
save him!'

The snake slithered over Edgy's shoulder, its coils
warm and dry, stroking the skin of his neck. He eased
his way over Henry, sliding under his belly and coiling
around him again and again, under and over, under and
over, until all Edgy could see was snake. The light faded
in the great domed hall and shadows shrouded the snake
and Henry. Edgy squinted to see what was going on. Dark
shapes swirled before his eyes. The snake's coils merged
into one. The darkness grew deeper until Edgy felt as if he
was staring into a bottomless well.

And then, gradually, the twilight returned. The
shadows slithered back behind the books and branches.

'He'll be fine now,' hissed the snake, bleeding back into
the darkness under the bookshelves. 'Remember your
promise.'

Henry stood before him, wagging his tail.

'Henry!' Edgy cried, scooping up his old friend. He gave

a yap and started licking Edgy's face as if it was smeared with jam. Edgy held him up. 'Look at you – not even a mark on you!'

Henry panted and shook with excitement. He looked bright and full of life, wagging his tail like a puppy. Even the dirty grey of his fur had become a brilliant white. Edgy spun around, hugging Henry to his chest.

'I just hope it was worth it, Edgy Taylor,' Sally muttered behind him.

Edgy turned on her. 'What's it to you anyway?' he snapped. 'It was you who shut him in the room in the first place. An' you never did answer the snake. Well, did you put the picture in my room?'

'Is that what you really think?' Sally gasped. Her voice echoed around the dome. 'If I was so keen to get rid of you, why did I pull you out?'

Edgy's face burned. 'I don't know, maybe you thought I'd be grateful an' give you your room back,' he said. Edgy knew he was wrong. It was the fact that she was right that annoyed him. Edgy didn't really know what he'd promised to the snake and, much as he loved Henry, it was a choice he might regret later.

'If you believe that, then next time I won't bother.' Sally's eyes narrowed and she leaned closer. 'And I bet there *will* be a next time, Edgy. Someone doesn't like you, and I can't say as I blame 'em.' She turned and slammed the library door, leaving Henry and Edgy alone with only the weeping lost souls for company.

Edgy sighed. She was right again. Someone had tried

to kill him. They'd quite deliberately taken a possessed painting from the wall and placed it in his room. And Edgy felt certain of one thing – anyone who went to those lengths would try again.

He opened her bosom all whiter than snow,
He pierced her heart and the blood it did flow,
And into the grave her fair body did throw,
He covered her up and away he did go.

'The Cruel Ship's Carpenter', traditional folk ballad

CHAPTER TWENTY-ONE

THE THREAT
IN THE SHADOWS

Anawald Milberry appeared at Edgy's door the next morning. She had blankets draped over her arm and a pale, concerned expression.

'Sally just told me about the picture,' she said. 'Have you any idea who put it in your room?'

'Haven't a clue, ma'am,' Edgy murmured sleepily.

'I brought you these.' She offered the blankets, then gave an awkward smile. 'Not quite sure what for but . . .'

'Thank you, ma'am,' he said, giving a tight smile. 'That's very thoughtful, like.'

'You were lucky that Henry was with you.' Milberry bent down and scratched the dog behind the ear. Henry wagged his tail. 'He's a brave little chap. Amazing that he wasn't hurt.'

'Yes, ma'am,' Edgy muttered.

'I don't know who did this, Edgy,' Milberry said, her face worried, 'but I'll investigate it. It's far from perfect but one day the Society will be a better place, I promise you.'

'Thanks, ma'am.' Edgy smiled again. Milberry was all right in his book.

He watched her disappear into the gloom of the corridor and went back to his bed. His whole body throbbed after being pulled and tugged between Sally and the demon in the portrait. Absent-mindedly, Edgy sat on the edge of the bed, gripping the thin, straw-filled mattress. His fingers grazed something underneath. A small notebook. Plain, not snakeskin like *A Demon a Day*. He opened it and read the spidery handwriting on the page:

Don't know why I'm writing this. Maybe a century of being alone has forced me to do it. To confess.

I was twelve when little Molly was born. All bright eyes, squeals and smiles, she was from the start. A proper bundle of mischief.

Mam worked herself to a scrap at the local mill and goodness knows where me da went. Off to the alehouse one night an' never came back. So I looked after Molly. Hard times, they were. She leadin' me a merry old dance around the house and street. An' many's the time I wished her gone. Wished myself free to go an' see me friends, not be stuck in the dark, damp room all day.

I can still remember her cry, harsh and piercin', it fair split my head. An' her snotty nose, it never stopped drippin'. Such a burden. Holdin' me back, keepin' me where I didn't want to be.

Until the fever came. Mam an' Molly took bad. Sunken eyes and rattlin' coughs. Pale, fevered skin. I can still hear her cryin' out my name, all hoarse and feeble, like.

Doctor Lustenbrück said he 'ad a cure. Came to our door. Just had to go with him, he said. He had medicine, he said. I could bring it back an' make Molly an' Mam well.

An' now I remember the feel of Molly's soft fingertips on my lip when I picked her up. The plump warmth of her cheek as she nestled into the curve of my neck. Her chubby knees an' brown curls.

'Course, he never had no cure for 'em. Just this livin' death. He gave me a potion. Told me it was to keep me well. When I woke up, I was so cold, so tired, so dry an' hungerless.

I took meself home but fever had taken Molly an' Mam. I never saw them again. Maybe one day I will, when I can rest.

But I never forgot 'em, you can rest assured. An' neither did Doctor Lustenbrück.

Till the day he died. I made sure of that.

Edgy slammed the book shut. It was Sally's. He gave a guilty sigh. He shouldn't be reading her personal journal and he shouldn't have judged her last night, either. She had saved his life and he accused her of trying to kill him. Henry stared up at him with reproachful eyes.

'I'll apologise,' Edgy murmured. 'Soon as I can.'

*

In the evening, Edgy searched for Sally but instead found Spinorix in the exhibition hall. He sat polishing what looked like glass eyes, rattling them down on to a display cabinet as he cleaned each one. Henry settled, watching him carefully, licking his lips and shifting from paw to paw.

Edgy twirled the bone triangle in his fingers, feeling the sharpness of the corners. 'The boy cut this out of the skull. To stop Mr Janus using the map,' he murmured.

Lines crawled across its brown surface. *If it's a map, one side of a line should be sea, the other land*, Edgy thought. *Surely they can't be roads?* But without the rest of the skull it was meaningless.

'Not just an act of vandalism then?' Spinorix said, squeezing one of the eyeballs until it popped out of his grasp and went clattering across the floor. Henry scurried off too. Spinorix had been appalled when he'd discovered that the hole had been cut out of the skull in the first place. It had taken Edgy a lot of explaining when he'd shown him the triangle and told him how he had come by it.

'Nah!' Edgy said, whistling to call Henry off as Spinorix scrabbled after the eye. 'Bernard would've just thrown it away and wouldn't have been so keen for me to 'ave it when he died.'

'Well then,' Spinorix gasped, retrieving the eyeball. 'Like you said, maybe he did it to stop someone from using the map on the skull. Maybe he was working for Salomé.'

'No, otherwise he would've taken the whole skull to her, surely,' Edgy said.

'So, Salomé is trying to find Moloch's body.' Spinorix

looked as if his head would explode with so much thinking. 'We want to stop her but someone else wants to stop us? That's confusing!'

'I know,' Edgy said. 'It could be anyone in the Society.'

'Lord Mauldeth,' Spinorix said, his eyes wide. 'He doesn't like anyone.'

'He's the chancellor, though,' Edgy said, shaking his head. 'Surely not him. What about Plumphrey? He's greedy enough to do something for money perhaps.'

'It could be any of them,' Spinorix sighed. 'We'll have to keep our eyes peeled.' He plopped the eyeballs back into a jar full of fluid.

'What are they?' Edgy asked, bringing his face close to the jar.

'The eyes of Argus,' Spinorix sniffed. 'A guardian monster. There's a couple missing too.'

The eyes bobbed up and down in the jar. One swivelled round and stared at Edgy, making him jump back with a yell.

It had been another busy day and Edgy decided to get some sleep. Not that he expected to sleep well, with all the thoughts buzzing around in his head. But as they approached his room, Henry growled.

'What is it, boy?'

Henry growled again. The corridor was empty and quiet apart from the hiss of the heating pipes. Edgy squinted beyond the gloomy red glow of the hellfire lamps. Was something moving in the shadows? He padded down the passage, straining to see into the half light.

A sudden yowl sent Edgy scurrying back. Mauldeth's cat screeched, bolting out of the shadows and past him. Henry gave a sharp bark and vanished after the cat.

Edgy laughed and leaned against the doorframe. 'Leave it, Henry,' he said, breathless, recovering from the jump the cat had given him.

But Henry was nowhere to be seen.

'Henry?' Edgy called, taking a few paces back up the corridor.

A footstep scuffed the floor. Pain exploded in the back of his head as something struck him from behind and Edgy plunged into blackness.

Edgy came to slowly. A steady, rhythmic pounding rattled his head, mingling with the dull ache behind his ear. His eyes felt heavy and for a moment he lay with them shut. Then his whole body shuddered and jolted as whatever he lay on moved. Edgy snapped his eyes open and tried to sit up. Thick rope tied his feet tightly together. His hands were similarly pinned behind his back.

Ossified demons surrounded him – some quite old, judging by the moss and cracks that covered them. They wobbled and shuddered as the floor shifted and trembled. Edgy shook his head, trying to clear it. They were moving in a jerking dance. Move, one, two, three. Bang. Move, one, two, three. Bang. Wriggling and grunting, Edgy managed to get into a sitting position. The pounding hadn't stopped but seemed to be getting louder. His heart thudded three times to every loud thump that echoed around him. Leaning against a statue, Edgy worked his way into a standing position.

Panic seized him.

He was on a slow-moving conveyor belt about six to eight feet wide. Hundreds of ossified demons were crowded on to it, wobbling and rocking like milk churns on a wagon. Up ahead some twenty feet away, a huge machine straddled the belt, like a bridge over a stream of demons. Every three seconds the belt lurched forward bringing a clutch of demons under the bridge. Move, one, two, three.

Bang. A colossal metal plate slammed down from within the bridge, crushing the ossified demons to rubble and sending splinters of rock whizzing in all directions.

Edgy pulled at his bindings, falling back down and wriggling like some crazed worm. He had only a couple of minutes at the most to get free.

The rope seemed to tighten as he kicked and rolled in the tiny space between the wobbling demons. Edgy yelled in agony as one of them fell over his legs and the weight of solid stone pinned him down.

'HELP!' he screamed.

His stomach muscles burned as he tried to wriggle free from under the statue. Edgy could smell the oil and grease of the machine now. *It's so close. How long? Another thirty seconds?* Cursing, he tried in vain to roll free, thrashing his body from left to right. The thud of the hammer deafened him. He squeezed his eyes shut against the dust and shards of rock that stung his face as the demons directly ahead of him exploded.

She spoke no word, her tears
They fell a salten flood,
And from her draggled ribbons
Washed out the stains of blood.

'Oh, Mother, I am dying,
And when in my grave I'm laid,
Upon my bosom, Mother,
Then pin a green cockade.'

'Green Cockade', traditional folk song

CHAPTER TWENTY-TWO
DEATH AND STONE

Edgy slumped on to the conveyor belt. It was useless. Sweat chilled his back. He groaned in despair.

A sharp barking suddenly sounded above the commotion of the crusher. Henry popped up over the statues and leapt down on to his chest. He plastered his wet tongue all over Edgy's face.

'Henry?' Sally's voice cut through the hissing and pounding. 'Henry, where are you? Have you found him?'

'Edgy!' This time it was Spinorix. Henry barked again.

'Here! I'm here!' Edgy tried to lift his head up above the encircling statues. 'Help! I'm trapped.'

The conveyor belt shunted forward. Edgy coughed and spluttered as rock dust filled his mouth and nostrils. His ears rang with the blast from the hammer. The dog's yelps were frantic now.

Spinorix's huge eyes appeared over the top of the demon that pinned Edgy. 'Hold on!' he cried, pulling at the stone arm of the statue. He looked tiny and insignificant against its huge bulk. The pounding of the hammer sent him hurtling over the demon and above Edgy's head. Henry barked and wagged his tail.

Sally clambered up on to the conveyor next. She fumbled with the knotted rope at Edgy's wrists and his hands were free. She pointed at the statue pinning his legs. 'You'll have to push too, Edgy,' she yelled above the grinding of the machine. 'On my count.'

Life tingled back into Edgy's hands and as he focused on the count, the incessant clanking and crashing seemed to fade. Sally's voice was all he heard.

'ONE,' she cried.

Edgy drew his breath and gritted his teeth. He pressed his numb hands against the cold stone.

'TWO.'

Edgy tensed every muscle in his body, every fibre, to use it against the statue that crushed him.

'THREE!' Sally screamed.

Edgy's scream merged with hers, topped by a screeching falsetto from Spinorix. Edgy lunged forward with all his strength, sending the statue beneath the crusher. Sally, Henry and Spinorix tumbled in a free fall off the conveyor.

Edgy grabbed at the other statues around him, pulling himself to his feet. With another yell, he hurled himself backwards, his legs still tied. Pain lanced up his back and shoulders as he landed with a jarring crunch on the cavern floor, groaning in agony. For a moment, he lay, trying to catch his breath, listening to the clatter of the machine. Then, with a huge hiss of steam and a rather melancholy sigh, it stopped. Edgy dragged himself into a sitting position.

Across the cave, Sally stood with a lever in her hand, looking rather pleased with herself.

'Edgy, are you all right?' Spinorix bounded over and, in his excitement, ended up crashing straight into him. Edgy fell back, winded once more. Spinorix slapped his hands to his head. 'By Beelzebub's bulbous buttocks, I've killed him! Oh, Edgy, I'm so sorry, so, so sorry!' Tears began to trickle down his long nose.

'Behave, I'm not dead yet,' Edgy gasped, rolling on to his side and sitting up again. Henry started up, scouring his face and jumping up at him.

'You're lucky that Henry's so fond of you,' Sally said. 'I found him outside your room, barking and whining. So I followed him –'

'*We* followed him,' Spinorix cut in. 'Though he's hard to keep up with – that hellhound can run!'

'Thanks,' Edgy said, groaning as he picked himself up. 'Y'know . . . for savin' me.'

''S all right,' Sally said, giving a white-lipped smile and looking at her feet.

Spinorix concentrated on twisting his fingers together and rocked from one foot to the other. An awkward silence descended on the trio for a moment.

Edgy coughed, breaking the spell. 'Someone clobbered me from behind.' He put a hand to the back of his neck, feeling a lump just behind his ear. Every joint ached, every muscle complained and his head pounded. 'Where are we?'

'We're deep beneath the Society – a cavern in the tunnels,' Sally told him.

'On the wrong side of the brass door.' Spinorix shuddered.

Now the machine was off and Edgy wasn't in immediate danger of being squashed flat, he took the time to look at his surroundings.

'What is this place?' Edgy asked, staring around him and slowly beating the rock dust from his clothes.

They stood in a large cavern. The massive stone-crushing machine filled one half and the other, apart from the space they stood in, was crammed with ossified demons. Hundreds of them. Tall, short, incredibly thin and hugely fat; every shape met Edgy's eye as they stretched off into the gloom. Some had horns and tails, others cloven hoofs; yet more had all three. But what united them all, what made Edgy's blood run cold, were their pained and horrified expressions.

They were pleading, begging, down on their knees.

Henry gave a whine and shuffled close to Edgy. There wasn't one defiant gesture in the whole room. These creatures hadn't been ossified as an act of self-defence. They'd been grovelling for their very existence just before someone turned them to stone.

'The not so attractive side of the Royal Society,' Sally muttered, not looking at the statues.

'It's horrible. What happened?'

Sally gave a sigh. 'There was a time when the Royal Society of Daemonologie was nothing more than a hunting club. Retired generals, frustrated clergymen with no interest in gathering knowledge or understanding at all. It was just a competition to them – who could kill the greatest number of demons.'

'It was terrible,' Spinorix said breathlessly, gathering up his tail and holding it in front of his face as if to ward off the awful vision. 'Demons were ossified by them like rich folks shoot grouse . . .'

'Then Lord Mauldeth and Mr Janus joined,' Sally continued. 'They were taught by the best demon hunters in the Society. They'd always been competitive but their rivalry got worse as the years rolled on. Lord Mauldeth would "bag" a demon, then Mr Janus would have to ossify two the next day.'

'The Stonemason,' Edgy whispered. 'That's what Belphagor called Mr Janus. And Talon did too. This is what they meant – Mr Janus has killed so many demons, turned them to stone.'

'Lord Mauldeth knew he could never beat his younger brother,' Sally said, looking darkly at Edgy. 'So, like a spoilt kid, he changed the game. He started searching for the scattered bones of Aldorath. Left Mr Janus high and dry. By the time Mr Janus realised what he was up to, Lord Mauldeth had found the skull.'

'How d'you know all this?' Edgy asked.

'I've been around for a bit, y'know. I was there.' Sally's

pale face seemed to go greyer when she said this. Edgy remembered the journal. She added, 'They were keen to get rid of these statues and set up this room to dispose of the embarrassing reminder. I thought it'd been sealed off years ago, though.'

'Anyway, even if it is true, it wasn't just Mr Janus.' Edgy frowned. 'And he's not like that now.'

'No?' Sally said, raising her eyebrows. 'A leopard don't change 'is spots, I reckon. Besides, he's always lookin' for a new way to outdo his big brother.'

'Well, Lord Mauldeth always puts 'im down, doesn't he?' Edgy said, looking at his boots. He picked Henry up.

'I don't see much difference in 'im.' Sally put her hands on her hips and glared at Edgy.

'His mind's on bigger things,' Edgy muttered. It sounded stupid.

'Like what?' Sally asked, her head raised in a challenge.

Edgy's temper flared. She had a nerve. Who was she to question him all the time? 'The body of Moloch, that's what,' Edgy snapped. His voice echoed through the chamber. Spinorix gave a yelp and dived behind the leg of the nearest statue. 'I reckon Mr Janus is tryin' to find it before Salomé does. She's got Moloch's heart and if she finds him first, then Moloch will come back and that'll be an end of everything, including you, missy! So if I wanna do my bit and help him save the world then I will. So there.' Henry gave a sharp yap and bared his teeth at Sally, punctuating Edgy's outburst.

Sally stood dumbfounded. Her hands fell from her

hips and hung limply by her sides. Spinorix peered from behind the statue. Edgy had never seen his eyes so huge. He exhaled slowly. There. That had told them. They wouldn't go questioning him so quickly next time.

But their gaze extended beyond Edgy. He glanced over his shoulder, then turned slowly to stare himself.

'Blimey!' Edgy croaked, stifling a scream.

Two eyes stared back, swivelling in the sockets of a mildewed demon skull. A skull with a triangular hole cut in its top. The skull sat on the smashed remains of an ossified demon torso. Two demon arms, rather desiccated and decomposed, had been lashed to the sides of the body with string. The whole hideous effigy sat on a flat trolley that was piled with jewellery, bones, watches, old candlesticks, cups and saucers. All manner of objects cluttered the base of the trolley.

'It's horrible,' Sally whispered, putting a hand to her mouth.

But Spinorix jumped up and down on the spot, his head wobbling with joy. 'The eyes of Argus!' he cried and ran forward. Henry wriggled out of Edgy's grasp and scurried over to the trolley, jumping up at the effigy and licking his lips at the eyes so tantalisingly close.

'In the skull of Aldorath, if I'm not mistaken,' Edgy murmured, looking at the intricate lines and blotches that scored the bone between the curved horns on the skull.

'It's all stolen from the collection.' Spinorix frowned. 'Thrown together to look like a demon.'

'Or placed around it,' Sally said. 'Like some kind of offering.'

'It does look 'orrid,' Edgy grimaced, watching the eyes of Argus swivel around in the dead sockets of Aldorath.

'It's not all here,' Spinorix said, scampering around the frightful pile, picking up pieces and dropping them again.

'How d'you know?' Edgy asked.

'I just know,' Spinorix snapped, holding up a milk jug shaped like a dragon. 'There's something missing . . . I just can't quite remember . . .'

'But we've got the most important piece, Spinorix,' Edgy said, allowing himself a grin. Janus would be so pleased to see the skull and the map. 'We just don't know who swiped it all.'

'Well, whoever brought you down 'ere is probably the same one who's been thievin' from the collection,' Sally said, turning away from the gruesome pile and looking around the cavern.

'But why didn't they hang around to make sure the job was done?' Edgy muttered. 'An' why not just kill me right off, instead of draggin' me all the way down 'ere?'

'You think the one who's been stealing from my collection has been trying to kill Edgy too?' Spinorix goggled at Sally.

'I do,' Sally whispered. Her face seemed paler than usual. 'And if I'm not mistaken, they're at the door right now . . .'

ENVY EATS NOTHING BUT ITS OWN HEART.

TRADITIONAL PROVERB

CHAPTER TWENTY-THREE

REFLECTIONS OF HORROR

As the heavy iron door squealed on its hinges, Edgy scooped up Henry and followed Spinorix and Sally across the cavern. They threw themselves behind the clutter of ossified demons. Edgy crouched down and held his breath.

'Do you think this is wise?' whispered Spinorix, trembling. 'I mean, it could be anyone. I know of some particularly vicious associate demons . . .'

'We don't 'ave much choice, do we?' Edgy hissed back. 'Let's just watch.'

He slowly raised his head and peered through the crook of a stony arm. The cavern was red in the dim twilight of the hellfire lamps. Clutching a cracked mirror, Madame Lillith shuffled across the floor towards the pile of stolen artefacts like an ancient spider. Her narrow, suspicious eyes, sunk deep in her face, flicked left and right.

Spinorix opened his mouth but Sally was quicker,

clamping her hand over his face and dragging him to her lap. Edgy put a finger to his lips.

'There,' Madame Lillith said, dropping the mirror on to the pile that surrounded the grotesque mannequin. 'Something more for you,' she said, barely opening her cracked lips.

'She's taken the mirror,' Spinorix whispered through Sally's fingers. His eyes bulged with indignation and Sally's grey knuckles whitened as she held him down. 'The magic mirror.'

'Did you miss me, eh?' Madame Lillith whined at the effigy, her voice sounding like the grating of the rusty hinges. 'Busy day, ooh, yes. Sweep, sweep, sweep. But that idiot imp wasn't anywhere to be seen.'

Sally fell to one side as Spinorix tried to launch himself over the statues. Edgy just managed to grab him and drag him back down.

'So I just helped meself. Lovely mirror. Cloudy, though. I wish it wasn't cracked,' she croaked.

Spinorix went a deeper shade of crimson as Edgy held him firm and Sally clamped both hands over his mouth.

'He really should look after these things better.' Madame Lillith breathed on the mirror and rubbed it with her grubby forearm.

Spinorix looked as if he would explode. Edgy wrestled to contain the little imp.

'Wish I 'ad his job. 'Ere, what's this?' Madame Lillith said. She peered hard into the glass. Then, dropping the mirror, she let out a shrill and chilling scream.

Edgy froze and, in spite of themselves, he, Spinorix and Sally all shot their heads above the cover of the statues. Madame Lillith stood, hands over her face, trembling and sobbing. She had turned away from the mirror, which lay on the floor, reflecting the red glow of the hellfire lamps.

'Obviously didn't like what she saw in the mirror,' Spinorix gasped, standing up in full view before Edgy could stop him. Madame Lillith still had her face covered.

'What d'yer mean?' Edgy frowned, standing too. 'I mean, she's no looker but . . .'

'It's a Mirror of Portent,' Sally whispered. 'It tells the future.'

'That one tells of approaching ill fortune,' Spinorix murmured.

Madame Lillith didn't look frightening any more. She looked like a terrified old woman. They slipped from their hiding place, eyeing the moaning demon.

'What did you see? Madame?' Sally asked quietly.

Madame Lillith looked up at them from behind her shaking hands. 'Echolites!' she hissed. 'They're comin' . . . Echolites . . .'

Edgy frowned. She was clearly petrified. 'What kind of creature frightens demons?'

'The children of Moloch,' Madame Lillith wailed and pressed her fists to the side of her head. 'Devourers of flesh and spirit. They'll destroy us all.'

'Echolites don't normally come up to these levels of the caves,' Sally gasped.

'It's her,' Spinorix snapped. 'Coming and going all the

time with things she's stolen. It's bound to draw them.' He dashed across to the trolley and started piling all the artefacts from the floor on to it. 'We've got to get away,' he panted as he grabbed the mirror and tried to prop it against the side of the ossified torso that stood on the trolley.

Madame Lillith continued with her pitiful whimpering. She was rocking back and forth. Edgy could see her fingers knitting and weaving together. *Did she really try to kill me?* He placed a hand on her shoulder. She turned and shook it away.

'Get off me,' she glowered at him, her face like a wrinkled old turnip, the hatred etched into it. 'I 'ate you, Edgy Taylor, with yer friends an' yer cushy job an' Mr Janus fawnin' all over yer.' She pointed at the effigy. 'I 'ave no one, apart from 'im.'

Friends? Edgy glanced at Sally, pale and grim, and Spinorix, scrabbling once more with the junk on the trolley. She was right. Even if they did argue, they'd come to save him. He'd never had friends before. He looked from the withered, grimacing Madame Lillith to her 'friend'. The one she had made out of the bits and pieces stolen from the collection.

'Is that why you tried to kill me?' Edgy asked, narrowing his eyes. 'Cos you were jealous?'

The shrivelled demon gave a snort. 'I never,' she hissed and then leered at Edgy. 'Wish I 'ad, though.'

'Never mind that,' Spinorix squeaked in terror. 'We must get away – now!'

He wrestled with the trolley, which lurched forward an inch, sending its contents sliding from the ramshackle heap on to the floor again and an avalanche of clutter on top of him. For a second all fell silent.

A distant quavering note drifted into the cavern. A single, beautiful voice echoing around the chamber. Madame Lillith gave a shriek but the song had begun its charm. Edgy felt the familiar calm start to spread over him. Henry gave a bark.

Then Sally slapped his cheek.

'Don't listen,' she yelled, tearing a strip of cloth from her petticoat. She snatched up an old candlestick from the pile. 'Here,' she said, rolling the wax from inside the stick around in her palms. 'The song doesn't affect me – I'm dead already. But you . . .'

She grabbed Edgy's head and stuffed the wax into his ears. The singing stopped. Edgy could hear nothing apart from the blood thundering in his head. Sally waved the cloth from her petticoat and her mouth moved.

'What?' Edgy bellowed.

Sally rolled her eyes to the ceiling and wrapped the strip of cloth around his head. Spinorix fumbled with half a candle, trying to soften its wax to fit it into his large, floppy ears.

Edgy grabbed Madame Lillith by her scaly arm. 'We've got to run!' he shouted.

'No!' Madame Lillith shrieked back. Edgy could hear her despite the wax in his ears. 'I don't need your stinkin'' help!' She wrenched her arm from his grip and scurried across the cavern towards the door with amazing speed.

'After 'er, quick!' Edgy boomed.

Spinorix dragged at the handle of the trolley with all his might, his feet skidding on the rock floor of the cavern. Edgy gave a growl of exasperation and snatched the skull of Aldorath by its curved horns and the imp by his ear.

'But we can't just leave it all!' Spinorix whined, scrabbling for Argus's eyes as they rolled out of the skull's sockets. Henry gave a yelp and pounced on one, Spinorix grabbed the other.

'There's a whole network of tunnels down here. The Echolites will come from all directions. We'll be trapped in here,' Sally snapped, pinching Spinorix's elbow and marching him towards the door with Edgy. 'The singing is getting louder. We have to run!'

Edgy's whole body ached as he pounded through the cavern door and out into the darkness of the tunnels. His breath rumbled through his throbbing head, amplified by the fact that his ears were bunged up. The world seemed strange, devoid of any external sound. Sally ran ahead and he could see her pale outline in the dark. She was shouting something but he couldn't make it out. Free of Edgy's grip, Spinorix scurried alongside him. But Sally skidded to a halt so quickly that Edgy ran into her, catching Spinorix with his elbow and sending him sprawling to the floor. Henry scampered back and hid behind Edgy's heel.

And then he saw Madame Lillith.

She stood in the centre of the tunnel, swaying to and

fro. Her eyes looked drowsy, heavy lidded, and a slight smile played across her thin, cracked lips. Even with his ear plugs, Edgy caught some higher notes of the Echolites' song and shuddered.

He froze.

Edgy twitched, barely able to breathe at the sight before him. Above Madame Lillith stood the strangest and the most hideous creature Edgy had ever seen. Like an enormous spider composed of bone, its fat, bloated body was poised on eight long and delicate legs. Each leg ended in a sharp point. The Echolite bobbed slightly in time with Madame Lillith. In time with its own deadly song. Thick hairs poked out of the creature's parchment-thin skin like black spines. Edgy's flesh prickled. A human head poked out of the front of its body. It had a man's face screwed up in an expression of agony. Its mouth opened and closed with the words of its song.

And then it went still.

Its lips stopped moving.

Madame Lillith swayed for a couple of seconds and then her eyes flickered as if she were waking from a dream. Edgy stood mesmerised, the blood thumping through his skull. Madame Lillith looked up and let out a chilling scream. The Echolite's mouth opened too, but from it came a long, bony needle, like another leg only much thinner. It flashed down, striking Madame Lillith in the temple and puncturing her head. She stood transfixed by the long spine that slowly turned from a creamy yellow into a pink then red.

Edgy felt the bile rise in his throat. The creature was sucking the very blood and brains from Madame Lillith. Edgy watched in horror as her cheeks sank and her body slowly crumpled like a deflated balloon. Soon only a few scraps remained of the envious demon.

For a moment, the Echolite stood still, as if savouring the feast it had just consumed. Its face twisted into a frown then a grimace of pain. Its features buckled and shrank, only to re-emerge a second later. Spinorix gave a yelp that Edgy heard through the wax in his ears. He felt Sally's hand cold in his but gripping him tightly. Madame Lillith's face now leered down at them from the creature's head. It slowly lifted a spindly leg and took a step towards them. Henry put his ears back and barked, baring his teeth.

'Come on, Henry,' Edgy called and turned to run.

Two more Echolites scuttled out of the darkness, cutting off their escape route, the tips of their bony legs clicking horribly on the rock floor. Edgy could see the faces of an old man and a boy hideously grafted on to the front of the monsters.

'We're trapped,' he said.

Henry gave a whining growl as, step by step, the Echolites closed in on them.

She stooped down unto the ground,
To pluck the rose so red.
The thorn it pierced her to the heart,
And this fair maid was dead.

'Dead Maid's Land', traditional folk song

CHAPTER TWENTY-FOUR
CORNERED

The Echolites clicked forward. Edgy looked at Sally, desperately trying to think of something that could get them out of this corner. But Sally looked as helpless as Edgy felt. He could see the Echolites' mouths moving. If he took out his ear plugs, the song would soothe him. He wouldn't be so afraid.

Spinorix fell to his knees. 'I don't want to die,' he sobbed. 'I don't want that . . . thing to steal my face!'

The first Echolite gave a fierce grin, stolen from Madame Lillith.

Edgy hurled himself at it, flailing the skull in a circular arc. 'Get back!' he screamed. Henry barked and howled. Edgy squeezed his eyes shut and swung the skull again, blind and deaf, spinning towards his own destruction, waiting for the horns to clatter ineffectively against the spiny shins.

But the skull met thin air and he overbalanced, falling

on to his chest with a groan as the breath was thumped from his diaphragm. The Echolites had stepped back. Edgy looked up into the eyes of what was once Madame Lillith, and saw confusion and maybe a little fear. The three Echolites had stopped singing and stood silently staring at Edgy. He picked himself up, their strange response making him brave.

'Garn!' he yelled, waving his hands again. 'Get back, I said!'

The creatures took another step back.

'They're afraid of you,' Sally shouted, stepping to his shoulder.

'Or the skull,' Edgy said, waving it in front of him. He held the skull towards the Echolites but it was him they were looking at. Their eyes bored into his until he had to look away. Were they afraid or was it something else? *Respect?* Edgy wondered. 'Go away,' he said. 'Leave us alone.'

They stood for a moment, staring intently at him, then backed away slowly, each step measured and reluctant.

'They're leaving,' Spinorix said, standing still and pointing.

'They did what you told them to,' Sally gasped as the Echolites receded further into the shadows of the tunnel. 'But why?'

'I don't care why.' Spinorix shivered, clinging to Edgy's sleeve. 'Let's just get away before they decide they're not scared.'

'All right but just back away slowly,' Edgy said, his

voice sounding painfully loud with his ears so blocked
up. He passed the skull to Spinorix and scooped up
Henry.

'Take the next left,' he heard Sally say. They shuffled
backwards down the tunnel, not daring to take their eyes
off the shifting blackness, but the Echolites had vanished.

The tunnels twisted and turned. Sally called out
lefts and rights until Edgy could have sworn they were
doubling back on themselves. His head ached and his
eyes felt heavy. *How long have we been walking?* He longed
to see his room and his bed.

'Soon be there,' Sally said, glancing at him.

'How do you know your way around so well, Sally?'
Edgy asked as he trudged after her.

'When you've been around as long as me, you get
to know a thing or two,' she grinned. Edgy could have
sworn her cheeks went a slightly deeper grey, as if she
were blushing.

They walked on in silence for a while. Edgy drilled the
end of his little finger into his ear. He'd removed the wax
but a few bits remained, making his ears itch. He watched
Sally walk in front of him.

'What's it like?' he said at last, catching up with her.
'Y'know, bein' . . . well, dead?' He cringed, wishing he
hadn't asked. It was a rotten question.

But Sally just gave a sigh. 'I don't really know,' she
said. 'My kind of dead is cold. Tired but never sleeping.
Hungry but never eating. Sad. Lonely. Dry. D'you know
how much I'd love to spit?'

Edgy shook his head. 'No,' he said, not knowing quite what to say.

'It's like havin' an itch and never bein' able to scratch, or thinkin' you can remember a name but it's just out of reach. There's no rest.' Sally sighed again. 'No peace . . .'

'I'm sorry,' Edgy muttered.

'What?' Sally asked, looking puzzled.

'That you're dead an' that . . . I'm sorry,' Edgy said and cleared his throat noisily.

'It was a long time ago,' she said, giving a thin smile. 'A very long time. Maybe one day I'll meet my family again and find peace. But thank you . . . That's a nice thing to say.' She reached out her hand and stroked Henry's ear. Henry tilted his head, accepting the caress.

'Hey, he's got used to you.' Edgy gave a grin and felt his face burning.

Friends. That's what Madame Lillith had said. For the first time in his life, Edgy had friends. His tiredness lifted and he quickened his step. Ahead, he saw a dull glow.

'It's the door, the way out!' he laughed. Henry gave a bright yap and leapt from Edgy's arms, his claws clattering on the rocky surface as he scampered to the exit. Then he remembered. 'It'll be locked. We're stuck inside.'

'That's one advantage of hanging around a dump like this for one hundred and nineteen years,' Sally smirked, conjuring a key from her apron pocket with a flourish.

Edgy gave a cheer but stopped as he caught a glimpse of Spinorix's long face. 'What's the matter, Spin?' Edgy said.

'The artefacts from the collection,' Spinorix sighed, staring down at the skull in his hands. 'They're lost . . . I'm useless.'

'Don't worry, Spin,' Sally said. 'We'll get them back at some stage and it's not your fault anyway.'

'There was so many things there,' Spinorix muttered. 'I should've reported the thefts sooner.'

'It's a big collection,' Edgy said, patting the imp's skinny shoulder. 'Nobody could remember it all.'

'I could,' Spinorix said, his eyes burning. 'I could name every item in that collection. I knew things were missing – it was all small stuff – I just tried to ignore it. I hoped nobody noticed, hoped I could catch someone in the act.'

'A bit harder when the skull went missing, eh?' Edgy said. 'Anyway, you did tell Mr Janus, remember?'

'A bit late,' Spinorix mumbled.

'Well, it's all there,' Edgy said, trying to cheer Spinorix up, 'in the cave. Like Sally says, we can go and get it later.' He tried to sound convincing but who in their right mind would go back into the tunnels for anything?

'That's it!' Spinorix jumped up, excited. 'That's what was missing. The Devil's Dagger.'

'What?' Edgy said, catching Sally's eye. She shook her head, obviously having trouble keeping up too.

'Remember I said that not everything that was stolen was in the cave?' Spinorix said, his eyes wide. 'Well, there was one thing missing – the Devil's Dagger.'

'I read a story about that,' Edgy said. 'Was it kept here?'

'The only blade that could kill the great Satan himself.

It was said to be the blade used to cut out the heart of Moloch.' Spinorix nodded. 'Razor sharp . . . nasty. I didn't miss it for months cos it's kept locked away.'

'Maybe Madame Lillith hid it somewhere else,' Edgy muttered. 'D'you think she was the one that tried to kill me?'

'She said she didn't,' Sally replied. 'She was a demon of envy, not really the kind of demon that kills. Stealing was about her limit.'

'Do demons have limits?' Edgy said, looking doubtful.

'There are all kinds of demons, Edgy,' Sally said. 'Some would tear you apart without a second thought, others are more timid and devious. Madame Lillith was so eaten up with jealousy she was nearly mortal.'

'Besides,' Spinorix said, with an embarrassed cough, 'from a demon's point of view, having gone to all the trouble of getting you into that cave and under that machine, I would have wanted to watch you get squashed . . . If I were a demon who liked that kind of thing – which I'm not – if you see what I mean . . . Madame Lillith wasn't there when you were tied up on the conveyor belt.'

'So you don't think it was a demon who tried to kill me?' Edgy said, narrowing his eyes and staring off into the distance.

'I don't think it's a demon's way to knock people out, either,' Sally said. 'They're more complicated than that. They can't do things the easy way. It's not in their nature. They have to set traps and go around the houses to catch someone out. No, if you ask me, whoever put you on the crusher wanted to be far away from the scene of your death when it happened.'

'So we still don't know who it was and they're still out there,' Edgy said as Sally turned the key in the lock. 'Maybe I'd be safer down here.'

IF MEAT AND DRINK THOU GAVEST NONE,
EVERY NIGHT AND ALL,
THE FIRE WILL BURN THEE TO THE BONE,
AND CHRIST RECEIVE THY SOUL.

'LYKE WAKE DIRGE', TRADITIONAL FOLK BALLAD

CHAPTER TWENTY-FIVE
FITTING THE PIECES

Surprise and amazement pushed Janus's eyebrows ever upwards as he listened to everything that had happened. He pushed the triangle of bone back into its place and traced a skinny finger along the ridges and grooves carved into the skull of Aldorath.

'I've not heard the full tale of the skull before,' he mused. 'And it was in the book from Scrabsnitch? Remarkable.' He swung away from Edgy, Sally and Spinorix and, stretching high, dragged rolls of charts from a shelf cluttered with scrolls and papers. A small bottle fell to the floor with a shrill tinkle but Janus was completely focused on unrolling the charts. 'It could well be the last piece of the puzzle.'

He ran his fingernail along the skull again, discarding several green- and brown-coloured sheets. Finally, he stopped on a chart coloured white and blue. One of the poles.

Edgy shivered – it looked cold even on paper. 'A land of snow and ice,' Edgy whispered. 'North or south, though?'

'If the story is true, Edgy, then we can match the outlines on the skull with those on the charts,' replied Janus.

'And find where Moloch lies . . .' Edgy said, his eyes wide. Sally and Spinorix stared back at Edgy in silence as Janus turned the chart round and round, tapping every now and then on the skull.

'Is that wise?' Sally asked, her voice hushed and hesitant.

'We 'ave to, Sally.' Edgy frowned. 'Salomé is probably only a step away from finding Moloch and that wouldn't do at all, would it, Mr Janus?'

Janus glanced up at them, his eyes vacant. 'What? Who? Oh, yes, quite, that wouldn't do at all,' he said and peered down again, lost in a land of icebergs and glaciers.

Spinorix gave a cough. 'The other exhibits, sir,' he said, staring at the floor, his voice subdued. 'They're still down below. We couldn't bring them with us –'

'And what do we do about Madame Lillith, Mr Janus?' Sally interrupted.

A spasm of irritation flashed across Janus's face. He waved a dismissive hand. 'Madame Lillith was a victim of her own greed. I have little sympathy with demons who steal from their employers.'

'But someone tried to kill Edgy,' Sally snapped back.

'Yes, yes,' Janus replied, frowning at Sally and glancing

back at the skull as if it was calling him. 'The governors will instigate a full investigation. Rest assured we'll get to the bottom of things. Now . . .' He returned to the patterns on the skull and the ice-blue chart.

A sudden weariness washed over Edgy. He had no idea of the time but he felt battered and bruised.

'I'm goin' to lie down now, Mr Janus, if that's all right with you, sir,' he called.

Janus looked up again and nodded. 'Yes, yes, you get some rest, my boy,' he beamed. 'You'll need all your energy for the coming days.' He fell back to tracking the grooves in the skull and muttering to himself. Edgy gave a backward glance as they left him deep in thought.

'*Thank goodness you're all right, Edgy,*' Sally said in a croaky impersonation of Janus the moment they were in the corridor. She put her hands on her hips and wobbled her head with indignation. '*Echolites, you say? How worrying! I've been frettin' about you all day . . .*'

'Leave it out, Sally,' Edgy grumbled, rubbing his eyes. 'I 'aven't got the energy for a scrap.'

'I'm just sayin' he could've shown a bit more concern about you,' Sally said.

'That's as may be but he's a busy man, Sally, a genius, like. Got 'is mind on higher things.' He smiled at her and she gave a *humph* of indignation and walked alongside him in silence.

'Well, I'm going back to the exhibition hall to make sure nothing else is missing,' Spinorix muttered, turning right as Edgy and Sally walked on.

'Don't worry,' Edgy called after him. 'I don't think anyone will be helpin' themselves to the collection now.'

They reached Edgy's door and Sally stopped, leaning on the threshold, her arms folded. Henry cocked his head as if to say, *'Right, what're you goin' to do now?'*

Edgy wasn't sure. It was easier in the old days, somehow – then he could've slammed the door in Sally's face. But now they were friends. What should he do? Invite her in? He stared at her, twitching, glancing right and left.

'Are you still after yer old room?' Edgy mumbled.

Sally smiled. 'Nah,' she said. 'But I'm not leavin' this door frame. Not while there's a killer about. You can rest peaceful, Edgy. I'll be watchin' over you!'

Edgy grinned. 'My own guardian angel,' he said, bowing and closing the door. He slumped on to the bed and fell into a deep and dreamless sleep.

Edgy awoke to find Janus standing over him and Sally peering over his shoulder.

'Come along, young man, get yourself dressed,' he said, pacing back and forth. 'It's a new day and we've got to meet the governors again if we're to get backing for this expedition.'

'Expedition, Mr Janus?' Edgy croaked, rubbing his aching head as he untangled himself from the sheets. He stopped and gave Sally a frown. 'D'you mind, Sal? I 'ave to get dressed, I'm not decent!'

Sally gave an impish grin and backed out of the room.

'Yes, expedition,' Janus continued. 'I've deciphered the

map and I think I've pinpointed the location of Moloch's remains –'

'We 'ave to find it before Salomé,' Edgy cut in, struggling to his feet and trying to get one leg into his trousers, 'or she'll put his heart back and that'll be an end of it!'

'Exactly, Edgy!' Janus said, rubbing his hands. 'And won't my brother hate it? Just think. We'll be the toast of the Society!' He thrust his face into Edgy's, making him lean back and stumble over, one leg still undressed. Janus seemed unperturbed. 'But it won't be easy, mind. They'll say it's a myth. They'll try to pour cold water on the whole thing. Come along, boy, look sharp. I'll need you to back me up.'

Edgy felt his heart sink. *Back him up?* 'The governors'll never listen to me, sir,' Edgy murmured, tucking his shirt in and pulling his braces over his shoulders.

'Nonsense, boy. You can see things they can't. Besides, you can show them the book. They can research that if they want.' Janus grinned. 'I've every faith in you.'

They left the room, Edgy hopping to put his boot on.

Sally smirked as they passed. 'Good luck,' she said.

'Keep Henry here, will yer?' he called back with a pleading look. Henry sat at Sally's feet, his head cocked quizzically.

Edgy's stomach rumbled and groaned as he followed Janus down the passage to the governors' room. His throat felt dry and tight. If only he'd had a chance to eat some breakfast.

'You must mention the book reference and tell them what happened in the tunnels,' Janus chattered on. Edgy felt so nervous he barely listened. He didn't want to let Janus down, that was why.

The governors' room was as stuffy as ever. The governors sat in their usual places; Plumphrey busily cutting into a fried breakfast, Mauldeth sneering over a cup of breakfast tea, Sokket with his fingers interlaced and his lips tight, and Milberry turning the pages of a thick book.

'Ah, Janus,' Plumphrey said, egg dribbling from the side of his mouth. 'What's all this about an expedition, eh? Moloch? All sounds a bit far-fetched.'

'Roland,' Milberry said, her voice quiet but firm, 'let's keep this official and not just leap in.' She closed her book and leaned over it. 'Envry, you have made a request for funds to mount an expedition to the frozen North. Can you explain?'

Janus's eyes shone and he gripped his lapels. 'Indeed I can, Professor Milberry. I intend to charter a ship to take us into the Arctic Circle –'

'Frozen North, little brother – she already said that.' Mauldeth stared at Janus over the rim of his cup, his pointed features set and stony. 'Just tell us what for.'

Janus gave a little nod. Edgy could see the red spots growing on his cheeks. 'It is my intention to uncover the long-lost remains of the arch-demon Moloch –'

'Told y'so,' Plumphrey said, spitting globs of bacon fat

across the table. 'Barking mad, ready for Bedlam – take him away.'

'Moloch is a myth, Envry, you know that,' Sokket said, screwing his face up. 'We've no more evidence that he exists than Satan himself!'

'He exists all right,' Janus said. He took Edgy's shoulder and pushed him forward as if he were presenting him to the governors. 'Edgy has had something of an adventure down in the tunnels. The Skull of Aldorath was stolen and he recovered it. But there's more – tell them, Edgy.' Janus nodded at him.

Edgy cleared his throat. He heard his voice, thin and dry, and cringed. Why did he sound so stupid and unconvincing? 'Well, in Mr Janus's book, *The Legends of Moloch*, I found a tale –'

'Not a pointed one, I hope, eh, lad?' Plumphrey roared with laughter at his own joke and elbowed Sokket, who winced as if he were in pain. 'Pointed, oh deary me!'

Milberry glared at him, quelling the tide of mirth in an instant.

Edgy gave another cough and continued, 'The markings on the top of the skull are a map –'

'I thought you had decided they were mere tribal marks, carved so deep into the thin flesh that they etched the skull, Mauldeth?' Sokket said, giving his fellow governor a sly grin.

'They are. This is all total nonsense – one of my little brother's wild goose chases, you mark my words,' Mauldeth said, pouring more tea.

'Show them, Edgy,' Janus said, passing the book to him.

Edgy flicked through the pages, searching for the right story, praying it would come to him. The book seemed to have a mind of its own, like everything else in this place. Title after title flickered past Edgy's gaze: *Moloch Creates the Echolites* followed by *Salomé and Moloch*. Despair seeped into Edgy's heart – there was nothing, no mention of Aldorath. He was going to look a right idiot and Janus would be laughed out of the room.

'Trouble, lad?' Sokket smirked at him. Edgy's fingers felt numb, sweat trickled down his back and the room seemed to close in. He gave a squint and a shudder.

'Really, Envry, you didn't tell us the lad was illiterate when we let you take him on,' Mauldeth drawled, stirring his drink and grinning at Edgy.

A stab of annoyance tightened Edgy's lips. *Illiterate? Cheeky beggar*, Edgy thought. His thumb slid into the book and he opened the page. 'Here we are,' he said, grinning back at Mauldeth. *The Legend of Aldorath and Moloch*. Edgy passed the open book to Mauldeth, who scanned the pages before thumping it on to the table with a snort.

'And that makes it true?' Mauldeth said.

Milberry picked up the book and peered closely at it, turning the pages and rubbing the cover. 'This is an old text. Ancient, I should say. You know how reliable they usually prove to be.'

'Old texts are ones written by demons themselves, Edgy,' Janus explained. 'They're often histories.'

'But extremely accurate in certain details,' Milberry added. 'Very useful. It's funny, I have a similar copy but I've never seen that passage. Very curious.'

'Well, it doesn't help us to decide about the damnable expedition,' Plumphrey said with a belch. 'It'll cost a pretty penny.'

'As my illustrious brother is forever pointing out,' Janus said with a humourless grin, 'we aren't short of money, Plumphrey.'

'An' with all due respect, sirs, and ma'am,' Edgy croaked, 'the map on the top of Aldorath's skull – it matches Mr Janus's charts.'

'It's a fool's errand, I say,' Sokket murmured, turning his mouth down. 'Better staying close to home and not risking all on the high seas. I should know, I was a ship's doctor for long enough.'

'On the other hand,' Milberry said, turning Edgy's book over and over, squinting at the cover, 'it may just settle the arch-demon debate once and for all . . . I mean, if he did find the remains of Moloch, then that would be proof perfect.'

'Some members of the Society speculate that demons are just another species of creature on earth, Edgy, and not supernatural at all,' Janus explained, seeing his confused frown. 'No human has ever encountered an arch-demon. Even some demons don't believe in them.'

'Or in Satan himself,' Plumphrey said, raising his eyebrows.

Edgy thought about the snake in the library. *Don't*

*they know? Was that why the snake made me promise to keep
quiet?*

'Edgy also managed to bind Belphagor with a riddle
and he told us that Moloch's corpse lies in a land of ice
and snow,' Janus said.

For a moment the governors studied Edgy closely – all
except Mauldeth, who steadfastly glared into his tea.

'Suppose you did find Moloch,' Sokket said, closing
one eye and sucking his cheeks in. 'What do you propose
to do?'

'Bring him back,' Janus said, staring at Sokket. 'Bring
him here to the Society.'

'Bring him back here to show off to all and sundry, no
doubt,' Mauldeth spat. 'It's all for glory, isn't it? You just
can't accept that I made the discovery of the century and
that it will never be bested.'

'How dare you? I would bring Moloch back for scientific study,' Janus shouted, banging his fist on the table.
'I'm not interested in your petty glory-seeking.'

'Gentlemen, please!' Milberry snapped, jumping to her
feet and raising her hand. 'This has to stop!'

Janus froze, glaring at his brother. Edgy stared from one
to the other.

Mauldeth dropped his gaze and clinked his cup back
into its saucer. 'I propose to the governors that Envry's
request to lead an expedition be rejected –'

'Wait,' Milberry interrupted. 'The enterprise does have
its merits, even though it is bold and probably reckless.'
She eyed Janus and then continued, 'However, if the

Society is funding it, then more than one fellow should go.'

Janus's eyes widened. 'Professor Milberry, I must protest –'

Mauldeth's eyes lit up. He jumped to his feet. 'Of course! Such an undertaking needs the close supervision of more than one fellow. As chancellor, I nominate myself to accompany Envry!'

'You'll kill each other,' Sokket said, his face grey and drawn.

'Which is why you should accompany them also,' Milberry said. Janus and Mauldeth turned to her in disbelief.

Sokket tried to speak, gaping like a landed codfish. 'Me?' he gasped at last.

'Why not? After all, you do have experience of the sea, Mortesque,' Milberry said archly. 'Didn't you just mention that you were once a ship's doctor?'

Edgy didn't know where to look – at Janus's furrowed frown, Mauldeth's gritted teeth or Sokket's slack-jawed stare.

'We'll all drown within the first week,' murmured Sokket.

PART THE SECOND

LORD BYRON'S MAGGOT

OUR MATE, HE IS A BULLY MAN.
LEAVE HER, JOHNNY, LEAVE HER,
HE GIVES US ALL THE BEST HE CAN.
AND IT'S TIME FOR US TO LEAVE HER.

'LEAVE HER, JOHNNY', TRADITIONAL SEA SHANTY

CHAPTER TWENTY-SIX
SETTING SAIL

Edgy's stomach churned as he stared from the side of the ship. The docks way below buzzed with activity as an army of workers scurried back and forth bringing last-minute items, checking ropes, shouting and whistling to each other. Edgy wrinkled his nose. The stink of the Thames mingled with tar and rope. The dock warehouses loomed above them. The blackened brick walls were dotted with square eyes and shuttered by metal doors. Here and there the swinging arm of a winch poked out as sacks and bales were heaved up to the darkness inside.

The ship bumped gently against the rope buffers that hung the length of the dockside. Its massive steam engine breathed slowly somewhere deep within its bulk. *A huge, black monster*, Edgy thought.

'Welcome aboard *Lord Byron's Maggot*,' Janus had declared, waving his arms to indicate the ship.

'Lord who's what?' Edgy had replied, forgetting himself. 'Beggin' your pardon, sir.'

'A strange name, I'll grant you, Edgy, but no finer ship could you find to take us on our mission!'

Janus had taken Edgy the length and breadth of the ship explaining each part but all Edgy could remember was that the front was called the bow and the back the stern. The other terms tangled together in Edgy's mind, a mass of bowsprits, mizzens and top gallants. The only thing that did make sense to Edgy was the huge funnel that jutted out of the centre of the ship.

'A steamship, Edgy,' Janus had beamed. 'One of the fastest and finest. With a hold big enough to carry a . . . well, you know what. An engineering marvel, boy, mark my words.'

'Like a railway engine, Mr Janus,' Edgy had said.

'In a manner of speaking,' he replied, putting his finger to his bottom lip. 'A steam engine turns the mighty paddles at the side of the ship. It still uses sail power too. We'll be at our destination in no time.'

Now Edgy sighed and stared down at the bustling dockside. He wondered what Henry was doing. If only he could have come – but Janus was strict on the matter.

'No place for a dog on a serious scientific expedition, young man,' he had said.

'Don't worry,' Sally had said, hugging the dog to her gaunt form. 'He's used to me now, he'll be fine.'

'Can't you come and wave me off?' Edgy had asked.

Sally's silver eyebrows had creased into a worried frown. 'You know I can't, Edgy. I'm tied to this place somehow. I can't set foot outside much as I'd love to wave you off.'

Milberry had come to see him the night before the voyage. She spread a thick fur coat across his bed.

'Finest reindeer skin,' she said. 'I had it imported. It'll keep you warm as toast. Take care, my dear.'

She had pulled Edgy to her and embraced him until he'd given an embarrassed cough.

'Yes, ma'am, I will,' he said, pulling away. Then he stopped, adding, 'And thank you for the jacket.'

But to think! A serious scientific expedition, and Edgy was going. Edgy, who just a couple of months ago was only good enough to scoop dog droppings from the street. The governors had all grumbled, of course.

'And why do you need the boy to go, Envry?' Sokket had said, massaging his temples and trying to regain his composure after Milberry had nominated him for the voyage.

'Edgy is crucial to this expedition.' Janus patted him on the back. Edgy couldn't help grinning. A warm glow of pride spread up from his stomach. Janus continued, 'The boy has shown his ability to riddle and to spot disguised demons. He outsmarted Salomé herself not too long ago. I need Edgy on this trip.'

Edgy had felt so proud then but now he felt nervous and lonely. The deck glistened black, worn by a thousand scuffing feet. Everything was black – the ropes, the wood, the warehouses, even the Thames. Soot, tar and the stinking, black river.

'Ye look a bit lost, young feller,' a soft voice said, making Edgy turn.

'Just takin' this case to Mr Janus's room, erm, cabin,' Edgy muttered, nodding down to the trunk by his feet.

A weathered, brown-faced man leaned against some packing cases, hands in the pockets of his stained, white trousers. A short blue jacket told Edgy that this man was a sailor. A round cap covered his greying, slicked-back hair. He looked thin, hook-nosed and seagull-eyed. Thick sideburns fringed his sunken cheeks.

He smiled but his eyes didn't join in as he extended a hand. 'Silky McFarland's me name. Able seaman.'

Somehow, his gentle voice made Edgy shudder. He shook the man's hand but didn't give his name.

'Been to sea before, boy?' Silky McFarland murmured.

'No, Mr McFarland.' Edgy shook his head, slipping his hand from the man's cold grasp.

Silky grinned, showing a gold tooth. 'Nothing to it,' he said. 'Once you get used to the roll o' the waves, we'll have ye up above.'

Edgy followed McFarland's gaze upwards to where the tops of the masts loomed. His stomach swirled and he remembered his rooftop adventure. McFarland's gentle chuckle snapped him to.

'Ye not so good with heights, are ye, boy?' he said.

Edgy frowned. *How does he know?* Or could he tell from Edgy's pale face?

'Seaman McFarland,' a stern voice called from behind them both. A tall, fierce-looking man in a naval officer's jacket stood scowling down at them. His black peaked cap shadowed his eyes, hardening his grimace. 'You have duties down on deck, sir. I expect you to be earning your keep, not chattering to children.'

Silky gave a half bow and tugged at the front of his cap. 'Aye, captain, beggin' your pardon. I'll see to it right away.' He turned and gave Edgy a wink. 'Don't worry. I'll be around, watchin' over ye,' he said and sauntered off to where men were throwing packing cases up from the dockside.

Edgy stared after him. There was something about the man he didn't like. *Could he be working for Salomé?* Edgy shook himself. He shouldn't be so silly. The man was just teasing him. All the same, Edgy made a note to mention it to Janus.

'I'm Captain Boyd,' he said. The man's voice had softened, but his ruddy complexion still made him look angry. 'Don't worry about McFarland. He delights in teasing youngsters. A bit of a practical joker too, by all accounts. He means no harm. Welcome aboard. I'll talk to you later perhaps. For now, I'd better check on your employer – he seems to be having problems down there.' A brief smile flickered over Boyd's face as he strode off amidships towards a growing crowd of dockers.

Edgy's gaze followed him and he could see Janus waving his arms and gesticulating as the sailors threw the remaining cases to each other in a chain that led up the gangplank.

'Careful, gentlemen, careful,' Janus cried, pressing his palms to his temples. 'They contain fragile equipment.'

Edgy smiled as the dockers made a pantomime of passing the boxes, almost dropping them but always catching them in time. He looked up. Straight into the eyes of Lord Mauldeth, who stood at the other end of the ship watching the same show. He smiled but there was no humour in his gaze. The captain barked a few orders, cuffed a couple of grinning dockers and soon all Janus's precious cargo was on-board.

Janus bounded across the deck and up the ladder to the poop deck where Edgy stood. 'Soon be off,' he cried, rubbing his hands and beaming. 'Just have to tow the ship into the Thames and then they'll get the engine turning and it'll be off to the open sea!'

'I don't think Mr Sokket is as keen to get away, sir,' Edgy said and nodded at Sokket. The tall, dour-faced governor stood on the gangplank, a suitcase in each hand. He looked like a condemned man heading for the gallows.

'Don't mind him,' Janus snorted. 'He didn't have to come. I'm surprised he did. Not really an adventurer, these days. More of an armchair collector, to be honest.'

'What kind of demon does Mr Sokket collect, sir?' Edgy asked. He realised now how Plumphrey was influenced by the demons of gluttony he kept around him. He wondered about Sokket.

'Sokket? Oh, he's interested in demons of wrath and envy,' Janus said, waving a dismissive hand. Then he leaned a little closer to Edgy and said in a lower voice, 'Some say he collects demons of despair too – which might account for his pessimistic outlook.'

'Despair?' Edgy said. 'Is that one of the sins?'

'Well,' Janus sniggered, 'it was until fairly recently but then the church replaced the sin of despair with the sin of sloth. Some demons adapted and changed but, as you can imagine with demons of despair, quite a few just gave up.'

'Does the church control demons then?' Edgy said.

'Not really, Edgy, but demons generally revel in the downfall of humans. If the church begins to view those who give up on life with sympathy rather than criticising them, then that particular game is ruined for the demons. And for demons, the game is everything.'

'The game, Mr Janus?' Edgy frowned. The demons he'd met didn't seem to be playing.

'The more complicated the better,' Janus explained. 'The more deadly the better. But to them it's a game.'

'I don't think I understand demons very well, Mr Janus,' Edgy sighed, shaking his head.

'Best not to, Edgy,' Janus muttered. 'Just remember, often they're full of pride and bluster, devious but easily tricked, as you've shown yourself. If there's a complicated way to do something, that's the way they'll do it and that is their weakness.'

'It's a wonder Salomé hasn't tried to interfere with all the preparations, Mr Janus,' Edgy said, glancing down at McFarland heaving on a rope with three other men.

'Hmm, you have a point, Edgy. I'd have thought she'd

have made an appearance by now.' Janus stroked his wispy white beard. 'I'd like to think that she hadn't got wind of this little jaunt but somehow I doubt that.'

'As you said, Mr Janus, if there's a complicated way to do it . . .' Edgy replied. 'Perhaps she's planning somethin'.'

'Oh, you can count on that, Edgy.' Janus nodded. 'But we'll soon be on our way. And then think, Edgy: every day takes us nearer to our goal!'

A crowd had gathered down below on the quayside. Women in grey shawls, scarves tied around their heads to ward off the cold. Ragged children quarrelled and bawled at their feet. A few of the younger seamen lingered with their sweethearts and then dashed up the gangplank just as it scraped across the cobbles back towards the ship. *Happy families.* Edgy watched some of the children waving, wives dabbing handkerchiefs to their eyes. *If I fell over the side now, who would miss me?* Edgy thought. He stopped and peered closer. A large, brown figure stood at the back of the crowd, hand half raised. Professor Milberry had come to wave them off.

Sokket appeared at Edgy's shoulder and gave a long sigh.

'Cheer up, Mortesque,' Janus beamed. 'We're on the expedition of the century.'

'We're on a fool's errand,' Sokket said. His face looked longer and greyer than ever. He shook his head.

Smoke began to belch from the ship's funnel and the great round paddles on either side of the boat began to thrash at the filthy water.

'One of the sailors told me that we'll get used to the sea,' Edgy said, watching the sailors scurrying about the deck.

'We won't need to worry if our bodies are rolling to and fro at the bottom of it,' Sokket muttered, staring wide-eyed into the water. 'To and fro . . .'

The ship's foghorn gave a blast, drowning out Sokket's mournful grumbling. The mighty paddle wheels thundered through the water, sending smaller craft bobbing away on the waves. Edgy watched the city float by behind a curtain of masts and sails, and soon the river widened and the banks became shrouded in grey mist. The ship reached deeper water and headed out to sea.

A POOR OLD MAN CAME RIDING BY,
AN' WE SAY SO, AN' WE HOPE SO.
A POOR OLD MAN CAME RIDING BY,
A POOR OLD MAN!
SAYS I, 'OLD MAN, YOUR HORSE WILL DIE.'
AN' WE SAY SO, AN' WE HOPE SO.
SAYS I, 'OLD MAN, YOUR HORSE WILL DIE.'
A POOR OLD MAN!

'THE DEAD HORSE', TRADITIONAL SEA SHANTY

CHAPTER TWENTY-SEVEN
DANGER IN THE RIGGING

Edgy awoke not knowing if it was night or day. The ship groaned around him and his head felt light with the rolling of the sea. The vibration of the engine rumbled through everything. He wondered what the others were up to back at the Society. He imagined Spinorix sorting through the collection, sticking his tongue out as he checked off every item. Edgy dragged himself off the bed and stumbled out of his cabin, grabbing on to the door-frames and beams as he made his way to the deck. He missed Henry.

A cold wind slapped Edgy's cheek and brought tears to his eye. The sky hung low and grey, stretched over the leaden water. The sails snapped and cracked. Edgy felt his stomach clench as the flat horizon swayed up and down. Now the sea surrounded them. He shuffled in a stumbling circle across the deck and fought the urge to vomit.

'Not found your sea legs yet then, Mr Taylor?' Captain

Boyd called down to him from the poop deck, his red face screwed up against the spray. 'Don't worry, a few days at sea and you'll be fine.'

Edgy staggered past the bustling crew towards the captain and clambered up the stairs. He tried to smile but a sudden swell brought his stomach up into his chest. He spun round and retched on to the deck. Straight on to a pair of fine black shoes. Edgy looked up into the unimpressed gaze of Lord Mauldeth. His pointed features twisted into a grimace of disgust.

'I can tell you're going to be such an asset on this expedition, Taylor,' Mauldeth snapped. 'I'll have these dropped by your room later. You can make sure they're clean.'

'Sorry, your lordship,' Edgy gasped, wiping his mouth with the back of his hand.

'It still puzzles me why my little brother was so insistent that you come,' Mauldeth continued. 'Mind you, you're not the only one whose presence I'd question on this voyage . . .' Edgy followed his gaze across the deck to where Sokket swayed and stared off into the horizon, slowly rubbing his hands and muttering to himself. 'Let's just hope no ill befalls you.'

He doesn't sound very sincere, Edgy thought.

Captain Boyd handed Edgy a scrap of paper, an amused twinkle in his eye. 'Take these bearings to Mr Janus, Edgy, then find yourself some food,' he said. 'A full stomach makes it easier.'

A full stomach? Edgy took the paper from Boyd and

crept around Mauldeth, avoiding his icy glare. He slipped
and stumbled down the steps and back below deck. Janus's
cabin and those of the other governors lay beneath the
poop deck at the stern of the ship. Edgy found his door in
the gloom and knocked hard. There was no answer. Edgy
waited and then knocked again. Taking a deep breath, he
lifted the latch and pushed on the door. It opened with
a creak.

Janus's cabin was much bigger than Edgy's but still
cramped. An oil lamp swung from the low beams of the
ceiling. A small pallet bed lay in one corner, a trunk was
open and spilling clothes across the floor, and a writing
desk was piled with books all huddled together, making
the floorboards almost impossible to see. Janus wasn't
there.

Edgy was about to leave but something caught his eye.
A book lay open on the desk – the book Janus had bought
from Scrabsnitch. *The Legends of Moloch*. Curiosity drew
Edgy back into the room. He knew the basic story of
Moloch but what were the other legends? What else
might the book tell them?

Edgy stepped carefully over the discarded clothes,
and settled himself on the stool in front of the desk. An
engraving of Moloch filled the left-hand page. Hatred
burned in his feline eyes, horns spiralled above his
frowning, wrinkled brow. He bared his teeth in a fierce
snarl that emphasised the pointed features, the sharp
nose, the goatee beard. Bat-like wings held him aloft in
a boiling black sky and he brandished a cruel spear that

seemed to point out of the page. Edgy tried not to look at the furious glare of the picture but read the caption: **My counsel is war**.

'Edgy, what are you doing?' Janus's voice made him start and slam the book shut with a thump.

'Nothing, Mr Janus. I mean, I saw the book – it was open.'

Janus stepped forward. 'What did you read?' he asked, his voice low. Edgy had never seen him like this – almost threatening.

'Nothin' much, sir, just somethin' about Moloch wantin' war,' Edgy said, his words running together as Janus snatched the book up from the desk.

'Yes, well. Isn't that why we're stopping Salomé from placing his heart back in his body?' Janus seemed to relax but he kept the book hugged to his chest. 'You mustn't handle this book again, Edgy, do you understand? It's very old and . . . fragile. If it were damaged, who knows what valuable information might be lost to the world.'

'Yes, Mr Janus. Sorry, sir,' Edgy said, looking down at the cluttered floor. How could he have been so bad-mannered?

'That's all right, Edgy, no harm done.' Janus gave a tight smile. 'Curiosity isn't a bad trait after all. It's what makes us go and find out about the world.'

'Yes, sir.'

'In fact, your demon-spotting skills are needed right away,' Janus said, placing the book on the bed, clapping his hands together and marching out of the cabin.

'They are?' Edgy said, scurrying after Janus.

'Indeed, Edgy. Follow me.' Janus was out on the deck and heading towards the bow of the ship. Throwing a glance over his shoulder every now and then, he continued, 'Of course, the ship employs a lookout at all times. Have to watch for obstacles, whales, other ships, all kinds of things really. But they don't have your talent for seeing demons.'

'Are there demons at sea, Mr Janus?' Edgy said.

'There are demons in all parts of the world.' Janus's voice had dropped as a couple of sailors had glanced up at him from their work. 'Sea demons are even more of a rarity than your regular demons. Not as many people to tempt, I suppose, but you never know.'

'So you want me to keep watch, sir?' Edgy asked, staring out across the grey sea.

'Exactly,' Janus beamed. 'If you see anything untoward, just let me know first.'

'Leave it with me, Mr Janus,' Edgy said, glad to see him smiling again.

'Excellent, young man,' Janus said and clapped Edgy hard on the back.

Edgy stood in the grey twilight. It hadn't occurred to him that standing at the front of the ship watching the sea would be hard work. The pounding of the steam engine and the rocking of the waves worked on his head and stomach. In the excitement of reading the book and being caught by Janus, Edgy had forgotten his nausea, but

now it returned. Standing still for so long proved diffi-
cult. Edgy leaned on the side of the ship, wriggling and
shifting position, stamping his numb feet in the cold. His
cheeks and the end of his nose had lost all feeling too.
The distant horizon stretched on, featureless, colourless
in the winter evening. It was so big. Edgy wasn't sure
where to look.

The decks were largely empty as most of the crew had
gone below in search of food from the galley. A smell of
gravy and stew tormented him. How long should he stay
up here? Janus hadn't really said. But Edgy couldn't stand
watch all night. He sighed and then froze.

Something shining and black slithered up out of the
water in the distance. It was hard to make out and it
vanished in an instant. *A seal? No, it's too big. A whale
then?* Edgy leaned over the edge of the ship and craned
his neck, squinting to see. If only Janus had given him a
telescope. He stepped back and turned to run to Janus's
cabin.

A dark figure flitted across the deck and Edgy heard
a rushing of air as something heavy swung towards him.
Silky McFarland appeared from nowhere, snarling and
running towards him. Edgy gasped, the air blasted from
his lungs as McFarland launched into him, knocking
him to one side. The deck was a tangle of wood and rope
crashing down on to them. A stab of pain lanced through
Edgy's temple as he tumbled back under McFarland's
weight.

They hanged my old father,
They hanged my old mother,
They say I hanged for money,
But I never hanged nobody.
And they call me Hangin' Johnny.
So hang, boys, hang!

'Hanging Johnny', traditional sea shanty

CHAPTER TWENTY-EIGHT
THE MERMAID INN

Edgy lay wheezing, trying to catch his breath. His back ached where he had hit the deck. Silky McFarland staggered to his feet, shrugging off a coil of rope.

'Edgy, are you all right?' Janus cried, dashing forward through the crowd that had gathered.

'He's fine. Just shaken, that's all,' Mauldeth sneered, staring at him down his pointed nose.

'What happened?' Edgy groaned. He lay on the deck staring up at the crowd of faces that surrounded him.

'Some of the rigging fell, Edgy,' Janus said, steadying him as he tried to stand. 'Mr McFarland here saved your life – you would have been crushed if he hadn't pushed you out of the way.'

'Thank you,' Edgy said, giving a weak smile. Had he misjudged this man?

The scrawny sailor grinned at him. 'You're welcome,

son. Though I wonder what you've done to make someone want to kill ye.'

'Are you saying someone sent that lot crashing down deliberately?' Mauldeth snapped.

'That's a serious allegation, Mr McFarland,' Captain Boyd said. 'What makes you think it?'

McFarland held up the end of a rope. 'It's been cut, captain. Not that you'd allow such shoddy seamanship on board, captain, sir, but if it *had* frayed, then the strands of the rope would be different lengths. Look – these are cut off square.' He triumphantly handed the rope to Boyd. 'Aye, someone's took an axe to that for sure.'

'By Gad, you're right,' Boyd murmured, twirling the rope in his thick fingers.

'But who'd want to do something like that?' Sokket muttered, staring intently at Edgy and rubbing his hands as if he couldn't get warm. He shook his head, whispering under his breath, 'I knew no good would come of this, no good at all . . .'

'With respect, sir,' Edgy croaked. His head pounded and he could feel his throat tightening with the roll of the ship again. 'Someone has tried twice before, back at the Society –'

'Yes, yes, yes. So you said,' Mauldeth cut in, dismissing the comment with a backward wave of his hand. 'I suggest that you get some rest, young man. The captain and I will conduct a thorough investigation in the morning –'

'You?' Janus interrupted, frowning. 'Why should you investigate?'

Mauldeth's heavy eyelids half closed in disdain at his younger brother. 'Because I am chancellor of the Royal Society and therefore leader of this expedition.'

Edgy winced as their voices rose, cutting into his head as keenly as the cold wind. Janus's face had reddened. 'You aren't the leader. This is *my* expedition.'

'Are you challenging my authority as chancellor?' Mauldeth snapped.

'You just want all the glory,' Janus shouted, stamping his foot. 'You've been desperate from the outset to stop me from making a greater discovery than you.'

'Gentlemen, please!' Captain Boyd said, taking a step forward. 'The boy is fit to pass out. Get him below and we'll discuss this further tomorrow.' He turned to the gaggle of sailors who had drifted up from below on hearing the commotion. 'Men, back to your duties or finish your supper. This ship won't sail itself, y'know. Seaman McFarland, well done. Your quick thinking saved the boy's life and I'll see you're amply rewarded. Now, everyone, back to what you were doing!'

Janus gave Mauldeth a cold stare and then turned to Edgy, shepherding him to his cabin. Edgy's head throbbed in time with the engines as he stumbled through the dark passages of the ship's hull. Sailors murmured and stopped to stare as he passed them. Janus got Edgy to his bed and sat him down.

'Don't worry, you're safe here. I'll have Captain Boyd put a man at the door,' he said.

'I saw somethin', Mr Janus,' Edgy groaned, laying his

head on the pillow. 'On the sea, just before the rigging came down.'

'What was it?' Janus asked, frowning.

'I'm not sure, sir. Somethin' black. I don't know if the lookout saw it too.' Edgy's eyelids felt heavy. 'It could've been a whale or a porpoise . . .'

'Don't worry, Edgy, I'll check. You rest for now,' Janus said, pulling the rough blankets over his shoulders. 'We need you fighting fit for this adventure, young man.'

Janus was right – he needed to sleep. He felt safe with the sprightly professor there, watching over him. Edgy smiled as sleep slowly drifted over him.

The following morning found Edgy pacing the deck with Captain Boyd. Silence had awoken him and at first he wondered what was missing as he had eased himself up in bed. The engines were still. No pounding pistons vibrated through the hull of the ship. All he could hear was the occasional cry of a sailor and the creak of the ship's planks as it rolled in the waves.

Clambering up on to deck, Edgy had met the captain.

'More problems, young Edgy,' Boyd said. 'Engine trouble. Not good.'

'Can it be fixed?' Edgy asked. This whole ship confused him with its tangle of rigging. And the language the men used was foreign to him with its ports and starboards, its mizzens and yardarms.

'Not sure yet,' Boyd sniffed. 'My men are checking it

now. It's almost as if someone somewhere doesn't want this expedition to go ahead.'

'D'you think someone's done it on purpose? Broke the engine, I mean?' Edgy gasped.

Captain Boyd shook his head. 'I'm not certain, Edgy,' he replied. 'But that rigging was badly damaged when it was cut. Maybe whoever did it didn't mean to get you. Just wanted to slow us down. Without the back-up of the sails we can't move as quickly. One thing's certain – we're going to have to put in at the next available port.'

A sailor appeared from one of the hatches at the centre of the deck. He held a bent, flat piece of metal.

'It's one of the rods, cap'n,' he called, his face grim. 'We'll need some time to hammer it out.'

'As I thought,' the captain muttered. He turned from Edgy, bawling commands down the ship. The crew scurried about, heaving ropes and preparing to turn the ship for shore.

Edgy scanned the deck, looking at the sailors as they worked. *It could be any one of them.* He shook his head and clambered down to his cabin.

Relief washed over Edgy as he set foot on the quayside. The ship had anchored off a small fishing village and a party was sent ashore in the ship's tender.

'It's still England, Edgy,' Captain Boyd had said. 'Though a far cry from the busy streets of London, I dare say.'

If Edgy had found the swell on the ship sickening, he

was green by the time he reached the shore in the smaller rowing boat. He clambered up on to the small stone jetty, almost standing on Lord Mauldeth's fingers on the gunwale of the boat.

'Careful, you stupid boy,' Mauldeth snapped. 'You'll have us all in the water!'

'Eager for dry land,' chuckled Silky McFarland. 'You not a lover of the sea then, eh, Edgy?'

'Not really.' He shook his head and twitched a little. McFarland still made him nervous, despite the fact he'd saved Edgy's life.

He glanced around at the scatter of nets and lobster pots that cluttered the jetty and the path that led steeply up to a village that seemed to cling to the side of the rocky cliff. Small cottages huddled together against the wind that moaned across the rumbling sea. The crew had taken most of the day getting to their mooring and preparing the tender. Now it was evening and a few lights shone in the tiny windows. It was a dismal place but better than the sea.

Boyd had suggested they spend a night onshore. Mauldeth jumped at the chance but Janus had been reluctant. Sokket wouldn't come out of his cabin, so Edgy had been sent to knock on his door.

'Away, boy!' came the muffled cry from inside. 'Leave me alone. You can all go ashore and never come back!'

Now Janus shook himself and stamped a foot on the quayside. 'Mauldeth might be glad of a night back on dry land, but I'm not pleased about this delay at all,' he muttered, clambering out of the rowing boat after

Mauldeth. 'Timing is everything with this expedition. February the fourteenth. We must be at our destination by then or all will be lost.'

Edgy frowned. *February the fourteenth? Why is that date so familiar?*

'There isn't much we can do,' Mauldeth sniffed, cutting through Edgy's thoughts. 'Anyway, a mug of good ale and a warm fire will be welcome after that damp ship. Captain Boyd said the Mermaid Inn was basic but comfortable.'

'If you wanted comfort, you could have stayed in London,' Janus spat and stalked off towards the village.

'Mr McFarland, you're to take the engine part to the smithy and find lodgings there for the night,' Boyd ordered. 'We'll meet on the quayside at dawn.'

'Aye, sir. We'll buy some rope too,' McFarland smiled, tugging his forelock. He turned to the other men who had rowed the boat ashore. 'Come along, gents, let's get this ship fixed.'

Edgy watched the sailors saunter off along the quay, then he grabbed Janus's bags, panting as he marched up the steep cobbled lane after him.

A faded sign swung above the inn door, showing a mermaid holding a tankard. The paint flaked from it and part of her tail was missing. Janus pushed on the heavy wooden door and the familiar smells of woodsmoke, tobacco and ale welcomed Edgy in.

The tiny room inside lay empty apart from a few thick-legged tables and chairs. A barrel filled one corner and bottles lined the shelves on the wall. An old man in a faded black jacket and trousers sat smoking a long-stemmed pipe by the fire. He looked up and nodded at them.

'Welcome to the Mermaid. Rooms are ready,' he wheezed, spitting into the flames. 'Saw t' ship heaving to. Reckoned there'd be some gents aboard. The name's Absalom, Christopher Absalom.' The fire flickered, reflected in his pale-blue, watery eyes. 'Landlord o' this 'ere pub.'

'Lord Mauldeth,' Mauldeth said, giving the slightest of nods. 'This is Professor Envry Janus and his servant.'

Absalom nodded back slowly and solemnly. 'There are two upstairs guest rooms with some good ale and beef waiting, y'lordship,' he said, looking up at the ceiling. 'The boy can sleep down here by t' fire.'

Edgy glanced around. The fire twisted their shadows on the walls of the tiny room, making tables and chairs appear to move and dance.

'Don't worry, young feller,' Absalom said, giving a brief smile that showed his few remaining yellow teeth. 'You'll be quite snug down 'ere. I've some thick blankets y'can borrow. There, in the trunk under the bench.' He pointed to a corner of the room. 'And there's some bread and cheese on the table – help yerself.'

'Never mind him, man,' Mauldeth hissed. 'Show us to our rooms.'

Absalom inclined his head. 'As you wish, y'lordship,' he said. 'Follow me.' He led them out of the room.

'Don't worry, Edgy, we'll be close at hand should you need us.' Janus smiled as Absalom led him away.

The latch rattled as he shut the door and Edgy suddenly

felt quite alone. He shivered and threw a log on the fire, watching the shower of sparks go up the chimney. The wind moaned outside and the room seemed to darken. Chewing at the crust of bread, Edgy found the trunk and dragged it from under the bench, pulling thick woollen blankets from it. Soon he had made himself a nest in front of the fire.

He could hear the brothers moving around upstairs, their feet thumping on the floorboards. Edgy could pick out Mauldeth's complaining nasal tones and Janus's muttering, gravelly voice. Soon they died down, leaving only the wind, a ticking clock and the spitting fire. Edgy squeezed his eyes shut.

Sleep came in fits and starts. A gust of wind slipped cold air under the door, waking him and making his legs numb. The ashes of the fire collapsed through the grate and the air cooled on Edgy's face. In his interrupted dreams, Janus leered at him and Salomé frowned, her green eyes hard and unforgiving. She held something in her clenched fist. Blood oozed from between her fingers, dripping on the floor. Edgy crept closer as Salomé extended her arm, opening her fist for him to see. A heart pumped in the palm of her hand, red and black, quivering with each beat.

With a gasp, Edgy awoke, sitting upright, bathed in sweat, his own heart pounding. The room lay in darkness apart from the feeble glow from the dying fire and the starlight through the window.

A floorboard creaked.

Edgy threw himself down and pulled the blankets right over his head.

The fire hissed.

Edgy curled up tightly in a ball, hugging the warm blankets to him.

Something moved in the corner of the room.

Edgy held his breath.

'Edgy?' a voice hissed. 'Edgy Taaaylor?'

Edgy froze. He couldn't move. Maybe if he stayed still whoever or whatever it was would go away and leave him alone. He tried to control his panting breath. The blood hammered in his chest and temples.

And then a footfall. Only it wasn't a foot. Edgy knew that. He could tell by the short, sharp rap. It was the sound Talon had made whenever he crept around the tannery. A cloven hoof.

There he met with Pretty Polly, all in the gores
   of blood,
In her lily white arms an infant of mine,
Such screaming and hollering, it all passed away.
A debt to the devil he surely had to pay.

'The Cruel House Carpenter', traditional folk ballad

CHAPTER TWENTY-NINE
A CURIOUS OFFER

Edgy opened one eye. A green glow from outside filtered through his blankets. The demon wouldn't just go away. He knew that. Trembling, he pulled the covers down. The room looked eerie in the emerald light that emanated from a pulsing rock in the demon's right hand. It stood over him, ram-headed, cloven-hoofed, glaring down with fiery eyes.

'Belphagor,' Edgy croaked, recognising the demon from their encounter at the Green Man Inn.

'You recognise me then,' Belphagor said mockingly. 'And you're right to be afraid, Edgy Taylor. I haven't forgotten my last humiliation at your hands.'

Edgy's heart pounded. He tried to cry out but his throat was dry. 'What do you want?' he whispered, choking out the words.

'There are many things I want, Edgy Taylor,' Belphagor spat. 'Your head on a chain around my neck would please me but I am bound not to harm you. I'm merely a messenger.'

'A messenger?' Edgy asked, swallowing hard but relaxing just a little. 'Who for?'

'Why, for Salomé, of course,' Belphagor said, sitting himself down in front of Edgy and throwing the glowing stone into the hearth. It flashed, setting a fire of crackling green flames and flooding the room with heat.

'Salomé?' Edgy said, confused. 'But I thought –'

'You thought what? That Salomé and I were enemies? Just because I wouldn't tell her what I knew about the location of Moloch's body? You've a lot to learn about demons, Edgy Taylor.'

Edgy sat silently, hugging the blankets around him.

Belphagor continued, 'After you found me at the Green Man Inn, I had nowhere to go. That was my home, I had friends there.'

Edgy hadn't really imagined that demons could enjoy friendship or value having a home. He thought of Trimdon and his pride in serving the Society. Spinorix was Edgy's friend.

'But you and your stonemason friends never consider that,' Belphagor sneered. 'To you we're just trophies, specimens to be collected. I took myself to Salomé, traded my information for her protection.'

'Was it you who damaged our engine?' Edgy croaked.

Belphagor shook his head. 'No, I didn't. You need to look closer to home for that. You are in danger, Edgy Taylor. Salomé says you should run. Flee this place now and she won't pursue you. Just go and lose yourself.'

'Why would Salomé say that?' Edgy spat, anger boiling up inside him. 'She's tried to kill me twice.'

'Could have killed you twice and many times besides, but didn't. Ask yourself why she hasn't visited you on that pathetic tub bobbing about on the sea,' Belphagor said, his voice cold and haughty. He held out his palm, revealing a gold charm shaped like a horned skull and tied to a leather lace. 'Take this if you will not flee. Just hold it and call Salomé's name. She'll come to your aid.'

Edgy didn't move. It had to be some kind of trick. But there was no disputing that his life was in danger. Slowly, he reached out to take it.

The door crashed open and Janus stood snarling at Belphagor. In his hands, Edgy could see the dull grey cylinder of an ossifier.

Belphagor launched himself to his feet and extended a hand but Janus had already pulled the trigger. A hollow thump sent the deadly dirty snowball hurtling across the room. It struck Belphagor in the side of the head. He dropped the charm into Edgy's lap and fell to his knees, hitting the floorboards with a crash, his entire body turned to stone.

Janus ran forward. 'What did he say?' he snapped, holding the ossifier in one hand, grasping Edgy's upper arm in the other. 'What did he tell you?'

Edgy had slipped the unseen charm under the covers. He stared at Janus's wild face, looking at a man he didn't recognise. His features were twisted, contorted with hatred. His eyes looked cold. It wasn't Janus. Not the one Edgy knew anyway. His grip was tight and hurt Edgy's arm.

'Nothin', he didn't tell me nothin',' Edgy said. 'He just told me to run away.'

Mauldeth appeared at the doorway in a long nightshirt. 'Edgy, what happened?'

'Belphagor . . . 'e told me to run away. Said Salomé wanted me to run away,' Edgy panted, pulling away from Janus's hold and massaging his arm. 'Said 'e wanted to kill me but Salomé wouldn't let 'im.' He stared at the statue kneeling on the floor.

'Well, he can't harm you now,' Janus said, heaving a sigh. He glanced at Edgy again, a frown flitting across his brow. 'You're sure he didn't say anything else?'

'For goodness's sake, Envry,' Mauldeth complained. 'Give the boy a chance to gather his wits. What else is the creature likely to have said?'

Janus shot Mauldeth a poisonous glance but kept quiet.

The first glimmers of dawn were beginning to break through the darkness outside. Edgy looked around. 'Where's Mr Absalom?' he said. Surely all the noise would have woken him. He'd want to know what was going on in his inn.

'I fear the Mr Absalom we spoke to last night may well have been Belphagor in disguise,' Mauldeth murmured, frowning and rubbing his chin.

'He nearly fooled me at the Green Man Inn,' Edgy remembered.

Mauldeth ignored his comment and continued, 'Strange that Salomé would send you such a message. And why would she stop Belphagor harming you?'

'Who knows? She's up to something and I don't like it,' Janus snapped. 'I suggest we get back to the ship as quickly as possible.'

McFarland and the other sailors looked sprightly and winked at Edgy as he and the two fellows trudged along the jetty to the boat.

'I trust the lodgings were to your satisfaction, sirs,' McFarland said, smiling.

Janus shot him a flinty glare. It was as if McFarland knew that something had happened, Edgy thought.

Edgy could see Captain Boyd waiting on-board as they rowed out to the ship. He paced back and forth, pulling a fob watch from his waistcoat pocket every few seconds as if that would make McFarland and his crew row any harder.

Mauldeth sat silently, his gaze wandering between Edgy and Janus. Edgy coughed and stared at the bottom of the boat when Mauldeth stared at him but his lordship was lost in thought.

'At last,' Boyd called as they clambered up the side of the ship and on to the deck. 'As soon as we get the engine part fitted we'll get under way.'

'Should we tell him about what happened last night, sir?' Edgy whispered to Janus, watching as the captain followed his men and the engine part down below.

Janus shook his head. 'I think not. Sailors are a superstitious lot.'

A few sailors glanced round at the word 'superstitious'. Janus stepped closer to Edgy.

'Don't they know what we're looking for?' Edgy whispered, eyeing the men as they strode up the ship to their duties. 'Not even Captain Boyd?'

'Captain Boyd knows. He told the crew we were looking for specimens of wildlife,' Mauldeth cut in. 'But I wouldn't mention it, all the same.'

'But we can trust Captain Boyd –' Edgy began.

'It was Boyd who recommended the lodgings. Trust no one, Edgy,' Mauldeth said, staring deep into Edgy's eyes. 'It's a good rule to live by when dealing with demons.'

Edgy didn't reply. How could you go through life not trusting anyone? He trusted Mr Janus. Didn't he? His fingers rose to the gold pendant that hung around his neck under his shirt. *Is that why I didn't tell him about the charm? Or was it the look on Janus's face after he had ossified Belphagor?* Edgy shivered.

By midday, the engines pounded once more and Edgy's stomach lurched as the ship cut through the rolling waves. Captain Boyd's face seemed more ruddy than ever as he breathed in the salt air.

'Inform Mr Janus that we are moving again, please, Mr Taylor,' he said, giving Edgy a nod. Edgy smiled back and hurried down below to pass the message on.

The door was ajar when Edgy arrived and he glimpsed Janus sitting hunched over *The Legends of Moloch*. He slammed the book shut with a thud as Edgy entered.

'Ah, Edgy. Just doing some more research, y'know,' Janus said. He rubbed his palms along the cover of the book.

'We're back on course, Captain Boyd says,' Edgy replied. 'Are you all right, Mr Janus?'

'What? Yes, fine, fine,' Janus said, clapping his hands together. 'Never better. Back on course, excellent! Time is pressing on – we only have five days to reach our destination. Now, you go about your duties, lad. I've got more research to do.' He sat, hands on his knees, staring at Edgy, waiting for him to leave.

'Righto, sir,' Edgy said, backing out of the room and closing the door behind him. He turned and almost walked straight into Lord Mauldeth. Edgy braced himself, waiting for the curses.

'Have you recovered from your encounter with Belphagor, Edgy?' Mauldeth said. Edgy half opened his mouth in surprise. Mauldeth continued without waiting for him to answer. 'I'm worried about Envry. I've seen him like this before . . . a long time ago. A little . . . preoccupied with his thoughts.'

'Yes, sir,' Edgy muttered, uncertain what else to say.

'Be careful,' Mauldeth said as Edgy clambered towards the deck.

The days passed quickly. Edgy began to find the rocking and plunging of the ship less sickening. The sea grew blacker and the sky white. He stood on deck staring at the icy water, wondering if all colour had been bleached from the world and if he would ever see land again. Shivering, he pulled the oilskin jacket closer over the thick jumper he had been given. Even with these extra layers, the cold gnawed at him. Breath steamed from his nose and mouth like the smoke from the funnel of *Lord Byron's Maggot*. From time to time, he spotted something black and glistening twisting up out of the water and then back under without a splash.

'Haven't seen anything myself,' Janus murmured when Edgy reported it. 'But we need to be vigilant.' He slammed his fist on the deck rail. 'Can't this damnable ship go any faster?' he spat.

'The sea and the cold play tricks, Edgy,' Captain Boyd said. 'Sometimes a diving seal looks huge and yet it's far away. Whales inhabit these parts and often you only see their backs or top fins. I wouldn't fret.'

The days grew shorter as the steamship powered its way north. Soon they seemed to be in perpetual night or, at best, a feeble grey twilight. Crystal flowers of ice bloomed on the railings and sails. Ropes turned white with frost. Only the black funnel repelled the white coating as it pumped out thick smoke and heat.

'We're into the frozen North now, Edgy,' Captain Boyd said to him one day. 'Be sure to keep well wrapped up. Don't let your bare skin touch anything here – hands, nose, cheeks or chin – or it'll freeze and be stuck fast. Try and free yourself then and you'll tear the flesh from your bones.'

Edgy threw himself into washing shirts, polishing boots – anything that kept him below decks and took his thoughts off the questions that jostled in his mind. *What is Salomé up to?* Edgy's hand went to the charm. *Why have*

I hung it around my neck? he wondered. *Does she honestly think I'm goin' to summon her after all she's done? Is someone on board tryin' to kill me or just stop the ship from gettin' to its destination?*

'Trust no one,' Mauldeth had said. But could he trust Mauldeth? Why was he so concerned about Edgy all of a sudden?

A rap on his door cut his thoughts dead. Mortesque Sokket's grey face appeared around it. His eyes glittered and his breathing was rapid.

'Are you all right, Mr Sokket?' Edgy asked. 'If you don't mind me sayin' so, sir, you look like you might 'ave a touch of fever.'

'Come with me,' Sokket said, his voice hoarse. 'I have to show you something.' He disappeared behind the door and Edgy jumped up, following him up on deck.

'Mr Sokket, if it's somethin' important maybe I should get Mr Janus,' Edgy began.

Sokket's eyes widened and he waved his hands in front of him, shaking his head frantically. 'No, no,' he croaked, his breath billowing in the cold air. 'Not him, not him. Just come with me.'

Edgy frowned and followed Sokket to the bow of the ship. Stars winked in the reddening sky; a brief dawn before the plunge back into darkness. Here, the full brunt of the sea hit the ship. Hissing streamers of foam leapt over the bow and into Edgy's face. The wind tousled his thick black hair and drew tears from his eye. The horizon swung up and down, movement exaggerated by the bowsprit, a huge pole that pointed out the direction they were heading in. Ropes rattled against the bowsprit, the sheets lashed to it snapped and cracked in the icy wind. Even the pounding of the engine was lost in this storm of wind and wave.

'What is it, Mr Sokket?' Edgy called.

Sokket leaned over the side of the ship, stabbing his finger at the thrashing tide. 'Porpoises! Edgy, have you ever seen porpoises running alongside the bow of the ship?' Sokket gave a forced smile. His eyes glowed as he gestured to the side. 'Porpoises, Edgy, look!'

Porpoises? Edgy thought about the black shape he'd seen writhing in the water. *Could it have been a porpoise? It's worth checking.*

Edgy shuffled next to Sokket, gingerly leaning over the side. The black water streamed past, cut by the sharp bow of the ship.

'I can't see –' Edgy began.

Then a bony hand gripped his ankles and the world turned upside down. For a split second, Edgy wondered quite what had happened and then he realised he was falling towards the water.

THEY SEWED HIS BODY ALL UP IN AN OLD COW'S HIDE,
AND THEY CAST THE GALLANT CABIN BOY OVER THE SHIP'S SIDE,
AND LEFT HIM WITHOUT MORE ADO ADRIFTING IN THE TIDE
TO SINK IN THE LOWLANDS LOW.

'THE GOLDEN VANITY', TRADITIONAL FOLK SONG

CHAPTER THIRTY
A SCRAMBLE FOR LIFE

Time seemed to slow for Edgy. He could hear the blood pulsing around his temples like the thumping of the ship's steam engine. Every breath roared in his ears like a rush of steam. He noticed the craggy blackness of the ship's hull, the barnacles that crusted the overlapping coarse planks. Huge tongues of water licked up the side towards him. Icy spray stung his cheek, the cold stealing his breath. Black, tarry ropes dangled in loops to his right and he glimpsed the criss-cross mesh of netting that swung beneath the bowsprit.

He snatched at the passing ropes. Fire seared across the palm of his hand and up his arm as he stopped with a jerk that threatened to break his grip. With a sob, Edgy snapped his other hand on to the rope, blotting out the grating pain as it cut into his hands. Seawater lashed at him, soaking him to the skin and threatening to pull him down. He scrabbled his feet against the crusty side of the ship and peered up.

Sokket stared down, his eyes wide and white against the grey of his face. He grinned mirthlessly, showing his yellowed teeth. Flecks of spit drooled down his chin.

'Damn your black heart, Taylor,' he snarled, leaning over. 'Why don't you just die?'

Gritting his teeth, Edgy swung himself to his left towards the net that rippled beneath the bowsprit. If he could get there, he might be safe. The sea slapped salty waves at him, numbing him even through his thick clothes and slamming him into the hull. The net came closer and then lurched away, grazing the tips of Edgy's extended fingers. Edgy looked up as he swung back.

Sokket still glared down but something silver flashed above his head. Edgy gave a cry as Sokket brought the axe down on Edgy's rope. He heard a distant, wooden *thunk* and felt his rope slacken. But he had already started on the arc of rope towards the net.

With a yell of defiance he released the useless coil that spiralled below him into the roaring sea and threw his body forward, stretching and grappling for the net. For a moment he felt weightless, blown by the wind like so much sea foam. Then the net struck him in the stomach. He had made it. For a second he lay, blinking up at the dark blue sky, desperately trying to get his breath back.

'No!' screamed Sokket, the axe still in his hand. He had clambered on to the bowsprit and now lay on top of it as he slid himself along towards Edgy. 'It's not fair. You escaped the demon in the picture and the stone crusher.

Even when I drop the rigging on you, some imbecile saves your skin. But you have to die!'

Edgy groaned and rolled on to his front, dragging himself along the net as Sokket leaned down, making futile swings with the axe.

'Don't hurt me, Mr Sokket,' Edgy gasped as he slipped and struggled along the net. 'I dunno what I done but you don't wanna kill me!'

'I don't *want* to kill you, poor child.' Sokket's face was twisted with torment. 'But believe me, it's best for all of us if you're dead.' He slipped off the pole and fell into the netting, rolling on to his back.

Clinging to the rope sapped Edgy's strength. He glanced down at the water rushing past them below as the ship forged ahead through the waves. Water soaked him to his skin and cold gnawed at his bones. He squeezed himself into the very corner of the net where it was lashed to the bowsprit. Sokket clambered towards him like some great grey, spindly spider on a web, axe in one hand, his eyes mad and staring.

'But why, Mr Sokket? It don't make sense,' Edgy panted. A crowd had gathered at the bow of the ship. Silky McFarland and some other sailors had begun to shin their way along the bowsprit to Edgy's rescue.

'Hold on, lad,' cried McFarland, oblivious to the spray from the bow of the ship.

'Nothing makes sense any more, Edgy Taylor,' Sokket gasped as he dragged himself across the net. 'But I'll not rest until you're safe at the bottom of the sea.'

He threw himself forward, raising the axe. Instinctively,

Edgy raised his feet, catching Sokket square in the chest and heaving him backwards and sideways. For a split second, Sokket teetered on the edge of the net, standing full height, staring at Edgy in disbelief.

'All you had to do was die,' Sokket wailed. 'Too much to hope for, I suppose . . .' Then with a scream he tumbled down, disappearing in the foam and spray that snapped and hissed around the sharp bow of the ship.

Edgy lay, panting for breath, fingers locked around the knots in the net. He stared down at the dark waves, slowly letting McFarland loosen his grip on the ropes and drag him back along the net.

'Steady now,' murmured a voice as Edgy felt himself being passed from hand to hand up to the deck level. His clothes felt heavy and wet. His body ached with the cold and his teeth began to chatter.

'Easy, lad, you're safe now,' McFarland said, planting him on his feet.

Edgy staggered a little and grabbed the nearest shoulder for support. Janus and Lord Mauldeth stood next to Captain Boyd, surrounded by sailors. Frost whitened their beards and hats.

'Edgy! Are you all right? What happened? What did Sokket say to you? Why did he try to kill you?' Janus asked, grabbing Edgy by the shoulders.

'I d-don't know, Mr Janus,' Edgy stuttered. He felt numb. Sokket's wild stare kept flashing into his mind – and the image of him tumbling into the sea. 'He said I'd be better off dead, at the bottom of the sea.'

'Madness,' Captain Boyd said, his normally red face pale and drawn. 'A terrible tragedy. But clearly Mr Sokket was unhinged. My men will put a boat out and search but I doubt very much if he survived. It wasn't your fault, Edgy. Now get the boy below – he's freezing to death!'

'Thank you, sir,' Edgy said through chattering teeth.

The cold gnawed at his aching joints and muscles now and his hands stung with rope burn. Hands dragged at his wet clothing, pulling it away as it stiffened and froze. Edgy's vision began to fade. Someone pulled him back and put a bottle to his lips. Brandy scorched his throat, making his eyes water. He coughed and retched, shaking.

'Edgy!' Janus cried. 'For God's sake, man, get him to his cabin. He's no use dead.'

'Don't go all blue on us, lad,' said a rough voice.

A hand slapped his cheek, bringing him to as McFarland dragged him down the steps into the pulsing warmth of the ship.

The night passed miserably for Edgy. Sokket's grey, staring face haunted his broken dreams. His hands ached and burned. He curled himself tightly into a ball on his bed, wrapping himself in blankets, shivering. The ship heaved and rolled and the engines beat time as they circled the area, searching for Sokket. Bells rang and men called to each other but there was no cry of success.

Edgy drifted in and out of sleep, tormented by questions. *Why would Sokket want to kill me? What had he meant when he'd said it would be best for all of us if I were dead? I wish Henry, Sally and Spin were here.* His head throbbed along with the engine, until he fell into a twisting dream in which the furnaces of the ship burned in his chest and pistons hammered inside him, threatening to burst out.

The cabin door crashed open, making Edgy sit up, tangled in blankets, his bedclothes clinging to him. Janus stood staring down on him. Edgy's mouth felt dry and tasted bitter.

Lord Mauldeth appeared behind Janus. 'You've been sick, Edgy. Delirious for the last twenty-four hours. How do you feel?'

'Stiff, your lordship,' Edgy groaned, swinging his legs out of bed. Pain lanced through his temples and he held his head in his hands, but gradually it subsided. 'A little better, I think –'

'Never mind that,' Janus interrupted. His eyes gleamed with excitement. 'We think we've found it.'

'Found what, sir?' Edgy screwed his face up and stretched his aching body.

'The cave of Moloch, of course,' Janus said, frowning a little as if Edgy should have guessed straight away. 'The coastline matches the map on the skull and our charts!'

Edgy dressed, groaning at every bend of his knee or elbow. The angry imprint of the ropes he had grabbed to stop himself falling still tingled across the palms of his hands but he was surprised at how strong he felt.

'That's it, that's it,' Janus murmured, hopping from one foot to the other as he waited for Edgy.

'Give him a chance, Envry,' Mauldeth snapped. He looked pale, worry etched into every line on his face. 'Don't know why you're so eager to show the boy anyway. There's nothing but ice.'

The cold wind slapped Edgy in the face as he emerged on deck behind Janus. Edgy gasped at the scene. The ship's engines beat a gentle tattoo, idling in a bay of black water. Mountains of ice surrounded them, illuminating the dark polar night.

'It's beautiful,' Edgy whispered, staring at the blues and greens of the ice where it thinned near the water's edge.

'So, sir,' Captain Boyd said, startling Edgy, 'we're at the destination you directed us to. I presume you'll want to get to shore to begin your investigations as soon as possible.'

'No, no, captain,' Janus said, smirking like a child with a secret. 'We'll wait a couple of days, if it's all the same to you.'

Some of the crew had gathered round and a murmur of surprise rippled through them. *A few unhappy frowns too,* Edgy thought. *Why do we have to wait? Doesn't Janus know where the cave is?*

'Can I ask why, sir?' Boyd said, his eyebrows arched in surprise.

'If my research is correct, then we should see a remarkable, erm, volcanic phenomenon in the bay.' Janus scanned the growing crowd of seamen that surrounded him.

Edgy frowned. *What's he on about?*

'What kind of phenom ... phen ... What kind of thing?' a voice called from the assembled men.

'Volcano?' muttered another. 'I remember one o' them in the South Seas. Smoke an' fire. Damn near sank our ship.'

'I trust that we aren't in any danger, Mr Janus,' Boyd said, gripping the lapel of his coat and frowning.

'No, no,' Janus beamed. 'No danger. But if my calculations are correct, then a small island of ice will rise up out of the sea at this point tomorrow, on February the fourteenth.'

'Island of ice?' said one of the seamen. 'Rise up? How's that possible?'

'Gentlemen,' Mauldeth called out. Edgy could see the fear spreading among them like a fever. 'The phenomenon you will see is perfectly natural –'

'Yes,' Janus butted in, still smiling genially. 'It happens, I believe, every thirteen years.'

'Thirteen?' cried a voice from the back of the scrum. Muttering and whispered conversation broke out.

'Envry, you aren't helping,' hissed Mauldeth through gritted teeth.

Silky McFarland squeezed his way through the men until he stood in front of Janus and Mauldeth. 'Not meanin' any disrespect,' he said, bowing his head, a slight smile playing about his lips, 'but me an' the men thought that it was seals an' the like you were after.'

'Thank you, McFarland,' Boyd said. 'Mr Janus, I suggest

you come below and discuss this with me so that I can reassure the men.' He turned to the crew. 'Gentlemen, I will not put a single life at risk needlessly. I will get to the bottom of this but for now, go about your duties.'

Janus and Mauldeth followed Boyd down to the cabins, leaving Edgy on the poop deck. He watched the men drift away, glancing over their shoulders and muttering. Last to leave was McFarland, who gave Edgy a grin. But there was no trace of genuine humour on his face and no warmth in his eyes.

'O, WHAT A MOUNTAIN IS YON,' SHE SAID.
'ALL SO DREARY WI' FROST AND SNOW?'
'O, YON IS THE MOUNTAIN OF HELL,' HE CRIED,
'WHERE YOU AND I WILL GO.'

'THE DEMON LOVER', TRADITIONAL FOLK BALLAD

CHAPTER THIRTY-ONE
THE ICE MOUNTAIN

Edgy stood at the stern of the ship, listening to the hollow lap of the waves against the hull. The engines lay silent and the anchors had been dropped. He watched the men working the capstan. It reminded Edgy of a huge cotton bobbin with holes in it to put thick planks of wood in. The men pushed against the planks, turning the bobbin and unwinding the chain. Usually, the men sang songs to keep them in time as they pushed. Some of the songs were rude and made Edgy snigger. But this time, they just grunted in time as they pushed on the capstan. Ice coated everything, making the men slip, stumble and curse.

'There's no doubt, Edgy,' Mauldeth murmured, appearing beside him. 'The men aren't happy. If only Envry hadn't spouted off about the island.'

'I 'ave to say, sir,' Edgy said, 'it was news to me.'

'Me too,' Mauldeth replied, raising his eyebrows. 'He

only told me after we met with Captain Boyd. According to legend, Satan hid Moloch's body on an island of ice and submerged it in the frozen waters. But every thirteen years, it rises from the sea.'

'On February the fourteenth,' Edgy murmured. 'My birthday . . .' Or so Salomé had said. Their first encounter seemed years ago now.

'Good Lord,' Mauldeth said, staring closely at Edgy. 'A strange coincidence.'

'I don't know, your lordship.' Edgy shook his head. He thought about Salomé. The way she wove her plans – a slipshod job here, a drunkard's bad decision there, all coinciding at the right moment to complete her schemes. And she'd made a point of telling him that date was his birthday. 'Is there any such thing as coincidence when demons are involved?'

'Good point, Edgy, but it's beyond me what your part in all this is,' Mauldeth replied.

'Why did Satan make the island rise every thirteen years?' Edgy wondered aloud. 'Why not just sink it for ever?'

'It's a game to them,' Mauldeth spat. 'Little clues and rumours, teasing mortals and fellow demons alike. Leading them on.'

Edgy nodded. *Nothing's simple*. He had thought Mauldeth was stuck-up and pompous, and had hated him. Yet he'd shown more concern for Edgy in the last few days than Janus had.

Mauldeth stared out into the darkness. The icebergs all

around reflected the moonlight, giving his face a bluish tinge. 'He's still my little brother, you know,' Mauldeth said quietly. 'We've always been competitive. Even as children we would fight for Mama's affection and Papa's approval.'

Edgy nodded and stared at the sea. *Happy families. Not all families are happy. Maybe I'm better off alone.*

Mauldeth continued, 'But I always watched over him. God, the number of scrapes I pulled him out of! Always chasing after the next demon to ossify.'

'But I-I thought you . . . killed just as many,' Edgy stuttered, choking back the words as soon as they had left his lips. It wasn't his place to criticise Lord Mauldeth.

Mauldeth shook his head. 'Most of the demons I killed, I did so to save Envry. When he first became involved with the Royal Society, I joined too to protect him. Once he becomes fixated on a goal, there's no stopping him.'

Something splashed in the water, snatching Edgy's attention away from the conversation. He peered into the blue twilight.

'What is it, Edgy?' Mauldeth whispered. 'What can you see?'

Edgy squinted hard into the dark water. 'I'm not sure, sir,' he hissed back. 'Down there – somethin' black an' shiny.' The water swirled and rippled as something slipped down into the depths. 'Captain Boyd says it's just a seal or somethin'.'

'But you think otherwise?' Mauldeth murmured.

Edgy nodded. 'It's just a feelin' but it gives me the creeps. An' anyway, wouldn't there be loads of seals round 'ere, not just one?'

Mauldeth shrugged, then turned as Silky McFarland emerged from the shadows. He scowled at Edgy, gave a short nod to Mauldeth and slipped down the steps to the main deck and his shipmates.

'Where in heaven's name did he appear from?' Mauldeth said. 'D'you think he was eavesdropping?'

'Without a doubt, sir,' Edgy muttered, staring after McFarland, who glanced back as he whispered to a gang of men by the mainmast.

The tension of the following day drove Edgy down to his cabin. Everywhere he walked in the ship, men stared at him and whispered to each other. Some crossed themselves and turned their backs to him. Fear tightened every jaw. He ate his meals in his cabin, avoiding the others. Up above where the men were muffled against the cold, eyes stared wide and angry over scarves rimed with frost. The perpetual night only served to heighten the feeling of foreboding that gripped the ship's crew.

Edgy lay on his bunk and flicked through *Everyday Daemonologie*. Questions flitted around his mind. His birthday. The island rising. What was their connection? Was it just coincidence? And what was it that prowled beneath them, slipping through the icy water? Edgy looked down at the page.

Leviathan:

A colossal beast of the sea, created by Satan to plague seamen. Its many heads, armed with row upon row of razor-sharp teeth, are capable of pulling a fully rigged man-o'-war to pieces and devouring its crew in a matter of minutes.

He stared at the rough woodcut print on the facing page, at the black body half out of the water. Hundreds of heads on long serpentine necks snapped and tore at a foundering ship. Was that what he'd seen? The necks twisting and writhing under the water?

He jumped up and ran to the foredeck where Janus, wrapped in furs, sat on a collapsible chair, peering out across the bay through a telescope. Edgy tried to ignore the hard stares as he barged his way up the steps to him.

'Mr Janus,' he hissed, clasping the book to his chest, his thumb stuffed between the pages of the book to keep his place. 'Mr Janus, I –'

'Not now, Edgy,' Janus said, not removing the telescope from his left eye. 'I'm expecting something to happen any minute. Don't worry, young man, you'll be able to play your part in this adventure soon enough.'

'But, sir, I think I know what it is that I keep seeing in the water,' Edgy hissed, trying to keep his voice from alerting the sailors, although one or two were frowning over at them even now. 'Look.' He thrust the book into Janus's free hand. He glanced down, eyes widening.

'A Leviathan, eh?' Janus said out loud.

Edgy screwed his eyes up in frustration but when he opened them, Janus and every man on deck stood, jaws slack, staring at the boiling water a hundred feet in front of them.

An icy point peeped out of the water, sending small ripples across the smooth surface. Gradually the waves grew bigger as more and more of the island forced its way out of the sea. The icebergs around them shook and flakes of ice sheared off, making the water more turbulent. Edgy gripped the side as the ship rocked. His ears rang with Janus's cries of victory. In the background, Boyd barked commands. The engine began to thump and Edgy felt them backwater away from the rising mass.

'Look, Edgy! Look, there.' Janus gripped Edgy's wrist, making him wince. Janus pointed with a trembling finger at the island.

It towered over them now, a huge cone of ice the size of a mountain. Edgy could just make out a narrow flight of carved steps twisting up into the heights of the island.

And then he flew forward as the whole deck tilted. Janus stumbled and tripped over him. The stern of the ship was rising, caught on the growing island. Barrels and boxes rolled and slid down the deck towards the bow. A seaman came running towards Edgy, unable to stop himself as gravity propelled him towards the sea. With a scream he sailed forward into the water that rushed up the bow of the ship. The bowsprit gave a deafening crack and slack lines swung back towards Edgy and Janus.

A loose pulley block whistled past Edgy's ear as he pressed his cheek to the freezing deck.

Then all was still.

Edgy could hear the engines pounding and the groans of the crew. The deck remained at a crazy angle. He pulled himself to his feet and peered over the side of the ship.

The island of ice had risen underneath them, grounding the stern of the ship and pushing its front into the sea. Water ran in rivers down the side of the island, pouring down on to the men on deck and into the heart of the ship. Steam boiled out of the ship's funnel, shrouding the deck.

'We've found it, Edgy!' Janus said, clapping his hands with glee.

'But, Mr Janus, we're trapped on the ice an' –' Edgy began.

'Yes, yes, yes,' Janus tutted, a scowl flitting across his face. 'First things first. We must explore the island.'

'You're not goin' anywhere,' McFarland said, stepping in front of him, a wall of angry-looking men behind him, all steadying themselves on the ridiculous tilt of the deck. The mist that closed around the ship made grey silhouettes of them in the eerie half-reflected moonlight.

Captain Boyd and Mauldeth were pushed through the crowd of sailors that had gathered on the main deck and sent stumbling next to Edgy and Janus.

'This is insubordination, McFarland,' the captain said, his voice calm and quiet. 'What d'you think you're playing at?'

'Beggin' yer pardon, captain, but the men aren't happy,' McFarland said, glancing from one sailor to the next. 'We want some answers.'

'Answers? Can't it wait?' Captain Boyd's voice rose a little. Edgy could see the back of his neck going red just above his cravat. 'In case you hadn't noticed, the ship has just been grounded.'

'That may be, captain,' McFarland said, 'and we'll attend to that soon enough. But the men are worried. All this ain't natural – islands risin' up out of the sea. There's been talk of demons too.'

Boyd let out a snort of derision. 'Demons?' he scoffed. 'You are a seaman on-board a modern steamship and you talk of demons?'

'That Professor Janus, he was talkin' about demons to the boy,' grunted a man behind McFarland. The crowd murmured.

'And look at this,' said one of the seamen, reaching forward and snatching Edgy's book in his huge brown hand. 'It says Everyday . . . Daemon . . . ol . . . ogie. Or a Demon a Day!'

The crew hissed and began chattering excitedly. Someone came up from below with an armful of Janus's books.

'Put those down – they're priceless.' Janus ran at the man but arms snaked out from the crush of sailors, pinning him. 'Let me go!' he bellowed. 'This is an outrage.'

McFarland took a book from the man and leafed through it, his skeletal features fixed in a frown. Edgy thought he could see him tremble a little as he held the book.

'Ye gods, would ye look at this,' he said, holding the book open.

Edgy glimpsed the words *Moloch* and *heart*, followed by *Salomé* and *Satan*. But it was the images that struck home. Satan pinned Moloch to the ground, his mouth twisted into a triumphant leer, a dripping heart beating in his hand. A babe lay on a stone altar, naked and help-less. Salomé towered over it, a long spiral blade in her hand, her green eyes flashing as she prepared to plunge the blade down.

'No!' Janus yelled, lunging forward so suddenly that he broke free. He crashed into McFarland, sending him sprawling and the book whirling across the deck. Uproar broke out as men pounced on Janus, dragging him back.

'Enough!' Captain Boyd barked. 'We've enough to deal with as it is. I'll not have it. D'you hear me? Not while I'm captain of this ship.'

McFarland dragged himself to his feet and wiped blood from his mouth with the back of his hand. 'Then we'll have to relieve you of that duty, sir,' he hissed. 'You said the mission was a scientific survey, but judging by these books it's evil and we'll have no part in it.' He nodded and Edgy found himself grabbed and held. Burly arms grabbed Boyd, Mauldeth and Janus too.

'Look around you, McFarland. We need to get this ship free somehow,' Mauldeth said coldly. 'Turning against us won't help matters.'

'We're not fools, your lordship,' McFarland said. 'Whatever you're seekin', it drove yon Mr Sokket mad and has brought ill fortune on this ship. I'll not stand by an' watch any more shipmates put in peril.'

'This is insubordination,' Boyd shouted, struggling against the two men holding him. 'You'll hang for this!'

'I'd rather hang than burn in the fiery pits of hell for all eternity,' McFarland said. He looked down at Edgy. 'I'm sorry it had to come to this, lad.'

A strange chirping sound echoed across the bay.

Edgy raised his hand. 'Listen,' he whispered.

Everyone fell silent. The mist had thickened and blew across the deck. The only sound was the slow, pulsing hiss of the engine deep in the heart of the ship.

And the eerie sound again.

Edgy shuddered – the sound grated on him. It seemed to seep out of the mist from all directions.

'What is it?' McFarland murmured.

As if in answer to his question, a pointed snout on the end of a long, slender neck loomed out of the mist. Row upon row of needle teeth grinned at them and bulbous luminescent eyes glowed with a malevolent hunger. The narrow jaws clamped into the shoulder of a nearby sailor and whipped him up into the mist.

Edgy and the rest of the crew stood stunned, not believing what they had seen, and then the sailors' screams snapped them back to reality. Blood splattered down on the deck like rain. Edgy felt its warmth on his cheek and grimaced.

'Leviathan,' hissed Janus.

And then the deck erupted into chaos as heads darted down, snatching man after man, snapping and tearing with razor teeth. Edgy scanned the ship for a place of safety. But there was none.

It is too pale for that old grey mare.
Pray, son, now tell to me.
It is the blood of my youngest brother
That hoed that corn for me.

What did you fall out about?
Pray, son, now tell to me.
Because he cut yon holly bush
Which might have made a tree.

'Edward', traditional folk ballad

CHAPTER THIRTY-TWO

THE SINKING
OF *THE MAGGOT*

Men ran across the deck, huddling behind barrels, pulling tarpaulins over themselves, anything to get under cover, uncertain where the next attack would come from. With a splintering of wood, the mainmast came crashing down, pinning an unfortunate seaman. Almost immediately a drooling snout plunged down out of the mist towards him. Edgy turned his head away from the screams and fell to his knees, grabbing *Everyday Daemonologie* from the blood-splattered deck. The book felt warm and strangely comforting.

McFarland scurried up the deck towards the stern, barging past Janus and leaping over the back of the ship on to the island of ice.

'Edgy!' Janus called. He too had run up to the stern and was now busy stuffing *The Legends of Moloch* into his shoulder bag, oblivious to the slaughter that continued around him. 'We have to get off the ship. The safest way is up.' He pointed to the steps that wound up the side of the island peak and vanished into the mist.

Edgy scrambled to his feet and froze.

A pointed head bobbed in front of him. The Leviathan's nostril slits blew sea foam and putrid slime in his face as it sniffed at Edgy. Its teeth packed its mouth, forcing it into a wicked smile. Edgy panted, his breath condensing on the monster's gory snout. Lumps of flesh, fabric and wood poked from between the Leviathan's teeth. Edgy's heart hammered at his ribs as the creature drooled blood and swayed inches from his face. It slid forward, letting out a low, menacing hiss.

Edgy fell back, sobbing. *This is it. It's going to eat me*, he thought, catching his breath. Any second now he would be yanked into the air and torn apart.

A sudden rush of air startled Edgy from his paralysis. An axe buried itself in the side of the monster's neck, making it rear up, screeching with fury.

Captain Boyd appeared by his side, a pistol in his hand. 'Run, Edgy!' he yelled, pushing him aside.

'Thank you, captain,' Edgy gasped.

'You're welcome. Now you get to shore. I'll not go down without a fight,' Boyd snapped, pushing him towards the stern of the ship.

Edgy staggered on, tripping and stumbling. He glanced back to see Boyd balanced on the shattered mast, pistol pointed skywards.

'Come and get me, you evil devil,' he howled.

The pistol roared, the creature screamed and a head

crashed down on to the deck, the light in its eyes dying. Boyd quickly fumbled with the pistol, desperate to reload. Another of the Leviathan's heads lowered itself down level with the captain.

Boyd stopped struggling with the gun. 'Oh well,' he murmured.

And the Leviathan snapped its jaws forward, whipping him up into the mist with a roar.

Edgy screwed his eyes shut. Boyd was gone.

The ship gave a shudder and Edgy looked round. The Leviathan had dragged itself half out of the water, over the bow, ten of its heads clamped on to the railings and fittings of the ship. Other heads snaked to and fro, snapping at fleeing seamen. Slowly it heaved on the bulk of the ship, dragging it into the sea. *The Maggot* groaned in protest as its timber splintered and cracked on the ice but it slowly began to move.

Edgy turned back and scrambled up towards Janus, who now clung precariously to the stern railing of the ship. More cargo, barrels and boxes bounced and lurched towards Edgy, making him swerve left and right as the ship tilted further. He threw himself at Janus, who grabbed his arm at the elbow.

Others had obviously heeded Janus's advice and clambered over the stern rails of the ship and slid down its exposed hull on to the island of ice. Janus climbed up on to the railing and wobbled, waving his hands to steady himself. Then he beckoned to Edgy, reaching out to him. Edgy climbed up beside him and looked down.

'We have to slide down, Edgy. It's our only hope,' Janus yelled over the grating of steel as the Leviathan tore at the funnel, ripping a huge chunk from it.

Edgy shook his head. He wasn't sure he could.

The ship juddered again as the Leviathan struck at it. More men screamed from the bow of the ship.

'Edgy!' Lord Mauldeth clung to the splintered stump of the mainmast at the back of the main deck. A beam of wood pinned his legs to the bloody deck. His face was blackened with soot from the shattered funnel and blood trickled down his brow.

'Mr Janus,' Edgy said. 'It's Lord Mauldeth. He's your brother – we have to save him!'

Janus pursed his lips and frowned, pausing and looking back.

'Mr Janus, we can't leave him,' Edgy gasped, grabbing his sleeve.

'Edgy!' Mauldeth called again. 'Beware. He's after . . .'

The whole ship lurched and the rest of Mauldeth's words were lost as Janus gave Edgy a sharp shove, sending him slithering down the hull of the ship. He bounced and rolled as his clothes snagged and caught on the rough surface. The sounds of rending steel and fracturing timber filled his ears as the ship slid away from him. For a moment, he fell free of the ship, the cold air whipping his cheeks. Then he gasped as he landed on the compacted ice.

Edgy watched as the Leviathan dragged *Lord Byron's Maggot* into the sea. Steam boiled and waves steadily pounded the shore of the island as the ship sank into the foaming water. A few heads snaked about, snapping up floundering sailors who had jumped into the water at the last moment. Then both the Leviathan and the ship vanished, leaving nothing but a bubbling black stain on the surface.

'Lord Mauldeth,' Edgy gasped. He couldn't believe it. Everything had happened so quickly. Tears froze on his cheek.

'Come along now, Edgy. Stiff upper lip,' Janus said, stretching and dusting ice from his trousers.

'But he's dead,' Edgy said. 'Your brother. He's dead. Don't you feel sad?'

A shadow crossed Janus's face and his mouth tightened. 'If we'd gone to save him, we'd be down there now too,' he muttered. He turned his back on Edgy. 'Come on, let's get up these steps before that beast comes back.'

Edgy glanced around at the shore of the island. Everywhere the blue ice reflected the moonlight. His breath plumed in the frozen air as he pulled his jacket tighter.

'That's far enough, Mr Janus,' Silky McFarland called. Edgy spun round. McFarland stood with two other sailors by the water's edge, a vicious knife in his grasp. 'You're not goin' anywhere.'

'Fool!' Janus spat. 'Do you suggest we just stand here and wait for that monster to return?'

'If it stops you goin' up those stairs, that'll do me,' McFarland said.

'You're in her employment, aren't you?' Janus hissed.

'Aye, I was told it'd be worth my while watchin' over

the boy,' McFarland said. 'An' if I stop you from goin' up those steps then she'll rescue me from certain death here.'

'Salomé paid you to protect me?' Edgy said, frowning. 'It don't make any sense.'

'Maybe not,' McFarland said, 'but I did a damned good job, laddie –'

An explosion of water and oil behind McFarland cut short any response. The Leviathan burst out of the sea, snapping up the two seamen behind him before they could even scream. McFarland threw himself forward, another set of jaws smashing down into the ice just behind him.

Janus bundled Edgy towards the stairs, slipping on the ice.

'Come back!' McFarland yelled, racing towards them. Janus skidded, gasping as the air blew from his lungs.

For a moment, McFarland towered over them, his knife raised to strike. And then he vanished, snatched away by the jaws of the sea monster. Edgy watched, mute as the sailor hurtled backwards, a trail of blood spattering the ice, marking his passage towards the sea. And then he too was gone.

More heads reared from the icy waves. Janus had picked himself up but was still struggling for breath. Acting on instinct, Edgy dragged the gasping old man towards the steps. Teeth snapped the air behind him. The smell of blood and seawater surrounded them. Janus regained his breath somewhat and began to run alongside Edgy.

'If we can get up the first few steps, we'll be out of its reach,' Janus panted. 'It doesn't seem keen to come out of the water.'

There was no time to think as Janus pushed Edgy on to the first narrow step. Each step felt like polished glass under his feet. He slipped and stumbled against the wall of the mountain they were climbing. Higher and higher they staggered, leaving the Leviathan and the bloody ice behind.

The mist had cleared up here and Edgy could see the stairs of ice twisting higher and higher up the side of the island. The wall to their left shone cold and white, offering no handhold or support. Edgy's heart battered at his ribs with every slick step. He could hear Janus's laboured breath, out of time and ragged.

Further they climbed. The world became a narrow strip of white. Edgy kept his eyes on the wall side of the steps so as not to look down at the dizzying drop. His bulky clothes hampered him, making movement even more awkward. Sometimes the edges of the steps blurred into one, making him stumble and curse. The wind prodded him, whipping his breath away. Edgy's body ached with the cold and his head began to spin. He squeezed his eyes shut and paused for a second.

'Don't stop, boy,' Janus hissed behind him.

Mist still shrouded the sea below. All Edgy knew was the black night sky above them and the wall of white that they clung to. Every individual step took an effort of concentration.

'We're nearly there,' Janus said.

Edgy risked a glance upward and saw a gaping dark-blue cave mouth above them. Another ten steps and

Edgy threw himself to the ground at Janus's feet. It felt so good to be off the treacherous stairs. Sitting up, he pressed his head to his knees, panting for breath. Far below, Edgy could see the black stain at the edge of the island – all that was left of the ship. The sea stretched out to the distant curved horizon, eerily illuminated by starlight and ice.

The cave entrance was dark and uninviting. Gripping the cave mouth, Edgy peered in and could see nothing but blackness. A sharp push sent him stumbling into the cave. He gave a scream as his feet found no floor. Suddenly, Edgy became weightless. The floor had vanished beneath his feet. He was sliding down a chute of blue ice.

With a grunt of pain, he came to an abrupt halt as he hit the floor. He groaned and looked up. He hadn't travelled far. The shock of the fall had been worse than the landing.

Edgy dragged himself to his feet and looked around, gasping at the sight before him.

See ye now that narrow road
Up by yon tree?
That's the road the righteous goes,
And that's the road to heaven.
An' see ye now that broad road
Down by yon sunny fell?
That's the road the wicked go,
An' that's the road to hell.

'The Queen of Elfan's Nourice', traditional folk ballad

CHAPTER THIRTY-THREE
MOLOCH'S CAVE

A cathedral of ice. Pillars soared above Edgy's head to the ceiling, jagged with stalactites that pointed down like teeth ready to snap. The walls of the cavern pulsed with a cold, blue light, making everything as clear as daylight. Every now and then, a *plop* of dripping meltwater echoed in the silence.

A demon stood encased in the ice of the wall. It dwarfed them. Its head reached the ceiling. Edgy's heart hammered at his ribs until he thought it would explode. Anger and hatred twisted the creature's face. Deep furrows carved their way across its green brow. Dark eyes glittered with an evil fire. Edgy shivered. It looked alive. Needle teeth filled the snarling mouth beneath its hooked nose. Its limbs bulged with sinew and muscle. Each claw in each thick finger stood as tall as a man. Every inch of the demon's body looked built for violence.

Edgy's reverie was shattered by a soft *thump* as Janus landed on the ice floor. He stood and stared up at the colossal demon.

'Moloch,' Janus hissed, his eyes wide and excited. 'Look at the wound . . .'

Edgy felt a wave of disgust wash over him as his eyes tracked down the demon's powerful, green torso, studded with boils and sores, to the gaping raw hole where its heart should have been. Edgy's chest felt tight, as if an iron band had been wrapped around it. He panted for breath.

'It's horrible,' Edgy gasped, looking away from the scales that crusted the green skin, the leathery bat's wings folded behind its broad back. Sweat trickled down Edgy's back despite the coldness of the cave. *What's wrong with me?* He could feel the blood pumping through his head and neck.

'A terrible beauty,' Janus whispered, shivering. He rummaged around in his pack and pulled out a small folded-up object. 'This is a mattock,' he said, opening it out into what looked like a small spade with a pick blade on the other side. 'You must climb up to the chest and break through the ice that covers the hole.'

Edgy's head spun. 'Up there, Mr Janus?' He gazed up to the demon's dark scar. It had to be a hundred feet at least. His whole body pulsed now. Every beat of his heart felt like an explosion. 'But why?'

'The ice is thinner there. If we begin to strip it away from the top then the job will be easier. Don't worry – look, there are footholds,' Janus said. His voice stayed low but trembled with anticipation. 'Use the mattock to deepen any crevices that you can stand in.'

'No,' Edgy said, twitching and blinking.

'What?' Janus's voice was barely above a whisper. He stared at Edgy in disbelief.

'It's horrible, Mr Janus,' Edgy said, holding the professor's stern gaze. 'So many people have died. We're trapped. We should be findin' a way to escape instead.'

'After all I've done.' Janus shook his head then rubbed his eyes and groaned through his hands. 'After my poor brother's sacrifice. We treated you like family.' Janus threw his hands down. 'And this is how you repay us,' he spat.

'No, Mr Janus, I didn't mean –'

'What did you mean, eh?'

'I just –'

'Do you think I would leave us marooned?' Janus hissed, shaking with emotion. 'Do you think I'm some kind of madman? Do you think I wanted all those people to die?'

'No, I'm sorry.' Edgy took a deep breath, grasping the mattock and digging his foot into the first toehold in the ice.

The wall didn't turn out to be as sheer as Edgy had imagined. That didn't make it any less slippery though. Each step required careful thought. His head throbbed and pulsed. Edgy hacked into the ice, trying to ignore the hideous form that lay inches beneath. The mattock splintered the smooth surface, gripping and reassuring Edgy. He paused at one point, hanging on to the mattock and staring down at the green mottled skin at his feet.

'Keep going, Edgy,' Janus called from below, his voice echoing across the chamber.

Edgy heaved on the mattock and kicked his toes into

the freezing hold underfoot. Finally, he looked down to see a dark gap, red and ragged, beneath the ice.

'I've found it, Mr Janus,' he called down.

'Break all the ice over the hole. It should be quite thin by now, if my research is correct,' Janus called up.

What research? Edgy pushed his toes further into the footholds he had carved. He bent his knees against the ice and then raised the mattock above his head. His heart thundered, making the cavern spin.

Edgy smashed the mattock down. The ice shattered like a pane of glass, sending shards tinkling around the cavern. His stomach lurched as the stench of rotten flesh took his breath away. For a second, the gory pit in front of him filled his vision and his left foot slipped. He whacked the mattock into the ice at the side of the hole as he fell backwards. The grating screech of the metal gouging the ice tore at Edgy's ears as he plummeted down the side of the wall. Splinters of frozen water showered him, burning his face as he scrambled against the slick wall, trying to get some purchase. The mattock kicked and jarred, numbing his hand and arm, but it slowed his descent.

With a yell of defiance, Edgy threw himself backwards as he neared the floor and landed on his feet, panting for breath. The whole cavern echoed with his cry.

'Excellent, excellent,' Janus said, hopping from one foot to the other. 'That's saved a lot of work.'

Edgy looked back at the huge furrow that ran down the wall. The whole cavern creaked ominously. Cracks appeared along the ice that encased the demon.

'One sharp blow and we'll have the whole lot down.' Janus beamed. His smile made Edgy shiver despite the pounding of the blood through his body and the sweat that slicked his temples. Edgy slumped down on the ground, exhausted. He didn't care that it was cold. His whole body felt drained.

'I don't feel too right, Mr Janus,' he said, rubbing his eyes.

'That's to be expected,' Janus murmured. He set his pack down and reached inside it with shaking hands. Edgy watched flatly as Janus drew something from the bag, concealing it with his jacket cuffs. 'I'll be back in a minute,' he said. 'Just need to make a few preparations.'

Edgy frowned. *Preparations?* He watched Janus stride off behind the ice pillar. *What does he mean?* He dragged himself to his feet. Janus's bag lay on its side, open. Its contents hung out. The book lay there. *The Legends of Moloch.* Edgy leaned over and picked it up. He flicked through the pages. Janus could be back any second.

The page flopped open and Edgy recognised the pictures straight away. They were the ones he'd seen just before the Leviathan attacked – Satan cutting Moloch's heart out, Salomé with a babe on an altar, preparing to kill it with the spiral knife. Edgy read the text.

Salomé, her wish granted, feared Satan's distrust. She knew that only if she held the heart of Moloch could she keep the ear of Satan. So Salomé hid the heart where nobody would ever find it. Not even Satan himself.

A scraping sound brought Edgy back to the cave. Janus was grinding something. Sharpening it. Edgy frowned and looked down at the book again.

> Salomé tricked men into lying with her and bore children by them. She took the heart and placed it in the chest of her cleverest, strongest child.

The scraping of metal on stone continued, drawing Edgy's attention, making it hard to concentrate on the book.

> This way, she thought, the heart would never be still but would roam the earth. Not even Satan would think to look into the heart of a young one. But every thirteen years, Salomé had to show Satan that she still had the heart.

The grinding sound stopped.

> So every thirteen years Salomé would seek out her cleverest and strongest child and cut its heart out, placing it in a new child after she had shown Satan that it was still safe.

'Happy Birthday, Edgy.' Janus stood before him, a long spiral blade in his hand. Edgy glanced down at the book.

The same blade as in the pictures. The same knife that Satan held to cut out the heart of Moloch. The same knife that Salomé held to cut out the heart of the babe.

The same heart that pounded and hammered in his chest now.

Eager to burst out and rejoin its true master.

Edgy scrambled to his feet as Janus stepped forward with the Devil's Dagger.

'Mr Janus, what're you doin'?' Edgy whispered, his voice dry and quaking.

'Think about it, Edgy,' Janus hissed, wide eyed. 'Once I put the heart of Moloch back into his chest, he will awaken. And I will be the greatest daemonologist in the world.'

'But what about me?' Edgy gasped. A vague, half-formed thought buzzed around in the back of his mind. If he carried the heart, it meant something else. *What is it?*

'You'll be famous too, don't you see?' Janus raised his eyebrows as if to show it was an easy and obvious conclusion. 'You'll always be known as the last boy to carry Moloch's heart!'

'You can't, Mr Janus. If you bring Moloch back, he'll destroy everything.'

'Not if I ossify him before he truly wakes.' Janus beamed, his face an insane mask of excitement. 'Imagine me, Envry Janus, the captor of an arch-demon! They'll make me chancellor of the Society. My brother's so-called achievements will be forgotten.'

'No, Mr Janus. This is madness,' Edgy panted, backing away. 'Think about what yer doin'.'

'Oh I have, Edgy. I've thought long and hard.' He moved closer, the knife reflecting the blue light of the cavern on to his face. 'I've sat and watched my brother take all the credit for my hard work. I've thought about his patronising, pompous ways.'

'But you said yerself, he died for us.'

'Ha!' Janus spat. 'I only said that to get you to break the ice on Moloch's body.'

'But he cared about you. He saved your life so many times,' Edgy pleaded.

'Is that what he told you? Poisoned your mind against me as well, eh?' Janus's mouth tightened and his eyes narrowed. 'Well, Mauldeth won't win.'

'He's dead, Mr Janus, you saw him on the ship.' Edgy's back pressed against the creaking cave wall. 'You mustn't do this.'

Janus wasn't listening. He threw himself at Edgy, knife-point first.

TALK OF THE DEVIL AND HE'S SURE TO APPEAR.

TRADITIONAL PROVERB

CHAPTER THIRTY-FOUR
NO SAVIOUR

Janus's strength surprised Edgy. The old man was small but his whole weight bore down on him. Janus sat on Edgy's chest, pinning him. Edgy clamped both hands around the professor's skinny wrist, panting and sobbing as the sharp tip of the blade inched towards his chest. Edgy's heart boomed, his body aching with every massive pulse.

'You can feel it, can't you, Edgy?' Janus hissed. 'The heart is growing. It wants to return to Moloch. It's not yours. Give up.'

'No,' Edgy grunted, hurling Janus away from him. The professor stumbled backwards.

'Sokket knew,' Janus whispered, gathering himself up. 'He'd been following my research more closely than I thought. That's why he tried to kill you – to destroy your body entirely.'

'The picture, the crusher . . .' Edgy gasped. 'There would

have been no trace of me left if Sokket had succeeded. That's why he wanted me at the bottom of the sea.'

But Edgy had no more time to think. Janus lunged once again, slashing at him with the knife and cutting through his coat. The torn clothes flapped and tangled around his arms. Janus's knife slammed down inches away, burying itself deep into the ice. Janus cursed, tugging at the blade. Edgy staggered to his feet.

He put his hand to his chest, feeling something hard and metallic. Salomé's charm. *She wanted to protect me. Janus lied about everything. She doesn't want to put my heart back into Moloch.*

Edgy tore the charm from around his neck and held it high above his head. 'Salomé,' he cried, 'help me. Janus is tryin' to –'

But Janus launched into Edgy and dragged him to the floor, the knife in his hand once more. Edgy fell back, cracking his head on the icy ground. Pain lanced through his skull and bile filled his mouth. He retched and rolled to one side. Janus's twisted face filled his vision. The knife blade flashed blue and cold. And then Janus's weight vanished from on top of Edgy.

'Well, well, what have we here?' Salomé's voice echoed across the cavern. 'What are you silly boys fighting about now?'

Edgy never thought he'd be glad to hear that voice. He scrambled to his feet, wincing at the pain as he did.

Salomé stood, dressed in a flowing white summer dress, lace and bustles. Her broad sun hat looked incongruous in the ice-blue cavern. She twirled a parasol on her shoulder and flashed a white smile at Edgy. Janus lay at Salomé's feet, glaring up at her, his knife on the floor a few feet away from him.

'Salomé,' Edgy panted. 'It's Janus – he wants to put my . . . my heart into . . . that . . .' Edgy pointed at the demonic body that loomed over them. The ice that encased it had melted slightly, making it easier to see the green scales and the purple veins that wormed through its flesh. Edgy's own body pulsed with pain. He touched his nose. A circle of blood darkened the finger of his glove. Salomé would help him. She was . . . what? He couldn't think straight.

'That's not wise, Mr Janus, trying to bring Moloch back.' Salomé shook her head. Edgy thought he saw a flash of contempt in those perfect green eyes as she looked down on Janus. 'Here's a riddle for you, Edgy Taylor. Who is worse, demons or men?'

Edgy shrugged, making his neck and shoulders throb. He wiped at the blood at his nose. The whole cave seemed more red than blue now and it swung back and forth as if the sea rocked it. His head burned. He blinked at Salomé, who giggled and swam in and out of his vision. 'I don't care,' he slurred. Edgy fell to one knee.

'Quite right too,' Salomé smiled. 'Personally, I don't think there's much to choose between them these days. Men might even be a little bit worse.'

Janus had slipped his hand into his pocket. Edgy opened his mouth to warn Salomé but Janus flicked his finger and a demon pearl bounced out on to the ground, cracking open in a flash of light.

'Oh my,' Salomé said as the flash enveloped her.

And then she was gone. Only a small black pearl remained, dark and round against the frozen ground.

Janus hauled himself upright and limped over to the dagger, picking it and the demon pearl up. 'She couldn't stop me, Edgy,' he panted, smoothing his long hair back. 'She even sent that stupid boy, Bernard, to be my servant. He was trying to stop me. Oh, I had my suspicions about the skull of Aldorath. That's why the lad cut it up.'

Edgy's legs gave way and he fell flat. Janus had betrayed him. Tears stung his eyes. The man he'd trusted had always been a killer.

'Oh yes,' Janus sneered, holding the pearl up between finger and thumb before tucking it in his breast pocket. 'He was taking it to her when I caught him. And you thought he was running from Salomé when he died? It was me he was running from!'

Edgy saw Janus bend to pick up the knife. His left arm felt numb.

'How do you think I found you? I followed you back to the tannery after your encounter with the boy and your chat with Salomé. Her interest in you piqued my interest. I knew all about her long before you met her. And you brought me all the clues I needed . . . and the heart, of course. The big fat pumping heart,' Janus said, swinging the blade in his hand. 'Scrabsnitch's book just confirmed my suspicion – that you carried the heart.' Behind him, meltwater trickled down the cracked ice that was slowly giving up the body of Moloch. 'Thammuz knew what I'd come for. That's why I had to kill him. Him and those gormless demons that worked for me. That's right, Edgy, they weren't Salomé's demons – they were mine!'

'But I trusted you,' Edgy gasped. He peered around, looking for something to defend himself with. The mattock lay discarded a few feet away. Grunting with every movement, Edgy dragged himself along by one elbow towards it.

'That made it so much easier, you foolish boy.' Janus paced towards him, the blade loose in the hand by his side.

'I saved your life,' Edgy said, reaching for the handle of the mattock.

'It's true I didn't expect the demon to turn on me like that, but it was perfect. It made a bond between us. A bond that brought you here.'

Janus strode nearer, his face grim and determined. Edgy's hand closed on the handle of the mattock. *I've been tricked.* All these weeks, he'd idolised Janus, wanted to be like him, to be part of his 'big discovery'. Tears stung Edgy's eyes. It felt like the heart thundering within him would burst out.

'The heart is trying to reach its master,' Janus said, his face cold, his eyes steely. 'Give it back.'

'No,' Edgy hissed weakly. He swung his arm in a wide arc. His sweaty palm slid along the handle of the pick and left his fingers plucking at the air.

Janus flinched, covering his head with his arms. But
Edgy watched in despair as the mattock flew wide of its
target. Janus glanced over his shoulder and then raised the
knife. A metallic clang halted him as the mattock hit
the wall of ice encasing Moloch. The tool bent up against
the wall and rattled uselessly to the ground.

A second of silence followed, then the cracks in the
weakened ice where the mattock had struck the wall began
to open one by one, widening with snaps and fizzes. Larger
fissures began to race across the wall, chasing each other,
joining and growing, moving faster, groaning louder.

Janus swayed, hypnotised by the disintegration of the
wall. Slivers of ice clattered down to the ground, shower-
ing them. Edgy curled up into a ball as larger chunks
bounced down, thumping him in the back.

Janus rolled Edgy over on to his back and raised the
dagger. The shower of ice chunks grew heavier. Bigger
pieces rained down around them, shattering on the hard
ground. Edgy tried to shield his face but Janus pinned his
aching arm with his foot.

'I'm sorry to have to do this, Edgy,' Janus said. 'Really,
I am. You were a good companion but this was always
going to happen.'

And then the room exploded with a deafening boom
as the whole ceiling collapsed. Edgy suddenly found his
arm free and rolled aside as boulders of ice smashed down
from above like fists. The cavern rumbled as meltwater
poured down on Edgy, soaking and freezing him. The cold
revived him too.

Glancing up, he saw the huge demon body, exposed now, standing frozen to the bare rock of the cavern. He threw himself towards it, hoping to shelter beneath its gargantuan form.

Janus stood, knife in hand, blocking his path. He'd taken a blow to his temple from the ice and blood trickled from his nose, but his mad grin remained. He raised the knife and let out a chilling scream of rage.

Edgy stumbled backwards, dodging more blocks of ice. But Janus charged forward, slashing with the blade. He closed on Edgy face to face. Edgy gave a last shove and sent him staggering back. A crack and a rumble made them both look up. Janus gave a final scream as a massive icicle speared down from the ceiling. It plunged down, piercing Janus's shoulder, stabbing deep into his body. His fingers grazed Edgy's jacket as he fell face down to the ground and lay still. Blood pooled around him, staining the icy water red.

The cave looked smaller now – the floor had risen and become a choppy ocean of ice and rock. Janus's arm poked out of the icy blocks. The professor's bag lay trapped under a rock the size of Edgy's head. He rummaged in it and managed to pull out the ossifier. The long cylindrical barrel was slightly dented but otherwise it looked in good order. The dial on the side told Edgy it had one more charge. He slung it over his shoulder. Not that it was any use. In fact, it was the cause of all the trouble, Edgy thought. If Janus hadn't been so trigger-happy, so intent on 'bagging' Moloch, then none of this would have happened. Edgy shook his head. No, the ossifier wasn't to blame – it was Janus himself. Edgy stared numbly at the pale hand sticking up out of the ice. *Who is worse*, he wondered, *demons or men? Maybe Salomé is right. Maybe there is nothing to choose between them.*

Salomé! She didn't want the heart after all. She had been trying to stop Janus all along.

Grimacing, Edgy rummaged in Janus's breast pocket and pulled out the pearl. He smashed it down on the ice.

Salomé appeared in a flash of red light, slightly dishevelled. Her hair hung down under her skewed hat and dirt smudged her creamy cheek. She smoothed her dress down and shook her parasol open.

'That wasn't very dignified at all,' she said, reminding Edgy of Sally in one of her more petulant moods. 'You freed me,' she said, a note of surprise in her voice.

'Why not?' Edgy croaked. 'You're the only one who can save me, I reckon.'

'Save you?' Salomé gave a little laugh and twirled her parasol. 'Why, my dear little boy, *I'm* going to have to cut your heart out now!'

Pull off, pull off your woollen shirt,
And tear it from gore to gore,
And wrap it around this deathless wound,
And it did bleed no more.

'Two Brothers', TRADITIONAL FOLK BALLAD

CHAPTER THIRTY-FIVE
THE ANSWER

Salomé stood gazing up at the frozen form of Moloch. Her parasol twirled to and fro.

'I sometimes wonder what would have happened,' she said, her voice distant and thoughtful, 'if I hadn't sided with Satan. Would Moloch have taken on the Hosts of Heaven?'

Edgy groaned and tried to stand but his legs folded beneath him, leaving him lying on his chest.

'All in all, I think Satan's done a better job than Moloch ever could have, don't you?' She flashed him a perfect smile. 'After all, it was Satan who thought to corrupt mankind. Can you tell the difference, Edgy? The difference between man and demonkind? I can't.'

'You're the one who cuts out children's hearts,' Edgy gasped, rolling on to his side and levelling the ossifier at her.

Salomé's face hardened. 'Now that's not very friendly,'

she said through clenched teeth. 'Anyway, don't be such a silly boy. I have to cut your heart out. I have to show Satan that it's safe.'

'Then I'll have to use this,' Edgy gasped, raising the tube. His vision blurred. Two Salomés swam in front of him. He shook his head and staggered to his feet, leaning heavily on a boulder behind him.

'You can't ossify me,' she sneered.

Edgy frowned, blinking sweat from his eyes. 'Why not?' he slurred.

'Did you ever work out my riddle? The one I asked you all those months ago.' She raised her eyebrows. 'Remember? What is it that everyone is born with, some die with, but most die without?'

Edgy's head swam. The cavern seemed to turn slowly. Salomé's words rolled around in his mind. *What is it that everyone is born with, some die with, but most die without?* His heart thumped, punching at his ribs. *Why is she asking stupid riddles?* The blood roared in his head. *She'll cut out my heart anyway. Like she does all her children. Think of all those kids down through the centuries. Murdered by her – their own . . .*

Edgy fixed his eyes on Salomé.

His mind cleared a little as the realisation sank in.

He looked down at his ossifier and at Salomé again.

'Well?' Salomé asked, a frown of impatience creasing her face. 'What is it that everyone is born with, some die with, but most die without?'

Edgy raised the ossifier, managing to smile at the look

of discomfort on her face. The answer to the question that had been bothering him since he realised what Janus was up to flooded into his mind.

'A mother,' he said. 'You're my mother.' He pulled the trigger and swung the gun to her left.

The last sludgeball in the ossifier flew over Salomé's shoulder and splattered wetly on the thigh of the frozen Moloch. Edgy dropped the ossifier and fell forward into darkness. Salomé's scream of rage echoed in his ears.

The cavern lay in a dim twilight when Edgy awoke. His head ached and every muscle protested as he pulled himself to his feet. Salomé sat on a pile of rubble, staring up at the grey, ossified body of Moloch – a massive gruesome statue. Edgy put a hand to his chest. His heart thumped gently, calmly.

'When you ossified him, the heart became yours,' Salomé said, resting her chin on her hand. Her hair hung loose and her hat lay discarded at her side. 'If you knew the effort I'd gone to. The tricks and traps I'd laid to stop Janus. What a waste.'

'But it's sorted now. You don't need to show Satan that the heart's safe,' Edgy said, 'cos there's no Moloch.'

'No,' Salomé sighed. 'Very clever. I thought you were going to ossify me.'

Edgy shook his head. 'I should've done. All those children you must've killed over the years . . .' Rage boiled up inside him.

'It doesn't matter now,' she said flatly. 'It's over. You've spoiled the game.'

'Game?' Edgy spat. 'Everyone that's died, everyone who's suffered cos of this an' you call it a . . . a . . . game?' He snatched up the ossifier that still lay buckled and dented by his side. 'I wish I 'ad another shot. I'd let you 'ave it and not worry about 'ow I got 'ome.'

'I wish you had another shot,' Salomé said. For the first time, Edgy noticed tearstains on her cheeks. 'Then you could end it all for me. It's over, Edgy Taylor. The time of demons is finished. It's mankind's turn now. But I suspect he's more than capable of destroying himself.'

'What do you mean?' Edgy frowned. *Is this some kind of new riddle?*

'Your precious stonemasons have hunted us to the verge of extinction. Either that or demons have become so earthbound that they're virtually human. Who's to say where demons end and humans begin?'

Edgy stood mute. He thought about Slouch, paralysed by sloth, and Madame Lillith, reduced to a shrivelled husk of envy.

Salomé sighed. She suddenly sounded old and weary. 'This was the last game. The last challenge. This island will sink soon and I think we'll go with it. It won't rise again.'

'You can drown if you want to,' Edgy said. 'But you owe me – I freed you from the demon pearl. I command you to send me back to the Royal Society.'

'See?' Salomé smiled. Her black hair had strands of

grey in it now. Worry and age lined her face. 'So selfish, humans. They don't know when it's time to give up. That might be one difference. Very well.' She rummaged in her skirts and produced the spiral dagger that Janus had tried to kill Edgy with. Edgy's heart gave a lurch.

'What's that for?' Edgy took a step back.

'Don't worry, I'll do what you ask. You might find this useful, that's all. It's the Devil's Dagger. Made by Satan himself. Janus sharpened it to a razor's edge but it could be blunt as a mallet and still do its job.' She handed the dagger to him, handle first.

'Which is?' Edgy murmured, taking it gingerly.

'To kill Satan himself,' Salomé sighed. 'You know the story. He always wanted to be mortal.'

'One of his games,' Edgy said, remembering the tale of the hunter.

'Yes,' Salomé smiled, something of her old looks flaring back for a second, 'in happier times.'

'So what d'you want me to do with it?' Edgy asked, staring at the dagger in his hand.

'Whatever you see fit,' Salomé said. 'I don't care any more. But remember: if you decide to use it, then your life is forfeit.'

The cavern gave a shudder, dislodging a few loose shards of ice from the roof. Meltwater began to pour from the walls, trickling down the stone face of Moloch and spouting from between his teeth.

'You see,' Salomé shouted, her face twisted with anger as she stabbed a finger towards Moloch. 'That's what we've become. Gargoyles! Hideous statues stuck on buildings where once flew creatures of fire and light. Our riddles shall become no more than children's amusements, our tales forgotten, our songs unsung. So many dead, so many killed. Ask yourself who is to blame. Is it me? Janus? You, Edgy Taylor?'

Salomé cast a hand towards Edgy. In a panic, he turned to run but the water swirled and gushed into the cave, freezing him, sweeping him up and throwing him from left to right until he was blind and consciousness left him.

WHEN A SNAKE IS IN THE HOUSE YOU NEED NOT DISCUSS IT AT GREAT LENGTH.

TRADITIONAL PROVERB

CHAPTER THIRTY-SIX
PAYING THE PRICE

Warmth enveloped Edgy and he found himself lying on a hard marble floor. No, not warmth – heat. Burning heat. The smell of woodsmoke filled his nostrils. He opened his eyes a crack. *Is this heaven or hell?* The room swirled with smoke but Edgy could see the wall paintings and knew he was back in the entrance hall of the Royal Society of Daemonologie. But the paint bubbled as flames licked around the door frames and across the panelling.

Slouch leaned over the arm of his sofa, resting his long chin on his forearms, and stared down at Edgy.

'Been busy?' he yawned.

'Y'could say that,' Edgy replied, coughing on the smoke. 'Slouch, what's going on?'

'Change of management,' Slouch murmured, his eyes glowing orange and a malicious smile splitting his drooping face. 'The place is burnin' down, I reckon. I'd escape but . . . Well, what's the point?'

'What d'yer mean, "new management"?' Edgy's eyes watered and he pulled the hood of his ragged jacket around his face. 'Where's Sally and Professor Milberry? Where's Henry?'

Slouch heaved a huge sigh and slowly raised an arm, pointing off down the nearest blazing passage. 'Library, I s'pose.'

Edgy didn't wait to question him further. With a curse, he dashed down the corridor into the thickening smoke. The snake was behind this, Edgy was certain. He gripped the Devil's Dagger tightly. Glass crunched beneath Edgy's feet. Above his head, the hellfire lamps blazed, each one looking as if it had exploded. Fire roared from them, pooling across the wooden ceiling.

A little piece of knowledge at a time. That's what the snake said. He's been setting this up for decades. Edgy sweated in his thick coat but it shielded him from the burning flames as he staggered through the swirling smoke. He tried not to think of what might have happened to the others. *Just think of the library, the library . . .*

A beam crashed down behind Edgy, spitting sparks and sending him scurrying down the tunnel of flames. The smoke thickened, blinding Edgy and sending him stumbling onward. With an oath, he hit something solid and then fell forward as it gave way before him. Edgy found himself sprawled on the floor of the library. The dome of a dark summer evening sky arched over him. Nightbirds sang in the branches that sprouted from the bookshelves lined with black, scaly books. Dark apples clustered among the leaves and quivered gently. No fire invaded this room.

Milberry, Spinorix and Trimdon lay bound and gagged at the foot of a tall bookcase. Henry quivered next to Trimdon, too terrified to move. Above them, looped time and again about a thick overhanging branch, hung the snake.

'Hello, Edgy Taylor. Back so soon?' he hissed.

'What've you done?' Edgy snarled, taking a step forward. He held the dagger behind his back.

'First things first. How's Mr Janus?' the snake said, as if enquiring about an old friend.

'Dead,' Edgy said, narrowing his eyes at the snake.

'And Salomé?'

'Dunno,' Edgy murmured. 'Said she was goin' to stay on the island.'

'Aah,' said the snake. 'And did you find Moloch?'

'Ossified him,' Edgy said. 'He won't be trouble to no one again.'

'Excellent,' the snake said, slithering back along the tree to the main bookcase trunk.

'You knew all this would happen?' Edgy snapped, gritting his teeth.

'You never can tell with humans,' the snake hissed. 'But with my experience, I could make a good guess. Things were getting a little worrying here, what with Janus's obsession with Moloch and Salomé's growing arrogance, continuously making demands on me, talking about "the old days". Quite tiresome, really.'

'So you gave us clues and got poor old Madame Lillith to steal the skull of Aldorath,' Edgy said.

'Clues? Madame Lillith? No, I just trusted her to follow her nature. She was almost human after all.' The snake's eyes glowed. 'But all games have to come to some sort of a close.' The snake's tail uncoiled out of the shadows, whipping around Edgy's arms, pinning him and sending the dagger clattering off behind the bookcases. 'You've proved highly entertaining as well as useful, Edgy. But now it's over.'

The snake's coils began to tighten. Edgy cursed, struggling against the pressure. The dagger lay just out of reach. He could see the handle poking out. But what if he recovered it and used it? Didn't the legend say that he would perish himself?

A pale hand reached out and grabbed the dagger. Edgy's eyes widened. *Sally!* Edgy struggled again. Sally peered round the edge of the bookcase and put a finger to her lips. Edgy tried to shake his head. *Would she die all over again if she used the dagger?* He had to distract the snake and somehow get free before they found out.

'But if you wanted Moloch's body destroyed why didn't you just go and do it yourself?' Edgy said. Sally disappeared back behind the bookcase.

'Do it myself?' the snake hissed, shuddering. 'Do you know who I am? I rarely do things myself. That would be far too easy and where's the fun anyway?'

'The Leviathan wasn't fun,' Edgy snapped. He thought of Captain Boyd and the crew of *The Maggot*, Mauldeth,

Janus, Sokket. All dead. Sally appeared behind the snake, the dagger raised.

'Ah, yes,' the snake said, unaware. 'The sea monster was gilding the lily a touch, I admit, but nothing's valued if it isn't a challenge.'

'You killed all those innocent people,' Edgy scowled.

'Oh dear,' the snake mocked. 'You seem a bit put out. Maybe I shouldn't brag about the fact that I also managed to bag three members of the illustrious Royal Society in the process. It seemed the right time to destroy the rest of them. Poor old Plumphrey's heart couldn't stand the strain of the fire, thanks to my demons of gluttony. That just leaves the complacent Miss Milberry here. I'll finish her after I've finished you.'

Sally crept nearer, her eyes wide with fear. Edgy wriggled and kicked but the snake held him fast. 'The whole crew – and the others – dead,' Edgy spat. 'Just for your idea of a game?'

'Oh, come on. I'm Satan. What do you expect?' the snake chortled. 'Would you kill me now if you could, Edgy Taylor? Even though you promised never to hurt me?'

'It'd be more than you deserve,' Edgy hissed. Sally raised the dagger.

'Oh, I like that,' Satan said. 'You'd justify breaking a solemn promise. That's what I call the thin end of the wedge. The road to hell is paved with good intentions and well-meant excuses . . .' Edgy gasped as the satanic snake tightened its grip. 'Demons always keep promises, which is why humans are worse than demons.'

'But humans care for each other.' Edgy felt like he would burst as Satan squeezed his scaly coils. 'Which is why they'll always be better.'

Sally pounced, ramming the dagger deep into Satan's neck. With a screech of surprised rage, the snake reared up, uncoiling from around Edgy and dumping him on the library floor. Satan thrashed from side to side, smashing over bookcases, splintering the wood.

'Damn you all!' screamed Satan, trying to lunge at Edgy. Satan writhed around, hissing like a deflating balloon, lashing his tail to and fro. Then he stopped. He lay still and dead.

The evening sky faded, the branches and apples vanished, and Edgy stood in an ordinary panelled room, lined with normal bookshelves filled with ordinary books. Smoke began to billow in, clouding Edgy's view.

Sally stumbled back, her eyes glazed.

'Sally, no!' Edgy screamed, running forward to catch her. She shook, staring into the distance.

'It's all right,' she whispered. 'We did it. I'm dyin', that's all. Only a hundred or so years late.'

'But you can't die,' Edgy said, choking back tears. 'You're my friend . . . my family.'

Sally gasped, her face creasing with pain, and then smiled. 'My family are comin' for me. I can see them again . . . Edgy, you 'ave a family 'ere now . . . Look after them. Don't be sad . . . Molly, my little Molly . . .' She stared into another world, pressing her hand on Edgy's.

Then she lay still. Her face had uncreased, a contented smile frozen on her lips.

The smoke in the room thickened and fire began to leap from the door frames to the panelling, nibbling at the piles of old books. At first, all Edgy could do was hold Sally's cold hand and gaze. All around him, white spectral figures flitted and laughed as they weaved among the flames. The library's trapped souls were free.

Henry padded up to him, nuzzling and whining in fear. Edgy shook himself. The fire was spreading quickly, devouring its way through the dusty volumes.

Yanking the dagger from the snake's neck, Edgy sawed at Spinorix's bindings.

'Edgy, I was so scared, I thought –'

'No time now! Free Trimdon, I'll get Milberry,' Edgy barked. He sliced through Milberry's ropes while Spinorix chewed at Trimdon's with his sharp teeth.

Milberry staggered to her feet, mute with shock and grief. She hugged Edgy hard, sobbing.

The flames roared in their ears now, scorching them as they plunged through the doors of the library. Edgy carried Sally, stumbling on the burning spars and broken glass that clogged the floor. Impervious to the heat, Spinorix heaved burning beams aside and led the way as they scurried out, covering their mouths. Edgy glimpsed bubbling oil paintings, warped faces screaming in the backgrounds as they melted.

At the entrance hall Slouch still lay on his sofa despite it now being a roaring pyre. Huge beams from the upper floors had crashed down through the ceiling and molten copper dripped from the pipes.

'Slouch!' Milberry cried. 'Come with us, quickly.'

'Nah,' Slouch grinned through the flames. 'I quite like it here – it's warm for a change.'

Edgy pushed them on, gasping great breaths of air as they stumbled out on to the steps at the front of the Society. He lay Sally down gently and slumped next to her, letting exhaustion take him at last.

EPILOGUE

Edgy laid the flowers on Sally's grave. Pure white chrysanthemums. They reminded him of her somehow.

'We're startin' again, Sal,' he said. 'Professor Milberry, Spin, Trimdon an' me. We're goin' to start the Society again. Not like it was before, but properly this time. Collectin' evidence an' leavin' what precious few demons there are well alone. The old building's destroyed – every last ossifier, statue, skeleton an' mounted head. All gone. Milberry is sellin' the land an' we're goin' to live in the country, away from pryin' eyes. That way Spin an' Trimdon won't have to disguise themselves. You wanna see Spin! He looks proper strange disguised as a human, all knobbly elbows and bulgy eyes. He'd probably get fewer odd looks in the street if he stayed red, horns an' all.'

'Come along, Edgy, the carriage is waiting,' called Milberry, standing by the cemetery gates.

'Who're you, my mother or somethin'?' he called over his shoulder to her and then gave a secret smile. 'You were right, Sal. My family are 'ere. An' though I miss yer, I'm glad you're back with yours now.' He stood and put his bowler hat back on. 'I'll come an' visit regular as I can, like.' Edgy turned around.

Milberry, Spinorix and Trimdon stood by the waiting hackney carriage. Spin hopped up and down impatiently. Trimdon, disguised as an old gentleman with a walrus beard, tapped his cane on the pavement.

'Are you all right?' Milberry asked, her brown hair blown by the breeze.

Edgy nodded. She smiled and hugged him close.

'Let's get going then. The train leaves at twelve and we don't want to miss it,' Milberry said, climbing into the carriage.

Happy families, Edgy thought. *They're possible after all. Even if you do have the heart of a demon.*

FOR ANOTHER DEVILISHLY BRILLIANT
ADVENTURE, READ MORTLOCK...
IF YOU DARE

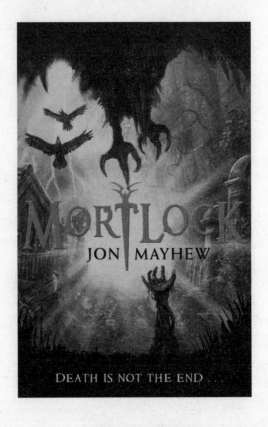

AVAILABLE NOW